The Clue of the
New Pin

HOUSE OF
STRATUS

This edition published in 2001 by House of Stratus, an imprint of
Stratus Books Ltd., 21 Beeching Park, Kelly Bray,
Cornwall, PL17 8QS, UK.

www.houseofstratus.com

Typeset, printed and bound by House of Stratus.

A catalogue record for this book is available from the British Library
and the Library of Congress.

ISBN 1-84232-666-X

We would like to thank the Edgar Wallace Society for all the support they have given
House of Stratus. Enquiries on how to join the Edgar Wallace Society should be addressed to:
The Edgar Wallace Society, c/o Penny Wyrd, 84 Ridgefield Road, Oxford, OX4 3DA.
Email: info@edgarwallace.org Web: http://www.edgarwallace.org/

Edgar Wallace was born illegitimately in 1875 in Greenwich and adopted by George Freeman, a porter at Billingsgate fish market. At eleven, Wallace sold newspapers at Ludgate Circus and on leaving school took a job with a printer. He enlisted in the Royal West Kent Regiment, later transferring to the Medical Staff Corps, and was sent to South Africa. In 1898 he published a collection of poems called *The Mission that Failed*, left the army and became a correspondent for Reuters.

Wallace became the South African war correspondent for *The Daily Mail*. His articles were later published as *Unofficial Dispatches* and his outspokenness infuriated Kitchener, who banned him as a war correspondent until the First World War. He edited the *Rand Daily Mail*, but gambled disastrously on the South African Stock Market, returning to England to report on crimes and hanging trials. He became editor of *The Evening News*, then in 1905 founded the Tallis Press, publishing *Smithy*, a collection of soldier stories, and *Four Just Men*. At various times he worked on *The Standard*, *The Star*, *The Week-End Racing Supplement* and *The Story Journal*.

In 1917 he became a Special Constable at Lincoln's Inn and also a special interrogator for the War Office. His first marriage to Ivy Caldecott, daughter of a missionary, had ended in divorce and he married his much younger secretary, Violet King.

The Daily Mail sent Wallace to investigate atrocities in the Belgian Congo, a trip that provided material for his *Sanders of the River* books. In 1923 he became Chairman of the Press Club and in 1931 stood as a Liberal candidate at Blackpool. On being offered a scriptwriting contract at RKO, Wallace went to Hollywood. He died in 1932, on his way to work on the screenplay for *King Kong*.

BY THE SAME AUTHOR
ALL PUBLISHED BY HOUSE OF STRATUS

1

The establishment of Yeh Ling was just between the desert of Reed Street and the sown of that great and glittering thoroughfare which is theatreland. The desert graduated down from the respectable, if gloomy, houses where innumerable milliners, modistes, and dentists had their signs before the doors and their workrooms and clinics on divers landings, to the howling wilderness of Bennet Street, and in this particular case the description often applied so lightly is aptly and faithfully affixed, for Bennet Street howled by day and howled in a shriller key by night. Its roadway was a playground for the progeny of this prolific neighbourhood, and a "ring" in which all manner of local blood-feuds were settled by waist-bare men, whilst their slatternly women squealed their encouragement or vocalized their apprehensions.

Yeh Ling's restaurant had begun at the respectable end of the street and he had specialized in strange Chinese dishes. Later it had crept nearer and nearer and nearer to The Lights, one house after another having been acquired by the unhappy-looking Oriental, its founder.

Then, with a rush, it arrived on the main street, acquired a rich but sedate facia, a French chef, and a staff of Italian waiters under the popular Signor Maciduino, most urbane of *maîtres d'hôtel*, and because of gilded and visible tiles, became "The Golden Roof." Beneath those tiles it was a place of rosewood panelling and soft shaded lights. There was a gilded elevator to carry you to the first and second floors where the private dining-rooms were – these had doors of plate-glass, curtained diaphanously. Yeh Ling thought that this was carrying respectability a little too far, but his patron was adamant on the matter.

Certain rooms had no plate-glass doors, but these were very discreetly apportioned. One such was never under any circumstances hired to diners, however important or impeccable they might be. It was the end room, No. 6, near the service doorway which led through a labyrinth of crooked and cross passages to the old building in Reed Street. This remained almost unchanged as it had been in the days of Yeh Ling's earlier struggles. Men and women came here for Chinese dishes and were supplied by soft-footed waiters from Han-Kow, which was Yeh Ling's native province.

The patrons of the old establishment lamented the arrival of Yeh Ling's prosperity and sneered at his well-dressed customers. The well-dressed customers being, for the most part, entirely ignorant that their humble neighbours had existence, ate their expensive meals unmoved and at certain hours danced sedately to the strains of The Old Original South Carolina Syncopated Orchestra, which Yeh Ling had hired regardless of expense.

He only visited the fashionable part of his property on one day of the year, the Chinese New Year, a queer little figure in a swallow-tailed coat, white-vested, white-gloved, and tightly, as well as whitely, collared.

At other times he sat at ease midway between the desert and the sown in a pokey little parlour hung about with vivid pictures which he had cut from the covers of magazines. Here, in a black silk robe, he pulled at his long-stemmed pipe. At half-past seven every night, except Sundays, he went to a door which opened on to the street, and was the door of one of those houses which linked the two restaurants, and here he would wait, his hand upon the knob. Sometimes the girl came first, sometimes the old man. Whichever it was, they usually passed in without a word and went up to Room No. 6. With their arrival Yeh Ling went back to his parlour to smoke and write letters of great length and beauty to his son at Han-Kow, for Yeh Ling's son was a man of great learning and position, being both a poet and a scholar. He had been admitted a member of the Forest of Pencils, which is at least the equivalent of being elected an Academician.

Sometimes Yeh Ling would devote himself to the matter of his new building at Shanford and dream dreams of an Excellency who would be its honoured master – for all things are possible in a land which makes education a test of choice for Ambassadorial appointments.

He never saw the two guests depart. They found their way to the door alone, and soon after eight the room was empty. No waiter served them; their meals were placed in readiness on a small buffet, and as No. 6 was veiled from the observations of the curious by a curtain which stretched across the passage, only Yeh Ling knew them.

On the first Monday of every month, Yeh Ling went up to the room and kow-towed to its solitary occupant. The old man was always alone on these occasions. On such a Monday, with a large lacquered cash-box in his hand and a fat book under his arm, Yeh Ling entered the presence of the man in No. 6, put down his impedimenta on the buffet, and did his reverence.

"Sit down," said Jesse Trasmere, and he spoke in the sibilant dialect of the lower provinces. Yeh Ling obeyed, hiding his hands respectfully in the full sleeves of his gown. "Well?"

"The profits this week have fallen, excellency," said Yeh Ling, but without apology. "The weather has been very fine and many of our clients are out of town."

He exposed his hands to open the cash-box and bring out four packages of paper money. These he divided into two, three of the packages to the right and one to the left. The old man took the three packages, which were nearest to him, and grunted.

"The police came last night and asked to be shown over the houses," Yeh Ling went on impassively. "They desired to see the cellars, because they think always that Chinamen have smoke-places in their cellars."

"Humph!" said Mr Trasmere. He was thumbing the money in his hand. "This is good, Yeh Ling."

He slipped the money into a black bag which was on the floor at his feet. Yeh Ling shook his head, thereby indicating his agreement.

"Do you remember in Fi Sang a man who worked for me?"

"The Drinker?"

The old man agreed to the appellation.

"He is coming to this country," said Mr Trasmere, chewing on a toothpick. He was a hard-faced man between sixty and seventy. A rusty black frock-coat ill fitted his spare form, his old-fashioned collar was frayed at the edge, and the black shoe-string tie that encircled his lean throat had been so long in use that it had lost whatever rigidity it had ever possessed, and hung limp in two tangled bunches on either side of the knot. His eyes were a hard granite blue, his face ridged and scaled with callosities until it was lizard-like in its coarseness.

"Yes, he is coming to this country. He will come here as soon as he finds his way about town, and that will be mighty soon, for Wellington Brown is a traveller! Yeh Ling, this man is troublesome. I should be happy if he were sleeping on the Terraces of the Night."

Again Yeh Ling shook his head.

"He cannot be killed – here," he said. "The illustrious knows that my hands are clean – "

"Are you a man-of-wild-mind?" snarled the other. "Do I kill men or ask that they should be killed? Even on the Amur, where life is cheap, I have done no more than put a man to the torture because he stole my gold. No, this Drinker must be made quiet. He smokes the pipe of the Pleasant Experience. You have no pipe-room. I would not tolerate such a thing. But you know places…"

"I know a hundred and a hundred," said Yeh Ling, cheerfully for him.

He accompanied his master to the door, and when it had closed upon him he returned swiftly to his parlour and summoned a stunted man of his race.

"Go after the old man and see that no harm comes to him," he said.

It seemed from his tone almost as though this guardianship was novel, but in exactly the same words the shuffling Chinaman had received identical instructions every day for six years when the thud of the closing street-door came to Yeh Ling's keen ears. Every day except Sunday.

He himself never went out after Jesse Trasmere. He had other duties, which commenced at eleven and usually kept him busy until the early hours of the morning.

2

Mr Trasmere walked steadily and at one pace, keeping to the more populous streets. Then at exactly 8.25 he turned into Peak Avenue, that wide and pleasant thoroughfare where his house was situated. A man who had been idling away a wasted half-hour saw him and crossed the road.

"Excuse me, Mr Trasmere."

Jesse shot a scowling glance at the interrupter of his reveries. The stranger was young and a head taller than the old man, well dressed, remarkably confident.

"Eh?"

"You don't remember me – Holland? I called upon you about a year ago over the trouble you had with the municipality."

Jesse's face cleared.

"The reporter? Yes, I remember you. You had an article in your rag that was all wrong, sir – all wrong! You made me say that I had a respect for municipal laws, and that's a lie! I have no respect for municipal laws or lawyers. They're thieves and grafters!"

He thumped the ferrule of his umbrella on the ground to emphasize his disapproval.

"I shouldn't be surprised," said the young man, with a cheerful smile; "and if I made you toss around a few bouquets, that was *faire bonne mine*. I'd forgotten anyway, but it is the job of an interviewer to make his subject look good."

"Well, what do you want?"

"Our correspondent in Pekin has sent us the original proclamation of the insurgent, General Wing Su – or Sing Wu, I'm not sure which. These Chinese names get me rattled."

Tab Holland produced from his pocket a sheet of yellow paper covered with strange characters.

"We can't get in touch with our interpreters, and knowing that you are a whale – an authority on the language, the news editor wondered if you would be so kind."

Jesse took the sheet reluctantly, gripped his bag between his knees,, and put on his glasses.

" 'Wing Su Shi, by the favour of heaven, humbly before his ancestors, speaks to all men of the Middle Kingdom…' " he began.

Tab, notebook in hand, wrote rapidly as the old man translated.

"Thank you, sir," he said when the other had finished.

There was an odd smirk of satisfaction on the old man's face, a strange, childlike pride in his accomplishment.

"You have a remarkable knowledge of the language," said Tab politely.

"Born there," replied Jesse Trasmere complacently: "born in a go-town on the Amur River and could speak the three dialects before I was six. Beat the whole lot of 'em at their own books when I was so high! That all, mister?"

"That is all, and thank you," said Tab gravely, and lifted his hat.

He stood looking after the old man as he continued his walk. So that was Rex Lander's miserly uncle? He did not look like a millionaire, and yet, when he came to consider the matter, millionaires seldom looked their wealth.

He had settled the matter of the Wing Su proclamation and was immersed in a new Prison Report which had been published that day when he remembered an item of news which had come his way, and duly reported.

"Sorry, Tab," said the night editor, "the theatre man has 'flu. Won't you go along and see the lady?"

Tab snorted, but went.

The dresser, hesitating, thought that Miss Ardfern was rather tired, and wouldn't tomorrow do?

"I'm tired, too," said Tab Holland wearily; "and tell Miss Ardfern that I haven't come to this darned theatre at eleven p.m. because I'm an autograph hunter, or because I'm collecting pictures of actresses I'm crazy about; I'm here in the sacred cause of publicity."

To the dresser, he was as a man who spoke a foreign language. Surveying him dubiously she turned the handle of the stained yellow door, and standing in the opening, talked to somebody invisible.

Tab had a glimpse of cretonne hangings, yawned, and scratched his head. He was not without elegance, except in moments of utter tiredness.

"You can come in," said the dresser, and Tab passed into a room that blazed with unshaded lights.

Ursula Ardfern had made her change and was ready to leave the theatre, except that her jacket was still hung on the back of one chair and her cloth cloak with the blue satin lining was draped over another. She had in her hand a brooch which she was about to put into an open jewel-case. Tab particularly noticed the brooch. A heart-shaped ruby was its centre piece. He saw her pin it to the soft lining of the lid and close the case.

"I'm extremely sorry to worry you at this hour of the night, Miss Ardfern," he said apologetically, "and if you're annoyed with me, you have my passionate sympathy. And if you're not mad at me, I'd be glad of a little sympathy myself, for I've been in court all day following the Lachmere fraud trial."

She had been a little annoyed. The set of her pretty face told him that when he came in.

"And now you've come for another trial," she half-smiled. "What can I do for you, Mr – ?"

"Holland – Somers Holland of *The Megaphone*. The theatre reporter is sick, and we got a rumour tonight from two independent sources that you are to be married."

"And you came to tell me! Now, isn't that kind of you!" she mocked. "No, I am not going to be married. I don't think I ever shall marry; but you needn't put that in the newspaper, or people will think I am posing as an eccentric. Who is the lucky man, by the way?"

"That is the identical question that I have come to ask," Tab smiled.

"I am disappointed." Her lips twitched. "But I am not marrying. Don't say that I am wedded to my art, because I'm not, and please don't say that there is an old boy and girl courtship that will one day materialize, because there isn't. I just know nobody that I ever wanted to marry, and if I did I shouldn't marry him. Is that all?"

"That's about all, Miss Ardfern," said Tab. "I'm really sorry to have troubled you. I always say that to people I trouble, but this time I mean it."

"How did this information reach you?" she asked as she rose.

Tab's frown was involuntary.

"From a – a friend of mine," he said. "It is the first piece of news that he has ever given to me, and it is wrong. Good night, Miss Ardfern." His hand gripped hers, and she winced.

"I'm sorry!" He was all apologies and confusion.

"You're very strong!" she smiled, rubbing her hand, "and you aren't very well acquainted with us fragile women – didn't you say your name is Holland? Are you 'Tab' Holland?"

Tab coloured. It wasn't like Tab to feel, much less display, embarrassment.

"Why 'Tab'?" she asked, her blue eyes dancing.

"It is an office nickname," he explained awkwardly; "the boys say that I've a passion for making my exit on a good line…really, I believe it is the line on which the curtain falls…you'll understand that, Miss Ardfern, it is one of the conventions of the drama."

"A tab-line?" she said. "I have heard about you. I remember now. It was a man who was in the company I played with – Milton Braid."

"He was a reporter before he fell – before he went on the stage," said Tab.

He was not a theatre man and knew none of its disciples. This was the second actress he had met in his twenty-six years of life, and she was unexpectedly human. That she was also remarkably pretty he accepted without surprise. Actresses ought to be beautiful, even Ursula Ardfern, who was a great actress if he accepted the general verdict of the press and the ecstatic and prejudiced opinion of Rex Lander. But she had a sense of humour; a curious possession in an emotional actress, if he could believe all that he had read on the subject. She had grace and youth and naturalness. He would willingly have stayed, but she was unmistakably ending the interview.

"Good night, Mr Holland."

He took her hand again, this time more gingerly, and she laughed outright at his caution.

On the dressing-table was the small brown jewel-case and a glimpse of it reminded him:

"If there is anything you'd like to go in *The Megaphone*," he floundered – "there was a paragraph in the paper about your having more wonderful jewels than any other woman on the stage…"

He was being unaccountably gauche; he knew this and hated himself. It did not need her quick smile to tell him that she did not wish for that kind of publicity. And then the smile vanished, leaving her young face strangely hard.

"No… I don't think that my jewels and their value are very interesting. In the part I am playing now it is necessary to wear a great deal of jewellery – I wish it weren't. Good night. I'm glad to upset the rumour."

"I'm sorry for the bridegroom," said Tab gallantly.

She watched him out of the room, and her mind was still intent upon this broad-shouldered towering young man when her dresser came in.

"I do wish, miss, you hadn't to carry those diamonds about with you," said the sad-faced dresser. "Mr Stark, the treasurer, said he would put them in the theatre safe for you – and there's a night watchman."

"Mr Stark told me that too," said the girl quietly, "but I prefer to take them with me. Help me with my coat, Simmons."

A few minutes later she passed through the stage-door. A small and handsome little car was drawn up opposite the door. It was closed and empty. She passed through the little crowd that had gathered to see her depart, stepped inside, placed the jewel-case on the floor at her feet, and started the machine. The doorman saw it glide round the corner and went back to his tiny office.

Tab also saw the car depart. He grinned at himself for his whimsical and freakish act. If anybody had told him that he would wait at a stage-door for the pleasure of catching a glimpse of a popular actress, he would have been rude. Yet here he was, a furtive and abashed man, so ashamed of his weakness that he must look upon her from the darkest corner of the street!

"Well, well," said Tab with a sigh, "we live and learn."

His flat was in Doughty Street, and stopping only to telephone the result of the interview, he made his way home.

As he came into the sitting-room a man some two years his junior looked up over the top of the armchair in which he was huddled.

"Well?" he asked eagerly.

Tab went over to a large tobacco jar and filled his polished briar before he spoke.

"Is it true?" asked Rex Lander impatiently; "what a mysterious brute you are!"

"Rex, you're related to the Canards of Duckville," said the other, puffing solemnly. "You're a spreader of false tidings and a creator of alarm and despondency amongst the stage-door lizards – whose ancient fraternity I have this night joined, thanks to you."

Rex relaxed his strained body into a more easy and even less graceful posture.

"Then she isn't going to be married?" he said with a sigh.

"You meant well," said Tab, flopping into a chair, "and I know of no worse thing that you can say about a man than that he 'meant well'! But it isn't true. She's not going to be married. Where did you get hold of this story, Babe?"

"I heard it," said the other vaguely.

He was a boyish-looking young man with a pink-and-white complexion. His face was so round and cherubic that the appellation of "Babe" had good excuse, for he was plump of person and lazy of habit. They had been school-fellows, and when Rex had come to town at the command of his one relative, his uncle, the sour Mr Jesse Trasmere, to take up a torturous training as an architect, these two had gravitated together and now shared Tab's small flat.

"What do you think of her?"

Tab thought before replying.

"She's certainly handicapped with good looks," he said cautiously. At another time he would have added a word of disparagement or would have spoken jokingly of Rex Lander's intense interest in the lady, but now, for some reason, he treated the other's inquiry with more seriousness than was his wont.

Ursula Ardfern stood for the one consistently successful woman management in town. Despite her youth she had chosen and cast her own plays, and in four seasons had not known the meaning of the word failure.

"She's quite…charming," Tab said. "Of course I felt a fool; interviewing actresses is off my beat anyway. Who is the letter from?" He glanced up at the envelope propped on the mantelpiece.

"From Uncle Jesse," said the other without looking up from his book. "I wrote to him, asking him if he would lend me fifty."

"And he said? – I saw him today by the way."

"Read it," invited Rex Lander with a grin.

Tab took down the envelope and extracted a thick sheet of paper written in a crabbed school-boy hand.

"DEAR REX" (he read). "Your quarterly allowance is not due until the twenty-first. I regret, therefore, that I cannot agree to your request. You must live more economically, remembering that when you inherit my money you will be thankful for the experience which economical living has given to you and which will enable you to employ the great wealth which will be yours, in a more judicious, far-seeing manner."

"He's a miserable old skinflint," said Tab, tossing the letter back to the mantelshelf. "Somebody was telling me the other day that he's worth a million – where did he make it?"

Rex shook his head.

"In China, I think. He was born there, and started in quite a humble way as a trader on the Amur River Goldfields. Then he bought property on which gold was discovered. I don't know," he said, scratching his chin, "that I ought to complain. After all, there may be a lot in all he says, and he has been a good friend of mine."

"How often have you seen him?"

"I spent a week with him last year," said Rex, with a little grimace at the memory. "Still," he hastened to add, "I owe him a lot. It may be if I wasn't such a lazy slug and didn't like expensive things, I could live within my income."

Tab pulled at his pipe in silence. Presently he said:

"There are all sorts of rumours about old Jesse Trasmere. A fellow told me the other day that he is a known miser; keeps his money in the house, which of course is a romantic lie."

"He hasn't a banking account," said the other surprisingly, "and I happen to know that he does keep a very large sum of money at Mayfield. The house is built like a prison, and it has an underground strongroom which is the strongest room of its kind. I have never seen it, but I have seen him go down to it. Whether or not he sits down and gloats over his pieces of eight, I have never troubled to discover. But it is perfectly true, Tab," he said earnestly, "he has no banking account. Everything is paid out in cash. I suppose he does have transactions through banks, but I have never heard of them. As to his being a miser" – he hesitated – "well, he is not exactly generous. For example, six months ago he discovered that the man and his wife who looked after Mayfield, which is a very small house, were in the habit of giving the pieces of food left over to one of their poorer relatives, and he fired them on the spot! When I was there this year, he was shutting up all the rooms except his own bedroom and his dining-room, which he uses also as a study."

"What does he do for servants?" asked Tab, and the other shook his head.

"He has his valet, Walters, and two women who come in every day, one to cook and one to clean. But for the cook he has built a small kitchen away from the house."

"He must be a cheerful companion," said Tab.

"He is not exactly exhilarating. He has a fresh cook every month. I met Walters the other day and he told me that the new cook is the best they've had," admitted the other, and there followed a silent interval of nearly five minutes.

Then Tab got up and knocked the ashes from his pipe.

"She certainly is pretty," he said, and Rex Lander looked at him suspiciously, for he knew that Tab was not talking about the cook.

3

Mr Jesse Trasmere sat at the end of a long, and, except in his immediate vicinity, bare table. At his end it was laid, and Mr Trasmere was slowly and deliberately enjoying a lean cutlet.

The room gave no suggestion of immense wealth and paid no silent tribute either to his artistic taste or his acquaintance with China. The walls were innocent of pictures, the furniture old, European, and shabby. Mr Trasmere had bought it second-hand and had never ceased to boast of the bargain he had secured.

If there were no pictures, there were no books. Jesse Trasmere was not a reader, even of newspapers.

It was one o'clock in the afternoon, and through the folds of his dressing-gown the grey of his pyjama jacket showed open at his lean throat, for Mr Trasmere had only just got out of bed. Presently he would dress in his rusty black suit and would be immensely wakeful until the dawn of tomorrow. He never went to bed until the grey showed in the sky, nor slept later than two o'clock in the afternoon.

At six-thirty, to the second, Walters, his valet, would assist him into his overcoat, a light one if it was warm, a heavy fur-lined garment if it was cold, and Mr Trasmere would go for his walk and transact whatever business he found to his hand. But before he left the house there was a certain ceremonial – the locking of doors, the banishment of the valet to his own quarters, and the disappearance of Mr Trasmere through the door which led from his study-dining-room to the basement of the house. This done he would go out. Walters had watched him from one of the upper windows scores of times, walking slowly down the street, an unfurled umbrella on one hand, a black bag in another. At eight-thirty to the minute he was back in the house. He invariably dined out. Walters would bring him a cup of black coffee, and at ten o'clock would retire to his own room, which was separated from the main building by a heavy door which Mr Trasmere invariably locked.

Once in the early days of his service Walters had expostulated.

"Suppose there is a fire, sir," he complained.

"You can get through your bathroom window on to the kitchen, and if you can't drop to the ground from there you deserve to be burnt to death," snarled the old man. "If you don't like the job, you needn't stay. Those are the rules of my establishment, and there are no others."

So, night after night, Walters had gone to his room and Mr Trasmere had shuffled after him in his slippered feet, had banged and locked the door upon him and had left Walters to solitude.

This procedure was only altered when the old man was taken ill one night and was unable to reach the door. Thereafter a key was hung in a small glass-fronted case, in very much the same way as fire-keys are hung. In the event of his illness, or of any other unexpected happening, Walters could secure the key and answer the bell above his bed-head. That necessity had not arisen.

Every morning the valet found the door unlocked. At what hour old Jesse came he could not discover, but he guessed that his employer stopped on his way to bed in the morning to perform this service.

Walters was never allowed an evening off. Two days a week he was given twenty-four hours' leave of absence, but he had to be in the house by ten.

"And if you are a minute later, don't come back," said Jesse Trasmere.

As the old man's valet Walters had exceptional opportunities for discovering something more about his master than Mr Trasmere would care to have known. He was for a very particular reason anxious to know what the basement contained. Once he had met a man who had been engaged in the building of the house, and learnt that there was a room below, built of concrete; but though he had, with the greatest care and discretion, searched for keys which might, during the daily absence of his employer, reveal the secret of this underground room, he had never succeeded in laying his hand upon them. Mr Trasmere had apparently only one key, a master-key, which he wore round his neck at night, and in the same inaccessible position in his clothing during the daytime, and Walters' search had been in vain, until one morning, when taking Mr Trasmere his shaving-water, the servant found him suffering from one of those fainting fits which periodically overcame him. There was a cake of soap handy, and Walters was a resourceful man…

Mr Trasmere looked up from his plate and fixed his servant with his grey-blue eyes.

"Has anybody called this morning?"

"No, sir."

"Have any letters come?"

"Only a few. They are on your desk, sir."

Mr Trasmere grunted.

"Did you put the notice in the paper that I was leaving town for two or three days?" he asked.

"Yes, sir," said Walters.

Jesse Trasmere grunted again.

"A man is coming from China; I don't want to see him," he explained. He was oddly communicative at moments to his servant, but Walters, who knew his master extremely well, did not make the mistake of asking questions. 'No, I don't want to see him.' The old man chewed a toothpick reflectively, and his unattractive face bore an expression of distaste. "He was a partner of mine, twenty, thirty years ago, a card-playing, gambling, drinking man, who gave himself airs because – well, never mind what he gave himself airs about," he said impatiently, as though he anticipated a question which he should have known never would have been put to him. "He was that kind of man."

He stared at the fireless grate with its red brick walls and its microscopic radiator and clicked his lips.

"If he comes, he is not to be admitted. If he asks questions, you're not to answer. You know nothing…about anybody. Why he's coming at all…well, that doesn't matter. He's just trash, a soakin' dope. He had his chance, got under it, and went to sleep. Phew! That fellow! He might have been rich, but he sold all his shares. A soak! Rather drink than sit in the Empress of China's council…she's dead. White trash… nothing…h'm."

He glared up of a sudden and asked harshly:

"Why the hell are you listening?"

"Sorry, sir, I thought – "

"Get out!"

"Yes, sir," said Walters with alacrity.

For half an hour old Jesse Trasmere sat where the valet had left him, the red end of his toothpick leaping up and down eccentrically. Then he got up and, going to an old-fashioned bureau, opened the glass front.

He brought to the table a shallow bowl of white porcelain half filled with Indian ink. His second visit to the secretaire produced a thick pad of paper. It was unusually large, and its texture of a peculiar character. From an open-work iron box he took a long-handled brush, and sitting down again dipped the fine point into the ink.

Another long interval of inaction and he commenced to write, beginning at the top right-hand corner and working down the page. The grotesque and intricate Chinese characters appeared with magic rapidity. He finished one column and commenced another, and so until the page was covered except for two spaces beneath the last and the penultimate line.

Laying down the brush he felt, with the slow deliberation of age, in his right-hand waistcoat pocket and pulled out an ivory cylinder as big and round as a large pencil. He slipped one end out and pressed it on the paper. When he took the stamp away there appeared within a red circle two Chinese characters. This was Jesse Trasmere's "hong," his sign manual; a thousand merchants from Shanghai to Fi Chen would honour cheques which bore that queer mark, and those for startling sums.

When the paper was dry he folded it into a small compass and getting up, went to the empty fireplace. Outside on the stairs a deeply interested Walters craned his neck to see what happened. From his position, and through the fanlight above the door, he commanded a view of at least a third of the room. But now Jesse had passed out of sight, and although he stretched himself perilously he could not see what was happening. Only, when the old man reappeared the paper was no longer in his hand.

He touched a bell, and Walters came at once.

"Remember," he rasped, "I am not at home – to anybody!"

"Very good, sir," said Walters, a little impatiently.

Mr Trasmere had gone out that afternoon when the visitor called.

It was unfortunate for the old man's scheme that the China mail had made a record voyage and had arrived thirty-six hours ahead of her scheduled time. Mr Trasmere was not a reader of newspapers, or he would have learnt the fact in that morning's paper.

Walters answered the bell after some delay, for he was busily engaged in his own room on a matter that was entirely private to himself, and when he did answer the tinkling summons it was to find a brown-faced stranger standing on the broad step. He was dressed in an old suit which did not fit him, his linen was stained, and his boots were patched, but his manner would not have been out of place in Lorenzo the Magnificent.

With his hands thrust into his trousers pockets, his soiled soft hat on the back of his head, he met the inquiring and deferential gaze of Walters with a calm and insolent stare, for Mr Brown was rather drunk.

"Well, well, my man," he said impatiently, "why the devil do you keep me waiting on the doorstep of my friend Jesse's house, eh?" He removed one of his hands from his pocket, possibly not the cleanest one, and tugged at his short grey beard.

"Mr – er – Mr Trasmere is out," said Walters, "I will tell him you have called. What name, sir?"

"Wellington Brown is my name, good fellow," said the stranger. "Wellington Brown from Chei-feu. I will come in and wait."

But Walters barred the way.

"Mr Trasmere has given me strict orders not to admit anybody unless he is in the house," he said.

A wave of anger turned Wellington Brown's face to a deeper red.

"He has given orders!" he spluttered. "That I am not to be admitted – I, Wellington Brown, who made his fortune, the swindling old thief! He knows I am coming!"

"Are you from China, sir?" blurted Walters.

"I have told you, menial and boot-licking yellow-plush, that I am from Chei-feu. If you are illiterate, as you appear to be, I will explain to you that Chei-feu is in China."

"I don't care whether Chei-feu is in China or on the moon," said Walters obstinately. "You can't come in, Mr Brown! Mr Trasmere is away – he'll be away for a fortnight."

"Oh, won't I come in!"

The struggle was a brief one, for Walters was a man of powerful physique, and Wellington Brown was a man nearer sixty than fifty. He was flung against the stone wall of the porch and might, in his bemused condition, have fallen had not Walters' quick hand grabbed him back.

The stranger breathed noisily.

"I've killed men for that," he said jerkily, "shot 'em down like dogs! I'll remember this, flunkey!"

"I didn't want to hurt you," said Walters, aggrieved that any onus for the unpleasantness should rest on him.

The stranger raised his hand haughtily.

"I will settle accounts with your master – remember that, lackey! He shall pay, by God!"

With drunken dignity he walked unsteadily through the patch of garden that separated the house from the road, leaving Walters a puzzled man.

4

At nine o'clock that night the bell of Tab Holland's flat rang long and noisily.

"Who the dickens is that?" he growled.

He was in his shirt-sleeves, writing for dear life, and the table was strewn with proofs of his industry.

Rex Lander came out of his bedroom.

"Your boy, I expect," he said; "I left the lower door open for him."

Tab shook his head.

"The office is sending for the copy at eleven," he said; "see who it is, Babe."

Mr Lander grumbled. He always grumbled when he was called upon for physical effort. He opened the door, and Tab, hearing a loud and unfamiliar voice, joined him. On the landing without was a bearded, swaying figure, and he was talking noisily.

"What is wrong?" asked Tab.

"Everything, sir," hiccupped the caller, "everything is wrong. A man, a gentleman cannot be robbed with impunity or assaulted by me – menials with – with," he considered a moment and added: "impunity."

"Bring him in, the poor soused herring," said Tab, and Mr Wellington Brown swaggered and staggered into the sitting-room. He was abominably intoxicated.

"Wish of you young gen'lemen is Rex Lander?"

"That is my name," said the puzzled Rex.

"I'm… Wellington Brown of Chei-feu. A pensioner at the mercy of a dam' ol' scoundrel! A perision'r! He pays me a pittance out of what he robbed me. I can tell you some'n about ol' Trasmere…"

"Trasmere, my uncle?" asked the startled young man.

The other nodded gravely and sleepily.

"I can tell you some'n about him. I was his book…keeper 'n sec'tary. I know! I'll tell you some'n about him!"

"You can save your breath," said Rex coldly. "Why have you come here?"

"Because you're's nephew. Thas why! He robbed me…robbed me!" he sobbed. "Took bread out the mouth of innocent child…thas what! Took bread out 'f orphan's mouth and robbed me, swin'led me out of my share Mancurian Trading Syn'cate, an' then gave me remittance 'n said, 'Dring yerself to death' – thas what he said!"

"And did you?" asked Tab sardonically.

The stranger eyed him unfavourably.

"Who's this?" he demanded.

"This is a friend of mine," said Rex, "and you're in his flat. And if the only business you have is to abuse my uncle, you can get out just as soon as you like."

Mr Wellington Brown tapped the young man's chest with a grimy forefinger.

"Your uncle is a rascal! Get that! A low thief!"

"Better write and tell him so," said Tab briskly; "just now I am engaged in churning out two yards of journalese, and you're disturbing my thoughts."

"Write to him!" roared Mr Brown delightedly; "write to him! Thas good…best thing I've heard for years! Why – !"

"Get out!"

Babe Lander threw open the door with a crash, and the visitor glared at him.

"Like ungle, like nephew," he said, "like nephew, like lackey… I'm goin'. And let me tell you – "

The door slammed in his face.

"Phew!" said Babe, wiping his brow. "Let's open the window and let in some fresh air!"

"Who is he?"

"Search me," said Rex Lander. "I've no illusions about Uncle Jesse's early friends. I gather that he's been a pensioner of the old boy's, and there is probably some truth in his charge that he was robbed. I cannot imagine uncle giving money away from charitable motives. Anyway, I'm seeing him tomorrow, and I'll ask."

"You'll see nothing," said Tab. "Do you ever read the fashionable intelligence or society news? Uncle is leaving town tomorrow."

Rex smiled.

"That is an old trick when he doesn't want to be seen – by Joab! It is the Wellington who has put his name in the society column!"

Tab paused, pen in hand.

"Silence will now reign," he commanded, "whilst a great journalist deals adequately with the Milligan Murder Appeal."

Rex looked at him admiringly.

"How you can stick your nose at the grindstone is a source of wonder to me," he said. "I couldn't – "

"Shut up!" snapped Tab, and the desirable silence was his. He finished the last page at eleven, sent off his copy by a punctual messenger, then filling his pipe, stretched himself luxuriously in his mission chair.

"Now I'm a free man until Monday afternoon – "

The hall telephone signalled at that moment, and he got up with a groan.

"Boast not!" he growled. "That is the office or I'm a saint!"

It was the office, as he had so intelligently foreseen. He snapped a few words at the transmitter and came back to the room. And Tab was very voluble.

A Polish gentleman concerned in certain frauds on insurance companies had been arrested, escaped again, and having barricaded himself in his house, was keeping the police at bay with the aid of boiling water and a large axe.

"Jacko is enthusiastic about it," said the savage Tab, speaking thus disrespectfully of his city editor; "says it is real drama – I told him to send the dramatic critic. Gosh! I did his job the other night."

"Going out?" asked Rex with mild interest.

"Of course I'm going out, you thick-headed jibberer!" said the other unkindly as he struggled into the collar he had discarded.

"I thought all that sort of stuff was invented in the office," said the young architect monstrously. "Personally I never believe what I read in newspapers…"

But Tab had gone.

At midnight he joined a little group of police officers that stood at safe range from the besieged house, whose demented occupant had found a shotgun. Tab was with them until the door of the house was stormed and the defender borne down and clubbed to a state of placidity.

At two o'clock in the morning, he and Carver, the chief of the detectives engaged in the case, adjourned to the police mess and had supper. It was half-past three and the streets were lit by the ghostly light of dawn when he started to walk home.

Passing through Park Street, he heard the whirr of wheels and a motor-car flew past him. It had gone a hundred yards when there came to him the explosion of a burst tyre. He saw the car swerve and stop. A woman alighted and examined the damage. Apparently she was alone, for he saw her open the tool-box on the running-board and take out a jack. He hastened his footsteps and crossed to the middle of the road. The only other person in sight was a cyclist down the road who had dismounted and was examining his wheel.

"Can I be of any assistance?" asked Tab.

The woman started and turned.

"Miss Ardfern!" he said, in astonishment.

For a second she seemed uncomfortable, and then with a quick smile: "It is… Mr Tab! Please forgive the familiarity, I cannot remember your other name."

"Don't try," he said, taking the jack from her hands; "but if you are very anxious to remember, I am called Holland."

She said nothing whilst he was raising the car. When he was knocking the torn wheel free, she said: "I was out rather late; I have been to a party."

There was light enough for him to see that she was dressed very plainly and that the shoes she wore were heavy and serviceable. He would have gone farther and said that she was dressed poorly. Inside the car on the seat by her side was a square black case, smaller but deeper than a suitcase. Perhaps she had changed her clothes – but for all their surprising agility in this direction, actresses do not change their clothes to go home from a party.

"I have been to a party too," he said, jerking off the wheel and rolling it to the front of the car: "a surprise party, with fireworks."

"A dance?"

Tab smiled to himself.

"I only danced once," he said. "I saw the gentleman taking aim with the shotgun and danced right merrily, yo ho!"

He heard the quick intake of her breath.

"Oh yes…it was the Pole. We heard the shots and I knew that he had taken refuge in his house before I left the theatre."

The wheel was replaced now, the tools returned, and the old wheel strapped to the car.

"That is OK," said Tab, stepping back. "Oh no, it was nothing," he said hastily as she began to thank him, "nothing at all."

She did not offer to drive him home. He rather hoped that she would; indeed, her method of going was a little precipitate, and she was out of sight before he realized that she was gone.

What on earth was she doing at that time in the morning, he wondered? A party she had said, but again it occurred to him that fashionable actresses did not go to parties in that kind of outfit.

Rex was awake when he reached home and came out to him. Strangely enough, although they discussed the happenings of the night, Tab did not mention his meeting with Ursula Ardfern.

5

"Ursula Ardfern." Tab woke with the words on his lips. The hour was eleven, and Rex had been out and was back again.

"L'ami de mon oncle has been – did you hear him?" asked Rex, stopping his towel-encompassed companion on his way to the bathroom.

"Who – Bonaparte?"

"Wellington is his name, I believe. Yes, he came rather subdued and apologetic, but full of horrific threats toward Uncle Jesse. I turned him out."

"Why did he come?"

Rex Lander shook his head.

"Heaven knows! Unless it was that he simply had to find somebody who knew uncle well enough to be interested in hearing him curse the old man. I've persuaded him to leave town until the end of next week. But I must say that I was impressed by the brute's threats. He says he will kill Uncle Jesse unless he makes reparation."

"Twiff!" said Tab contemptuously, and went to his tub. Over his breakfast (Rex had had his two hours before) he returned to the subject of Mr Jesse Trasmere and his enemy.

"When a man soaks he's dangerous," he said. "There isn't any such thing as a harmless drunkard, any more than there is a harmless lunatic. Carver and I had a talk on the matter early this morning, and he agreed. That man is certainly intelligent, which is more than you can say of the majority of detectives, poor fellows; they are the victims of a system which calls for a sixty-nine-inch brain."

"Eh?"

"A sixty-nine-inch brain," explained Tab, and there was really no excuse for Babe Lander to be puzzled, for Tab was on his favourite topic, "is the brain of a man who is chosen for the subtle business of criminal investigation; not because he is clever or shrewd or has a knowledge of the world, but because he stands sixty-nine inches in his stockings and has a chest expansion to thirty-eight. Funny, isn't it? And yet detectives are chosen that way. They have to strip hard, very hard, but they need not think very hard. Do you ever realize that Napoleon and Julius Caesar, to mention only two bright lads, could never have got into the police force?"

"It hasn't struck me before," admitted Rex. "But I've never had any doubt as to the size of your brain, Tab."

There were exactly seventy inches of Tab, though he did not look so tall, having thickness and breadth to his shoulders. He had a habit of stooping, which made him seem round-shouldered. This trick came from pounding a typewriter or crouching over a desk which was just a little too low for him. He was fresh-coloured, but brown rather than pink. His face was finer drawn than is usual in a man of his build, his eyes deep-set and steadfastly grey. When he spoke he drawled a little. Those who knew him very well indeed detected one imperfection of speech. He could not say "very" – it was "vethy," but spoken so quickly that only the trained and acquainted ear could detect the lisp.

He came to journalism from one of the Universities, bringing no particular reputation for learning, but universally honoured as the best three-quarter back of his time. Without being rich he was comfortably placed, and as he was one of those fortunates who had innumerable maiden-aunts he received on an average one legacy a year, though he had studiously neglected them because of their possessions.

It would be more true to say that Tab leapt into journalism, and to that peculiar department of journalism which he found most fascinating, when he dived off the end of a river pier and rescued Jasper Dorgon, the defaulting banker who had tried to commit suicide, and had extracted an exclusive story from the banker whilst both sat in a state of nudity before a night watchman's fire watching their clothes dry.

"Let it strike you now, Babe," he said. "The sixty-nine-inch brain, the generally accepted theory that anything under the sixty-nine-inch level is solid ivory, is the theory that keeps Lew Vann and old Joe Haspinell and similar crook acquaintances of mine dining in the Grand Criterion when they ought to be atoning for their sins in the Cold Stone Jug. But Carver is a good man. He thinks, though it is against regulations."

"What does he think about Wellington?"

"Didn't tell him," said Tab. "You ought to warn your uncle."

"I'll see him today," nodded Rex.

They went out together before the lunch hour. Tab had a call to make at the office and afterwards he was meeting Carver for lunch. Carver, a lanky and slow-speaking man, was ordinarily no conversationalist. On some subjects he was impressively interesting, and as Tab provided the subject, two hours slipped away very quickly. Before they left the restaurant, Tab told him of the drunken stranger and his threats against Jesse Trasmere.

"I don't worry about threats," said Carver, "but a man with a grievance, and especially a Number One grievance like this man has, is pretty certain to cause trouble. Do you know old Trasmere?"

"I've seen him twice. I was once sent to his house to make an inquiry about an action that the municipality started against him for building without the town architect's permission. Rex Lander, who is a kindergarten architect by the way, and rooms with me, is his nephew, and I've heard a whole lot about him. He writes to Rex from time to time; letters full of good advice about saving money."

"Lander is his heir?"

"Rex hopes so, fervently. But he says it is just as likely that Uncle Jesse will leave his money to a Home for the Incurably Wealthy. Talking of Trasmere, there goes his valet, and he seems in a hurry."

A cab dashed past them, its solitary passenger was Walters, a pinch-faced man, bareheaded, and on his face a tense, haggard look that immediately arrested the attention of the two men.

"Who did you say that was?" asked Carver quickly.

"Walters – old Trasmere's servant," replied Tab; "looks pretty scared to me."

"Walters?" The detective stood stock still, thinking. "I know that man's face… I've got him! Walter Felling!"

"Walter who?"

"Felling – he was through my hands ten years ago, and he has been convicted since. Walters, as you call him, is an incorrigible thief! Old Trasmere's servant, eh? That's his speciality. He takes service with rich people, and one fine morning they wake up to find their loose jewellery and money and plate gone. Did you notice the number of the cab?"

Tab shook his head.

"The question is," said the detective, "has he made a getaway in a hurry, or is he on an urgent errand for his boss? Anyway we ought to see Trasmere. Shall we take a cab or walk?"

"Walk," said Tab promptly. "Only the detectives of fiction take cabs, Carver. The real people know that when they present their cab bills to the head office a soulless clerk will question each item."

"Tab, you certainly know more about the interior economy of thief-catching than an outsider ought to know," responded the detective gloomily.

Between them and Trasmere's house was the better part of a mile. Mayfield, the dwelling-place of old Jesse, was the one ugly building in a road which was famous for the elegance of its houses. Built of hideously yellow brick, without any ornamentation, it stood squat and square in the middle of a cemented "garden." Three microscopic circles of earth had been left at the urgent request of the builder, wherein Mr Jesse might, if he so desired, win from the sickly earth such blooms and blossoms as might delight his eye. To this he reluctantly agreed, but only after there had been pointed out to him the fact that such an alteration to his plans would save a little money.

"It isn't exactly the Palace of the Fairy Prince, is it?" said Tab, as he pushed open the cast-iron gate.

"I've seen prettier houses," admitted Carver. "I wonder – "

So far he got when the front door was flung violently open and Rex Lander rushed out. His face was the colour of chalk, his big baby eyes were staring wildly. They fell upon the two men on the concrete walk, and his mouth opened to speak, but no words came.

Tab ran to him.

"What is wrong?" he demanded, and that something was badly wrong one glance at Babe Lander told him.

"My uncle…" he gasped. "Go…look…"

Carver rushed into the house and through the open door of the dining-room. It was empty, but at the side of the fireplace was a narrower door.

"Where is he?" asked the detective.

Rex could only point to the narrow aperture.

There was a flight of stone stairs which terminated in a narrow passage, barred by yet another door, which was also open. The corridor was well lighted by three globes set at intervals in the ceiling, and the acrid smell of exploded cordite filled the confined space of the passage, which was empty.

"There must be a room opening from here," said Carver. "Whose are these?"

He stooped and picked up an old pair of gloves that lay on the floor and pushed them into his pocket.

He looked round for Rex Lander. That young man was sitting on the top step of the stairs, his face in his hands.

"There's no sense in questioning him," said Carver in an undertone, "where is his uncle?"

Tab walked rapidly down the passage and came to a door on the left. It was a narrow door, painted black and deeply recessed in the thick wall. There was no handle, and only a tiny keyhole. Four inches from its top was a steel plate pierced with small holes for the purpose of ventilation. He pushed the door, but it was locked. Then he peered through the ventilator.

He saw a vault which he guessed was about ten feet long by eight feet wide. Fixed to the rough walls were a number of steel shelves, loaded up with black iron boxes. A brilliant light came from a globe in the vaulted roof, and he saw plainly.

At the farther end of the room was a plain table, but it was not at this he was looking, but at the figure crouched against one of its legs. The face was turned in his direction.

It was the face of Jesse Trasmere, and he was dead.

6

Tab gave way to the detective and waited whilst Carver looked.

"There's no sign of a weapon – but by the smell there has been some shooting," he said. "What is that on the table?"

Tab peered through the ventilator.

"It looks like a key to me," he said.

They tried the door, but it resisted their combined weight. "The door is much too thick and the lock too strong for us to force," said Carver at last. "I'll telephone headquarters, Tab. See what you can get out of your friend."

"I don't think he'll tell me much for some time. Come along, Babe," said Tab kindly, taking the other's arm. "Let's get out of this beastly atmosphere."

Unresisting, Rex Lander allowed himself to be led back to the dining-room, where he dropped into a chair.

Carver had finished his telephoning and had returned long before Rex had recovered sufficiently to give a coherent narrative. His face was blanched, he could not control his quivering lips, and it was a considerable time before he could tell his patient hearers all that he knew.

"I came to the house this afternoon by appointment," he said. "My uncle had written to me asking me to see him about an application which I had made to him for a loan. He had previously rejected my request, but, as had often happened, he relented at the last moment, for he was not a bad man at heart. As I was pressing the bell the door opened, and I saw Walters – Walters is my uncle's valet."

The detective nodded.

"He looked terribly agitated, and he had a brown leather bag in his hand. 'I am just going out, Mr Lander,' he said – "

"Did he seem surprised to see you?"

"He seemed alarmed," said Rex. "It struck me when I saw him that my uncle must be ill, and I asked him if anything was the matter. He said that uncle was well, but he had sent him on a very important errand. The conversation did not last more than a minute, for Walters ran down the steps into the road before I could recover from my amazement."

"He wore no hat?" asked Carver.

Rex shook his head.

"I stood in the hall for a moment, knowing that my uncle does not like people to come in upon him unless they are properly announced. You see, Mr Carver, the situation was rather a delicate one for me. I had come here in the rôle of a suppliant, and naturally I did not wish to prejudice my chance of getting the fifty which my uncle had promised me. I went to uncle's living-room, but he was not there; but the door which I knew led to the strongroom was open and he could not be far away. I sat down and waited. I must have been there ten minutes, and then I began to smell something burning, as I thought, but which was, in fact, the smell of gunpowder, or whatever they use in cartridges, and I was so thoroughly alarmed that I went down the steps and after a little hesitation, knowing how my uncle hated being overlooked, I went on to the door of the vault. It was locked, and I rapped on the ventilator but had no reply. Then I peeped through. It was horrible," he shuddered. "As fast as I could I ran up the stairs into the street, intending to call a policeman, and I saw you."

"Whilst you were in the house you heard no sound to suggest that there was anybody else present? Where are the servants?"

"There is only the cook," said Rex, and Carver went in search of her.

But the kitchen was closed and deserted. It was apparently the cook's day off.

"I'll make a search of the house," said Carver. "Come along, Tab, you are in this case now and you had better stay with it."

The search did not take a very long time. There were two rooms used by Mr Trasmere, the remainder were locked up and apparently unused. A passageway led to Walters' sleeping apartment, which had originally been designed as a guest-room and was larger than servants' quarters usually are. The room was meagrely furnished and there was evidence that Mr Walters had not anticipated so hurried a flight. Some of his clothing hung on pegs behind the door, others were found in a wardrobe, whilst a cup filled with coffee stood on the table. Carver dipped his little finger into the liquid. It was still warm.

A cloth had been thrown hurriedly over some bulky object at one end of the table, and this the detective removed. He whistled. Clamped to the edge of the table was a small vice and scattered about were a number of files and other tools. Carver turned the screw of the vice and released the object in its grip. It was a small key of peculiar shape, and the man must have been working upon it recently, for steel filings covered the base of the tool.

"Then friend Walters was making a key," said Carver. "Look at that plaster cast! That is an old dodge of his. I suppose he got an impression of the key on soap or wax and has been working at it ever since." He looked at the thing in his palm, curiously. "This may save us a great deal of trouble," he said, "for unless I am mistaken this is the key of the strongroom."

A few minutes later the house was filled with detectives, police photographers, and coroner's officers. They came on a useless errand, for the door remained locked. Tab took advantage of their arrival to escort his friend home.

Before he went Carver drew him aside.

"We shall have to keep in touch with Mr Lander," he said. "He may be able to throw a great deal of light upon this murder. In the meantime I have sent out all station calls to pull in Felling – who is Wellington Brown?"

"Wellington Brown? That is the man who has been threatening Trasmere – I told you about him at lunch."

Carver pulled an old pair of gloves from his pocket.

"Mr Wellington Brown was in that underground corridor," he said quietly, "and was sufficiently indiscreet to leave his gloves behind – his name is written inside!"

"You will charge him with the murder?" asked Tab, and Carver nodded.

"I think so. Either he or Walters. At any rate we shall hold them on suspicion, but I cannot be more definite until we've got inside that vault."

Tab escorted his friend to the flat, and leaving him, hurried back to Mayfield, by which fanciful name Trasmere had called his grim house.

"We've found no weapon of any kind," said the detective, whom Tab found sitting in Trasmere's dining-room with a plan of the house before him. "Maybe it is in the vault, in which event it looks like a case of suicide. I have been on the telephone with the boss of Mortimers, the builders. They say that there is only one key in existence for that vault – I was speaking to Mr Mortimer himself, and he knows. Trasmere made a special point about the lock, and had twenty or thirty manufactured by different locksmiths. Nobody knows which one he used, and Mortimer says that the orders were so imperative that there should be no duplicate key that it is unlikely – in fact, I think, impossible – that the murderer could have entered the vault except by the aid of Trasmere's own key. However, we shall soon know; I have the best workman in town working at the unfinished key in Felling's room, and he says it is so far advanced that he is in no doubt he will be able to open the vault tonight."

"Then it is useless in its present state?"

The other nodded.

"Quite useless; we have tried it, and the locksmith, who is an expert, says that it wouldn't fit into the keyhole as it was when we found it."

"Then you suggest it is a case of suicide? That old man Trasmere went into the vault, locked himself in and then shot himself?"

Carver shook his head.

"If the revolver is found in the vault, yours would be a very sound theory, though why Trasmere should shoot himself is entirely beyond me."

At a quarter to eleven that night three men stood before the door of the Trasmere vault, and the shirt-sleeved workman inserting the key, the lock snapped back. He was pushing the door open when Carver caught his arm.

"Just leave it as it is," he said, and the locksmith, obviously disappointed that he should be denied a full view of the tragedy which he had only half glimpsed, went back to gather up his tools.

"Now," said Carver, drawing a long breath, and pulling a pair of white gloves from his pocket he put them on.

Tab followed him into the chamber of death.

"I've telephoned for the doctor. He'll be here in a few seconds," said Carver, looking down at the silent figure leaning against the table legs. He pointed to the table. In the exact centre lay a key, but what brought the exclamation to the detective's lips was the fact that the one half was stained red. The fluid which had run from it had soaked into the porous surface of the table.

"Blood," whispered the detective, and gingerly lifted the flat steel.

There was no doubt about it. Though the handle was clean, the lower wards appeared as though they had been dipped in blood.

"This disposes of the suicide theory," said Carver.

His first search was for the pistol which had obviously slain the man. There was no sign of any weapon. He passed his hand under the limp body, and Tab shivered to see the head drop wearily to the shoulder.

"Nothing there…shot through the body too. Suicides seldom do it that way."

His quick fingers searched the silent figure. There was nothing of any value.

Carver straightened himself and stood, fist on hip, surveying the dreadful sight.

"He was standing here when he was shot – he never knew what killed him. As faked suicide it is inartistic – apart from the absence of weapon, the old man was shot in the back."

If there were any doubts on the subject they were set at rest when the doctor made his brief examination.

"He was shot at the range of about two yards," he said. "No, Mr Carver, it is impossible that he should have committed suicide; there is no burning whatever. Besides, the bullet has entered the back, just beneath the left shoulder, and of course death must have been instantaneous. It is impossible that the wound can have been self-inflicted."

Again came the police photographers, and after they had gone, leaving the vault thick with the mist of exploded magnesium, the two men were left to their search. The first boxes were, for the main part, filled with money. There was very little gold, but a great deal of paper of various nationalities. In one box Carver found five million francs in thousand-franc notes, another was packed with English five-pound notes, another was full of hundred-dollar bills fastened in packets of ten thousand. Only two of these boxes were locked and only one that they looked at that night contained anything in the nature of documents. For the most part they were old leases, receipts painted on thin paper in Chinese, characters, and which they only knew were receipts because somebody had written a translation on their backs. They were bracketed neatly in folders, on each of which was described in a fine flowing hand, the nature of its contents.

On one thick bundle fastened with rubber bands was an old label: "Trading correspondence, 1899."

In his search Tab, who was looking through the box, found a folded manuscript, which he brought out.

"Here is his will," he said, and Carver took it from him. It was written in the crabbed boyish hand which Tab had come to know so well, and it was very short. After the conventional preamble, it went on: "I leave all my property and effects whatsoever, to my nephew, Rex Percival Lander, the only son of my deceased sister, Mary

Catherine Lander *née* Trasmere, and I appoint him sole executor of this my will."

It was witnessed by Mildred Green, who described herself as a cook, and by Arthur Green, whose description of his profession was valet. Their addresses were Mayfield.

"I think those are the two servants the old man discharged for pilfering some six months ago. The will must have been executed a few weeks before they left."

Tab's first feeling was one of pleasure that at last his friend was a rich man. Poor Rex, little did he dream that he would come into his inheritance in so tragic a fashion.

Carver put the document back into the box and continued the examination of the door which Tab had interrupted.

"It isn't a spring lock, you notice," he said. "So, therefore, it couldn't have been slammed by a murderer who first shot Trasmere and then made his escape. It has to be locked either from the inside or the outside. If there was any reasonable possibility of Trasmere having shot himself, the solution would have been simple. But he did not shoot himself. He was shot here, the door was locked upon him, and the key returned to the table – how?" He took the key and tried one of the air holes of the ventilator. The point of the key scarcely entered. "There must be some other entrance to the vault," he said.

The sun was up before they finished their examination of the room. The walls were solid. There was neither window nor fireplace. The floor was even more substantial than the walls.

In a last hopeless endeavour to solve the mystery Carver called in an expert to inspect the ventilator. It was made of steel, a quarter of an inch thick, and fastened into the door itself. There were no screws with which it could have been taken out, and even if it had been removed, only the tiniest of mortals could have crept through.

"Still," said Carver, "if we could suppose that the ventilator was removable, we might have taken a leaf from Edgar Allan Poe and thought seriously of a trained monkey being introduced."

"There is the theory of the duplicate key – "

"Which I dismiss," said Carver. "I am satisfied that no duplicate key was used. If a duplicate key had been procurable, Felling, or Walters as you call him, would have found his way to it. He is the cleverest man in that business, and he has lived on duplicate keys all his life. He must have known that it was impossible to gain admission by such a method or he wouldn't have taken the trouble to make one. He is a specialist in that line of business, probably the finest locksmith of the underworld."

"Then you suggest that this key was used?" Tab pointed to the table.

"I not only suggest it, but I would swear to it," said Carver quietly. "Look!" He pulled the door open so that the light fell upon the outside keyhole. "Do you see the little blood spots?" he asked. "That key has not only been used from the outside, where it has left unmistakable markings, but the same has happened on the inside of the door."

He swung the door again and Tab saw the tell-tale stains.

"That door was unlocked from the inside after the old man was dead and locked again upon him."

"But how did the key get back to the table?" asked the bewildered reporter.

Mr Carver shook his head.

"A medical student was once asked by a professor whether Adam was ever a baby, and he replied 'God knows' – that is my answer to you!" he said. "We will leave the other boxes until tomorrow, Tab."

Carver led the way out of the vault, locked the door with the duplicate key, and put it in his pocket.

"My brain is dead," said Tab.

And it was then that he saw the new pin.

7

From where he stood the light caught it and sent up a thread of silvery reflection. He stooped mechanically and picked it up.

"What is that?" asked the detective curiously.

"It looks to me like a pin," said Tab.

It was a very ordinary pin, silvery bright and about an inch and a half in length. In that sense it was of an unusual size, though it was the kind that is commonly used by bankers, who delight in fastening large documents together by this barbarous method. It was not straight, there was a slight bend in it, but otherwise it had no remarkable features. Tab looked at it stupidly.

"Give it to me," said Carver. He took it in his white-gloved hand and walked to a position under one of the lights. "I don't suppose it has any significance," he said, "but I'll keep it." He put the pin carefully away in the match-box where he had put the key. "Now, Tab," he said more briskly as they went out of the house together into the bright sunlight, two unshaven, weary-looking men, "you have the story of your life, but go easy on any clues we have found."

"I didn't know we had found any," said Tab, "unless the pin is a clue."

"Even that I should not mention," said Carver gravely.

When he got back to his flat Tab found the lights of the sitting-room blazing and Rex Lander, fully dressed, asleep on the settee.

"I waited up till three," yawned Rex. "Have they caught Walters, or whoever it was?"

"Not when I left Carver, which was ten minutes ago," replied Tab. "They suspect that man Brown. His gloves were found in the passage."

"Brown, the man from China?…it was pretty awful, wasn't it?" asked Babe in a hushed voice, as though the fearfulness of those moments through which he had passed were only now appealing to him in their sheer terror. "My God, what an awful thing! I've tried not to think about it all night; that horrible memory persisted so that it nearly drove me mad."

"I have one bit of good news for you, Rex," said the other as he began to prepare for bed. "We found your uncle's will. That is unofficial."

"You found the will, did you?" said the other listlessly. "I am afraid I am not interested in his will just now. Who gets the money – the Dogs' Home or the Cats' Crèche?"

"It goes to a stout young architect," said Tab with a grin, "and I can see our little home breaking up. Maybe I'll come and see you when you are rich, Babe, if you'll know me."

Rex's impatient gesture silenced him.

"I'm not thinking about money – I'm thinking about other things," he said.

Tab slept for four hours, and woke to find that Rex had gone out. When he came into the street the special editions of the Sunday newspaper were selling, with stories of the murder.

The news editor had not arrived when Tab reached the office, but he turned in the rough narrative of the tragedy to guide the office in its general search for Walters and Brown.

He went on to Mayfield, but Carver was not there, and the police-sergeant in charge of the house was indisposed to admit him. Carver, being a single man, lived in lodgings. Tab surprised him in the act of shaving.

"No, there is no news of Felling, and Brown, who is a much more difficult proposition, has disappeared from view. Why is he more difficult? Because he is unknown. In comparison tracing Walters is child's play. Yet we haven't even found him," said the Inspector, wiping his face, "which is rather surprising, considering that we know his usual haunts and acquaintances. None of these say they have seen him. The cab-driver has come forward in answer to our hurry-up call, and says he set down Felling at the Central Station. They stopped on the way to buy a hat, apparently."

Carver had not been to the station that morning, and even if he had he could not have given the news which was to startle Tab later in the day.

"Have you formed any fresh theory, Carver?"

Carver looked out of the window and pulled his long nose thoughtfully. He was a tall thin man, with a lean face that was all lines and furrows. In repose it was melancholy in the extreme, and his gentle apologetic tone seemed somehow in keeping with his appearance.

"There are several theories, all more or less fluid," he said.

"Has it occurred to you," asked Tab, "that the shot might have been fired through one of the ventilator holes?"

Carver nodded several times before he answered. "It occurred to me after I left you and I went back to make sure, but there is no blackening of the grating such as there would be if a pistol of sufficiently small calibre had been pressed against one of the holes and fired, added to which there is this important fact: the bullet of the size the doctors found in Trasmere's body would not go through any such hole." Carver shook his head. "No, the murder was committed actually in the vault, either by Brown, by Walters, or by some third person."

Tab had a few independent inquiries to pursue, one of which related to the cook. She had already been questioned by the police, he discovered, when he reached her little suburban home. A quiet, motherly, and unimaginative woman, there was little she could tell.

"It was my day off," she said. "Mr Trasmere said he was going into the country, though I don't suppose he was. He had said that before, but Walters told me to take no notice. I have never seen Mr Trasmere," she said, to Tab's surprise. "All my orders came through Mr Walters, and practically I was never inside the house except once, when the cleaning woman did not turn up in the morning and I helped Walters to tidy the master's sitting-room. I remember that morning because I found a little black lid – well it was hardly a lid – I have got it here if you would like to see it. I have often wondered what it was for."

"Lid," said Tab. "What kind of a lid?"

"It was like the lid of a small pill-box," explained the woman, "about the size of a threepenny-piece. I picked it up and asked Mr Walters what it was for, and he said he didn't know. It was on the floor near the table and I brought it home, meaning to ask my husband what it was."

She went out of the room and returned with the "lid," which proved on examination to be a celluloid cap such as typists use to cover their keys.

"Had Mr Trasmere a typewriter?"

"No, sir," she answered, shaking her head, "not so far as I know. I have never seen one. As I say, I have only been that once into the house. The kitchen is built away from the living rooms, although it is connected; Mr Trasmere gave strict orders that I was to keep to my kitchen."

Tab looked at the little cap which he held between his finger and thumb. It was undoubtedly part of a typist's equipment, and yet Mr Trasmere had never employed a typist. He always wrote to Rex in his own hand.

"Are you sure nobody came during the day to take your master's correspondence?" he asked.

"No; I am perfectly sure Mr Walters would have told me. He used to complain how dull it was because nobody came to the house at all, and he was rather partial to young women, so I am sure I should have heard. Have they found Mr Walters? I'm certain he didn't do it."

Tab satisfied her on that point.

"Do you remember the Greens?" he asked, remembering just as he was on the point of leaving the house the witnesses to the old man's will.

"No, sir, not really," she said. "Mrs Green was cook before me and I saw her once, the day I came, and Mr Green too. They were a very nice couple and I don't think the master treated them very well."

"Where are they now?"

"I don't know, sir," she said. "I did hear that they had gone to Australia. They were middle-aged people, but very strong and healthy, and Mr Green was always talking about going to Australia, where he was born, and settling down there."

"Did Green or his wife have any hard feeling against Mr Trasmere?"

She hesitated.

"Well, they naturally felt sore because they had been accused of thieving, and Mr Green seemed to feel the disgrace terribly, especially when the master had their boxes searched because he had lost some valuable silver and a gold watch."

This was news to Tab. He had heard of the food pilfering, but he had not heard of the other losses. She could tell him very little more, except that Green had acted as a sort of butler.

"Was Walters there at the time?" asked Tab.

"Yes, sir; he was Mr Trasmere's valet. After Mr Green went Mr Walters was butler and valet, too."

Tab went straight to the office to write the story up to date, but he knew that it was a waste of labour, since some news was certain to come in before nightfall.

The news editor was at his desk when he pushed open the big swing doors and came into the news room to report.

"These front page crimes always come together in shoals," complained the news editor bitterly. "I have another very good story – "

"Well, give it to a good story writer," said Tab. "This case is going to occupy not only my time, but the time of half a dozen men very fully indeed. What is the new sensation?" he asked sarcastically.

"An actress has lost her jewels, which does not sound tremendously exciting," said the news editor, fishing for two slips of paper on which he had made a rough note of the case, "but you needn't bother about that. I'll put another man on the story as soon as I can get one."

"Who is the actress?"

"Ursula Ardfern," replied the editor, and Tab's jaw dropped.

8

"Ursula Ardfern! She is not the kind of person who would mislay her jewels for the sake of a few lines of advertising," he said. "Where did she lose them?"

"It is rather a curious story," said the editor, leaning back in his chair, his hands clasped behind his head. "She went into a post office on Saturday morning on her way to the theatre for the matinée, bought some stamps, putting the jewel-case down on the counter by her side. When she looked round, the case was gone. It happened so suddenly and in such a surprisingly short space of time that she could not believe her eyes, and did not even complain to the post office officials. Her own story is, that she thought she must be suffering from some kind of delusion and that she had not brought the jewel-case out at all. She went back to her suite at the Central Hotel and searched every room. By the time she was through, it was near the hour for her matinée, and she hurried down to the theatre – anyway, to cut a long story short, she did not report her loss to the police until this morning."

"She wouldn't," said Tab stoutly. "She's the kind of girl who would hate the publicity of it and would do all she could to make sure there was not a simple explanation of their loss before she put the matter in the hands of the police."

"You know her, eh?"

"I know her in the sense that a reporter knows almost everybody, from the Secretary of State to the hangman," said Tab, "but I'll take this story if you like. There will be nothing doing on the Trasmere case before the evening. She stays at the Central, does she?"

45

The other nodded.

"You will need to exercise a little ingenuity," he said, "especially if what you say about her hating publicity is true. I'd like to get a photograph of the actress who hated publicity and hang it up in this office," he added.

At the Central Hotel Tab found himself up against a blank wall.

"Miss Ardfern is not receiving callers," said the inquiry clerk. He was not even certain that she was in.

"Will you send my card up?"

The clerk very emphatically said that he would not send up anybody's card. Tab went straight to the supreme authority. Fortunately he knew the hotel manager very well, but on this occasion Crispi was not inclined to oblige him.

"Miss Ardfern is a very good customer of ours, Holland," he said, "and we don't want to offend her. I will tell you, in the strictest confidence, that Miss Ardfern is not in the hotel."

"Where is she?"

"She went away this morning in her car to her country cottage. She always spends Sunday and Sunday night in the country, and I know that she does not want to see any reporters, because she came back this morning especially to tell me that the staff were to answer no inquiries relative to herself."

"Where is this country cottage – come on, Crispi," wheedled Tab, "or the next time you have a robbery in this hotel I'll make a front-page item of it."

"That is blackmail," murmured Crispi, protestingly. "I am afraid I cannot tell you, Holland. Maybe if you get a Hertford directory – "

In the office library he found the directory and turned its pages. Against the name of "Ardfern, Ursula," was "Stone Cottage, near Blisville Village."

The distance from town was some forty-five miles, and the route carried him past an unfinished building which one day was to play its part in the ending of many mysteries. Tab covered the ground on a fast motorcycle in just over an hour. He leant his machine against a very trim hedge, opened the high garden gate, and walked into the beautiful little garden that surrounded Stone Cottage, which was not ill-named, though the stone which composed its walls was completely hidden by purple-flowering creeper.

In the shade of a tree he saw a white figure stretched at her ease, a figure which sat bolt upright in her deep garden chair at the click of the gate-lock.

"This is too bad of you, Mr Tab," said Ursula Ardfern reproachfully. "I particularly asked Crispi not to tell anybody where I was."

"Crispi didn't tell. I found you in a directory," said Tab cheerfully.

The sunlight was very kind to Ursula, and it seemed to him that she looked even more beautiful in these surroundings than she had in the generous setting and the more merciful lighting of the theatre.

She was slimmer than he had thought, and conveyed an extraordinary impression of hurt youth. Somewhere, some time, this girl had suffered, he thought, yet there was no hint of old pain in her unlined face, no suggestion of sorrow or remorse in her clear blue eyes.

"I suppose you have come to cross-examine me about my jewels," she said, "and I will allow you, on one condition, to ask me any question you wish."

"What is the condition?" he smiled.

"Bring up that chair." She pointed across the strip of lawn. "Now sit down"; and when he had obeyed, "The condition is this: that you will confine yourself to saying that I have no recollection of the jewels being taken, but I shall be very glad to have them back and pay a suitable reward; that they were not as expensive as most people thought and that I am not insured against loss by theft."

"All of which I will faithfully record," said Tab. "I am an honest man and keep my promises. I admit it."

"And now I will tell you, for your own private ear," she said, "that if I never see those jewels again I shall be a very happy woman."

He looked at her open-mouthed.

"You don't think I am posing, do you?" She looked round at him suspiciously. "I see that you don't. I am not in the least worried that I shall have to play the part with property jewels as I did last night."

"Why didn't you go to the police before?" he asked.

"Because I didn't," was her unsatisfactory but uncompromising reply. "You may put whatever interpretation you like upon my slackness. You may say that it was because of my humanity, my desire to save some person from being accused, or coming under suspicion of having stolen the pieces, when all the time they were snug in my bureau drawer, or you may think or say that I did not want to make a fuss about them. In fact," she smiled, "you can do or say what you wish."

"You don't remember who was standing by you – "

She stopped him with a gesture.

"I remember nothing except that I bought ten stamps."

"What was the jewellery worth?" he persisted. She shrugged her shoulders.

"I can't even tell you that," she said.

"Had they any history?"

She laughed.

"You are very persistent, Mr Tab." Her eyes were smiling at him, though her face was composed. "And now, since you have surprised me in my Abode of Quiet, I must show you over my little domain."

She took him round the garden and through the tiny pine wood at the back of the house, chatting all the time, and then after leaving him, as she said, to ensure that her room was tidy, she beckoned him into a large and pleasant sitting-room, tastefully, if not expensively furnished, a cool, quiet haven of rest.

He had arrived at two o'clock and it was five o'clock before he reluctantly took his leave. And all that afternoon they had talked of books and of people, and since she had not mentioned or spoken of the murder which had engrossed his thoughts until her soothing presence had made Mayfield seem very remote and crime a thing of distaste, he did not introduce so jarring a discordance into the lavender atmosphere of her retreat.

"What kind of story do you call this?" snapped the news editor when Tab handed him two folios of copy.

"From a literary point of view," said Tab, "it is a classic."

"From a news point of view, it is rotten," said the editor. "The only new fact you have discovered is that she loves Browning, and maybe even the police know that!"

He grumbled, but accepted the copy, and with his blue pencil committed certain acts of savage mutilation, while Tab was making his final round-up of the Trasmere case.

Here again very little new matter was available. Walters and the man Wellington Brown were still at liberty, and he had to confine himself to a sketch of Trasmere's life, material for which had, from time to time, been supplied to him by the Babe.

The new millionaire he had not seen all day. When he got home that night he found Rex Lander in bed and asleep and did not disturb him. He was tired to death and more anxious to make acquaintance with his hard pillow than he was to discuss Ursula Ardfern. In truth, he was not prepared to discuss Ursula at all with any third person.

"I just loafed around," said Rex the next morning, when asked to give an account of his movements. "I had a very bad night and was up early. You were sleeping like a pig when I looked in. I read your story in *The Megaphone* – by the way, you know that Miss Ardfern's jewellery has been stolen?"

"I know that very well indeed," said Tab, "I saw her yesterday."

Rex was instant attention.

"Where?" he asked eagerly. "What is she like, Tab – I mean off the stage? Is she as beautiful – what colour eyes has she?"

Tab pushed back his chair and frowned at the young man across the table.

"Your curiosity is indecent," he said severely; "really, Rex, I never dreamt that you were so interested in the lady."

Rex did not meet his eyes.

"I think she is very beautiful," he said doggedly. "I'd give my head to spend a day with her."

"Phew!" said Tab. "Why, you young devil, you are in love with her!"

Rex's babyish face went crimson.

"Stuff," he said loudly. "I am very fond of her. I have seen her a hundred times, I suppose, though I have never spoken to her once. She is my idea of the perfect woman. Beautiful of face, with the loveliest voice I have ever heard. I am going to know her one day."

This revelation of Babe's secret passion was, for some reason, which Tab could not define, an extremely disquieting one.

"My dear Babe," he said more mildly, "the young lady is not of the loving or marrying sort – "

Suddenly he remembered.

"Why, you are a millionaire now, Babe! Jumping Moses!"

Rex blushed again, and then Tab whistled.

"Do you mean in all seriousness that you are truly fond of her?"

"I adore her," said Rex in a low voice. "I got so rattled when I heard a fellow say she was going to be married that I had to send you to see her."

Tab interrupted him with a roar of delighted laughter.

"So that was why I was sent on a fool's errand, eh?" he asked, his eyes dancing. "You subtle dog! It was to bring balm to your bruised heart that an eminent crime specialist must stand, hat in hand, in the dingy purlieus of a playhouse, begging admission to the great actress's dressing-room." He was serious in a moment. "I hope this isn't a very violent attachment of yours, Rex," he said quietly. "In the first place it struck me that Ursula Ardfern is not of the marrying kind, that even your great possessions would not tempt her. In the second place – " he stopped himself.

"Well?" asked Rex impatiently. "Whatever other just cause or impediment do you see?"

"I don't know that it is any business of mine," said Tab, "and I certainly am not in a position to give you fatherly advice."

"You mean that an actress is the worst kind of wife a man can have, I suppose. I have heard all that rubbish before. Poor Uncle Jesse, when I spoke about it – "

"You spoke to him of your – liking for Ursula Ardfern?" asked Tab in surprise.

"Of course I didn't," said the other scornfully. "I approached it in a roundabout sort of way. Uncle Jesse foamed at the mouth. It was then he told me that he was going to leave all his money away from me. He said horrible things about actresses."

Tab was silent, a little puzzled at himself. What did it matter to him, anyway, that Rex Lander should be head over heels in love with the girl? Yet, for some mysterious reason, he regarded Babe's passion as a personal affront to himself. It was ridiculous, childish in him, and he laughed softly.

"You think it is darned funny, I daresay," growled Rex, getting up from the table in a huff.

"I was laughing at myself for daring to give advice," said Tab truthfully.

9

Tab was in his own room when Carver called.

"I have had a talk with some of the High Ones," he said, "and put it up to them that you might be of assistance to me. First of all they were horrified at the idea of a newspaper reporter being allowed even to smell inside information, but I persuaded them at last. I am on my way down to the house now, and I thought I would pick you up. I am going through those boxes that we didn't search on Saturday."

Tab heard with mingled feelings. To assist the police actively meant that his newspaper stories would suffer. He would not be allowed to use any of the information he secured, except in the tamest, most colourless form. If he remained outside, he was fairly certain to get a line to the crime, which he might use without laying himself open to the charge of breaking faith. There was no time to discover the mind of his chief on the subject – he had to make an instant decision.

"I'll go," he said. "This means, of course, that I shall only be able to write the punk stuff that the evening papers print, but I'll take a chance."

He was surprised, when he came out into Doughty Street, to find that a private car had been placed at Carver's disposal. Knowing the parsimony of headquarters, he expressed his surprise.

"It is Mr Trasmere's own. He has had it garaged for the past year, but Mr Lander gave us permission to get it out, and offered to pay the running expenses."

"Good old Babe," said Tab, sinking back into the carriage seat. "He didn't tell me anything about it."

Nearing the house, Carver broke the silence.

"I have something to show you later," he said. "Our men have been at the post office all night, making inquiries as to Mr Trasmere's correspondence. It appears that he has had a whole lot during the past year or two. We shall probably come across it in the boxes that remain unsearched. But that wasn't the big thing we found. Most of the telegraph staff were off duty yesterday. It was only this morning that we learnt a telegram had been received at Mayfield about ten minutes before Walters disappeared."

When they were in the sitting-room and the door was closed, Carver produced the telegram from his pocket. It was handed in at the General Post Office and ran:

"Remember 17th July, 1913. Newcastle police coming for you at three o'clock."

It was unsigned.

"I have been searching the newspaper files this morning," said Carver, "to discover the reference to that date. On the 17th July, 1913, I find that Felling was sent down at Newcastle for seven years, and the judge said that if he ever came before him again on a similar charge he would send him down for life."

"Then the telegram was despatched by some friend of Walters?" suggested Tab.

Carver nodded.

"It was delivered five minutes before he disappeared; that is to say, exactly at five minutes to three. I have seen the lad who delivered the telegram, and he says that Walters himself took in the message."

"Would that account for his disappearance?"

"In a sense it might, yet it does not necessarily follow that Walters is innocent of the murder. The telegram may have come to him immediately after the murder was committed and have decided him to get away. If he was responsible for the murder, there would be even more reason why he should leave in a hurry. The arrival of the police, who would find the body, would, of course, have been fatal to him."

"Did anybody see Wellington Brown go into the house?" asked Tab. It was a question he meant to have put before.

"Nobody," said the detective. "At what hour he arrived only Walters can tell us."

He folded the telegram and put it away, then unlocking the door from the study which led to the passage, he went down the steps and, stopping only to switch on the lights, made his way into the vault. One by one the boxes were taken down, emptied of their contents, and carefully examined.

Money was everywhere: banknotes, treasury bills, money in the greasy notes of a Chinese Government bank, money in the shape of Greek drachmas and Italian lira. Sometimes a box would contain nothing but these valuable squares of paper, sometimes a box held thick packets of correspondence addressed to Trasmere, at queer-looking towns in Northern China. All bore the same clerkly number, generally written in green ink, and none of them threw any light whatever upon the tragedy they were investigating.

In the last box of all, the correspondence was more recent. It was mostly typewritten copies of letters, evidently addressed by the dead man to various corporations with whom he had dealings, and these they went through letter by letter.

"Where were those typed?" said Carver. "And when? He doesn't seem to have kept a secretary."

Until that moment Tab had forgotten the discovery of the typewriter-key-cover. Now he referred to the find.

"But he used to go out every night at half-past six and remain away until half-past eight," said Tab. "Probably he went to some typewriting office – there are a few in the city which make a speciality of after-hours work."

"That is possible," admitted Carver. "There is nothing here. I have sent anything that looked important to the translators – I don't think it is worth while sending the trading accounts of '89." He put the papers carefully back into the box. "And that's the lot," he said.

Tab was standing with his back to the lower shelf to the right hand of the door, and his fingers were idly touching the plain strip of steel when he felt something underneath and, looking down, saw that the obstruction which his fingers had found was one of two slides on which hung a drawer. They had been pushed so far back that it was impossible to see it from where they had stood.

The detective stooped and picked it out. "Hullo," he said, "what are these?"

He brought out first a small box of Chinese workmanship.

It was exquisitely lacquered in pale green. Lifting off the lid he saw that it was empty.

"Nothing there – some curio he was hoarding," said Carver. Next he produced a small brown jewel-case from the drawer, and putting it on the broad shelf, opened it.

Even before he saw the heart-shaped ruby brooch that was pinned to the satin lining of the lid, Tab knew what it was.

"Those are Ursula Ardfern's jewels," he said, and they looked at one another.

"The jewels that were stolen on Saturday morning?" asked the detective incredulously.

Tab nodded, and the detective took out an emerald cross, turned it over, looked at its face, then put it back again.

"On Saturday morning," he said slowly, "if I remember the facts aright, and I only read them in the newspaper this morning, Miss Ursula Ardfern went into a post office to buy some stamps. Whilst she was there she put her jewel-case by her side, and looking round, discovered it was gone. Thinking she had made some mistake, she went back to her hotel and searched her room. She reported it to the police on Sunday morning."

"That is the case as I understand it," said Tab, who was as dumbfounded as his companion.

"And three or four hours after Miss Ardfern lost her jewels, Trasmere was murdered in this room. The jewels were here at that time, because obviously nobody has been in or out of this room since Trasmere was murdered, except possibly the murderer; in other words, in the space of two hours the jewels were stolen and conveyed to Jesse Trasmere and locked in his strongroom – why?" He stared at Tab.

Tab could only stare back. Carver scratched his head, massaged the back of his neck irritably, rubbed his chin, and then: "In other circumstances one would say that Trasmere was a receiver. I have known some very unlikely people who were receivers of stolen property and grew rich on the proceeds, and I have known very unlikely folk to lend money, not only to actresses, but very substantial people, on the security of their jewels. Had we not Miss Ardfern's report of their loss, the obvious explanation would have been that these had been pledged to Trasmere in security for a loan."

"I am perfectly sure she doesn't know Trasmere. I happen to be an – an acquaintance of hers," said Tab quickly.

Again the detective was giving contortional evidence of his perplexity. His long face was longer still, his downturned mouth more melancholy.

"Anyway, there is no question of pledge. The only thing we have to decide is, whether he was the kind of man who would receive stolen property." He glanced round at the black boxes which filled the shelves and shook his head. "The probability is all against that theory," he said. "Trasmere was too rich a man to run the risk. Besides, we should have found other property. It is not likely that he would act as receiver for one gang of thieves, and for only one of their crimes."

He hoisted himself to the top of the table, pushed his hands in his trousers pockets and, with his chin on his breast, considered.

"Now that beats me," he said at last. "I admit that I am thoroughly and absolutely beaten. You are perfectly sure that these are Miss Ardfern's jewels?"

"I am absolutely certain that it is her jewel-case. Probably at headquarters they have a description of the jewels which are lost," said Tab.

"Then we'll settle that little mystery at once."

He was telephoning for a quarter of an hour, taking notes all the time; and when he hung up the receiver he turned to Tab.

"Without having carefully looked at the pieces in that box," he said, "I think it is absolutely certain that those jewels are Miss Ardfern's. She gave a fairly complete list to the police, but could not remember every item. We will go along and check our inventory."

He had not been at work long before it was clear that the jewellery was Ursula Ardfern's property.

"Go along and see her, Tab," said Carver. "Take the empty box with you – we had better hold on to the jewellery a little longer – and ask her to identify the case."

10

Ursula had only arrived a few minutes before Tab reached the Central Hotel, and the ban against reporters must have been lifted, because Ursula saw him immediately.

She took the case from his hand slowly, and with a face from whence all expression had fled.

"Yes, this is mine," she said. She lifted the lid. "Where are the jewels?" she asked quickly.

"The police have those."

"The police?"

"It was found in the strongroom of Jesse Trasmere, the old man who was murdered on Saturday afternoon," said Tab. "Have you any idea how they came into his possession?"

"None," she said emphatically. "I did not know Mr Trasmere."

He told her about the murder, but apparently she had already read the details and seemed loath to discuss the matter until he told her the part that he himself was taking in the tracking of the murderer.

"Where did you find these?" she asked.

"In his strongroom. The curious thing is we turned out all the boxes, ran over all the papers, and found nothing of importance. It was only by accident that we discovered this case. It was in a little drawer pushed far under one of the shelves."

"You went through all the papers," she repeated mechanically. "What sort of papers – did he have – many?"

"Quite a number," said Tab, surprised that after definitely and decidedly changing the subject she had returned to it voluntarily.

"Old bills and accounts, copies of letters, and that sort of thing. Nothing of any very great importance. Why do you ask?"

"I had a friend once, a girl who was interested in Mr Trasmere," she answered. "She told me that he was keeping a number of documents connected with her family. No, I don't remember her name. She was an actress I met on tour."

"There was nothing in his papers except purely business records," said Tab.

Tab was very sensitive to atmosphere. He could have sworn when he came into the room that she had keyed herself up to meet him. There was no reason why she should, except the reluctance to discuss the robbery, and she maintained that tense attitude throughout the interview. Now he was as certain that she was relieved. He sensed, rather than saw, a relaxation of mind. Probably it was only his imagination, but imagination had never played such a trick upon him before.

"When are the police going to give me my beautiful jewels?" she asked, almost gaily.

"I am afraid they will retain those until after the court proceedings are through. There must be an inquest, you know."

"Oh," she said, and seemed disappointed. Then again she returned to the murder. "It seems all so dreadful and mysterious," she said quietly. "How do you account for it, Mr Holland? One of the newspapers says that it was impossible that any other hand than Mr Trasmere's could have locked the door, and yet they are equally certain that he did not commit suicide. And who is the man Brown for whom they are searching?"

"He is an adventurer from China who was at some time or other a sort of secretary to old Trasmere."

"A secretary?" she said quickly. "A man – how do you know that?"

"Brown told me himself. I saw him the day before the murder. Apparently Trasmere had treated him badly and had held him off for years by paying him a sum of money."

She bit her lip in thought.

"Why did he come back?" she said, half to herself. "He might have lived comfortably on the allowance. I suppose it was a good allowance?" she added quickly. "That is all you want to see me about, Mr Holland?"

"You may have to go to the police station to identify the jewellery," said Tab; "and they are pretty certain to ask you how the box came into Mr Trasmere's possession."

She did not answer this, and he left her with an odd feeling of uneasiness.

Going to report the result of his interview to Carver, he found that energetic man crawling about the vault on all fours. He looked over his shoulder at the sound of Tab's footsteps.

"Was Saturday wet or fine?" he asked.

"It was a particularly fine day."

"Then this must be a blood impression." He pointed to the floor, and Tab went on his knees at his side. There was a faint half-moon printed on the edge of the concrete. "That is the edge of a heel, and a rubber heel," said Carver, "which proves beyond any doubt whatever that somebody came into the vault after the old man was killed, probably went close to the body to see the effect of the shot, and in doing so got a little of the blood on a part of his heel. The rubber accounts for his coming on Trasmere without the old man hearing him. There is no other impression that I can find."

"Which brings us back to the question of the duplicate key."

"There was no duplicate key; you can cut that idea right out," said Carver, getting up and dusting his knees. "I have been into the matter very thoroughly with the manufacturers, and although they each claim to have the best kind of lock and are naturally inclined to take an uncharitable view of their rivals, they say that the maker of our particular key is reliable, and he says that it was in the hands of his most trustworthy man, and that no second key was ever made. Not only that, but no drawing of the key was kept. In fact, the lock, just before it was fitted, was altered by the manufacturer's expert here, on the premises. I am seeing him tomorrow, but from what I learnt on the telephone he says that we can dismiss from our minds the possibility of there being a duplicate."

"But Walters was making – "

"Walters hadn't finished his job, and even if he had, he could not have fashioned a key that would have unlocked this door, clever as he was. No; the bloodstained key is the key that locked the door. What is more, it is the key which the old man carried on a thin silver chain round his neck. We found the broken ends of the chain in his clothing after the body was searched. Then again, there are the bloodstains, both on the inside and on the outside of the door. That is the most remarkable feature of the case, that after the murder the door was locked both from the inside and the outside. At one period, after the death of Trasmere, the murderer must have been locked in this vault with him. If I did not know it was an absolute impossibility I should say that it was locked finally from the inside, the key was placed on the table, and the murderer disappeared through some secret entrance, which we know very well does not exist."

"Have you tested the roof?"

"I have tested everywhere – roof, walls, floor, and door," said Carver. "A fact which may or may not be important, is that there is about an eighth of an inch of space between the bottom of the door and the floor. If the key had been found on the floor there would be no mystery about the matter, because the murderer could have pushed it under and, with a flick of his finger, sent it into the middle of the room. Here is the situation in a nutshell." He ticked off the points on his fingers. "Trasmere is murdered in a vault, the door of which is locked. The murderer is either Brown, who has threatened him, or Walters, who has been robbing him. Inside the locked vault is found the only key which could open or close it. Note this particularly, that Trasmere was shot in the back."

"Why is that important?"

"As proving that at the moment of his murder Trasmere was in no fear. He was not expecting either to be shot or hurt. And now we add to the situation, which is sufficiently baffling, the discovery in the vault of a jewel-case belonging to an eminent actress, from whom it has been stolen on the very day of the murder. This is the case which I must take to a coroner's jury. It doesn't look very good to me."

It did not "look very good" to the coroner's jury which contented itself a week later with returning a verdict of wilful murder against some person or persons unknown, and added a rider expressing its dissatisfaction with the inefficiency of the police.

The day that verdict was returned, Ursula Ardfern fainted twice in the course of her performance and was carried home to her hotel in a condition of collapse.

11

A murder lends to the locality in which it is perpetrated a certain left-handed fame which those of its inhabitants who appear most disgusted most enjoy. Human nature being what it is, trouble and misery have a larger sale-value to newspapers than have comfort and happiness. Nothing makes a newspaper reader more conscious of the emptiness of his journal than to learn that his insignificant neighbour has unexpectedly inherited a fortune. Therefore it is only natural that when the average man or woman finds himself or herself promoted from mere observer to participant, however indirect, he or she experiences a queer satisfaction that is no less satisfying because it is queer.

The woman of the house may shudder and make unusual efforts to "keep it from the children," but she listens avidly to the cook's inside story of the crime that was committed next door, and presses for further details. The man may express his horror and indignation and talk of leaving his house and finding another in a less notorious neighbourhood, but for years he will point out to his visitors and guests the window of the room where the fell deed was done.

Opposite to Mayfield was the home of John Fergusson Stott, who, in addition to being a neighbour of the late Jesse Trasmere, was the employer of his nephew. This gave him an especial title to speak as an Authority. It supported him also in his determination to Say Nothing.

"It is bad enough, my dear, to be living in the street where this ghastly crime has been committed. I cannot afford to be dragged into the matter."

He was a small, fat man, very bald, and he wore spectacles of great magnifying power.

"Eline says – " began his buxom wife.

Mr Stott held up a podgy hand and closed his eyes.

"Servants' gossip?" said he. "Let us keep out of this business. I cannot afford to have my name in the papers. Why, we should have the house full of reporters in no time! And the police too. I had quite trouble enough over the dog's licence, without wanting to see the police again."

He sat soberly in his place before the window, glaring out at the darkening street. A light flitted to and fro in one of the upper windows of Mayfield, came and went and came again. The police were searching. He was interested. Tomorrow, when he met the men at Toby's, he would be able to say: "They are still searching old Trasmere's house. I saw them last night – the house is just opposite to mine."

Presently the light disappeared for good, and he turned to his wife.

"What did Eline say? Ring for her."

Eline was a parlour-maid, grown of a sudden from the merest cypher in the great sum of parlour-maids to an isolated and important factor.

"I'm sure it gives me the shivers to talk about it, sir," she said. "Little did I ever think I should be mixed up in a case like this. I'm sure that I'd die if I was ever called into court to give evidence."

"You will not be called into court," said Mr Stott decisively. "This must go no farther, do you understand that, Eline?"

Eline said she did, but she seemed in no way pleased that she was to be spared the painful publicity.

"I've had toothache for the past fortnight – "

"You should have it out," said Mr Stott. An opportunity for advising sufferers to have their teeth extracted is one which no normal man can miss. "It is always best to deal drastically with a decaying tooth. Out with it, my girl – well?"

"It comes on about half-past eleven and goes off at two. I could set the clock by it."

"Yes, yes," said Mr Stott testily, his interest in Eline's misfortune ended; "but what did you see at Mayfield?"

"I usually sit at the window until the pain has gone," said Eline, and Mr Stott resisted the temptation to tell her that that was the very last place in the world where she *ought* to sit, "and naturally anything that happens in the street I see. The first night I was sitting there, I saw a little motor-car drive up to the front of the house. A lady got out – "

"A lady?"

"Well…she might have been a woman," admitted Eline. "But she got out, opened the gates and drove into the garden. I thought that was funny, because Mr Trasmere hasn't a garage, and I knew there was nobody staying with him."

"Where did the car go?"

"Just into the garden. There is plenty of room for it, because it is not exactly a garden – more like a yard than anything. I think she took the car near the house and put out all the lights. Then she went up the steps and opened the door. There was a light in the passage the first night, and I saw her taking the key out before she shut the door. She hadn't been in the house a few minutes before I saw a man on a bicycle coming along the road. He jumped down and propped the machine against the kerb. What struck me about him was the funny way he walked. Sort of queer little steps he took. He was smoking a cigar."

"Where did *he* go?" asked Mr Stott.

"Only as far as the gate and leant on it, smoking. By and by he threw away his cigar and lit another, and I saw his face – it was a Chinaman!"

"Good God!" said Mr Stott. The mental picture she conjured of a Chinaman lighting a cigar in the vicinity of Mr Stott's stately home was a particularly revolting one.

"Just before the policeman came along he went back to his bicycle and rode away, but after the policeman had passed he came back again and stood leaning on the gate until the front door of Mayfield opened. Then he sort of slunk back to his bicycle and rode in the opposite direction – I mean opposite to the way he had come. He had hardly got out of sight before I saw the lady come down and open the gates. Soon after she brought out the car, got down, closed the gates again, and drove away. And then I saw the Chinaman riding behind and pedalling like mad, as if he was trying to catch up the car."

"Extraordinary!" said Mr Stott. "This happened once?"

"It happened every night – Friday was the last night," said Eline impressively – "the lady in the car, the Chinaman, and everything. But on Sunday night two Chinamen came, and one went into the garden and was there for a long time. I knew the other one was a Chinaman because he walked so curiously. But they didn't come on bicycles. They had a car, which stopped at the far end of the street."

"Remarkable!" said Mr Stott, and stroked his smooth face.

Eline had finished her story, but was reluctant to surrender her position as news gleaner.

"The police have been taking things away from the house all day," reported the observer, "boxes and trunks. The girl at Pine Lodge told me that they are leaving there tonight. They've been keeping guard on the house ever since the murder."

"Very, very extraordinary; very remarkable," said Mr Stott. "But I don't think that it is any business of ours. No. Thank you, Eline. I should certainly have that tooth out. You mustn't be a baby, and American dentistry has reached such a high level of efficiency that –"

Eline listened respectfully but nervously, and went up to her room to plug the aching molar with Dr Billbery's Kure-Ake.

It seemed to Mr Stott that his head had scarcely touched the pillow before there came a knock upon the panel of his bedroom door.

"Yes?" he asked fiercely, in case it was a burglar who was in this polite manner seeking admission to his chamber.

"It is Eline, sir…they're there!"

Mr Stott shivered, and, conquering an almost irresistible desire to pull the bed-clothes over his head and pretend that he had been talking in his sleep, he got reluctantly out of bed and pulled on his dressing-gown. As to Mrs Stott, she never moved. She went to bed, as she had often said, to sleep.

"What is it, Eline – waking me up at this time in the morning?" asked Mr Stott irritably.

"They are there – the Chinamen. I saw one getting through the window," said the girl, her teeth chattering, to the serious disturbance of Dr Billbery's Kure-Ake.

"Wait a moment until I get my stick."

Mr Stott kept hanging to his bed-rail a heavily loaded cane. He had no intention of going nearer to Mayfield than the safe side of his dining-room window, but the holding of the stick gave him the self-confidence of which he was in need.

Cautiously the girl let up the blind of the dining-room window and unfastened the catch. The sash slid up noiselessly and gave them an uninterrupted view of Mayfield.

"There's one!" whispered Eline.

Standing in the shadow was a figure. Mr Stott saw it plainly. They watched in silence for the greater part of half an hour. Mr Stott had an idea that he ought to telephone for the police, but refrained. In the case of ordinary burglars he would not have hesitated. But these were Chinese, notoriously clannish and vengeful. He had read stories, in which Chinamen had inflicted diabolical injuries upon men who had betrayed them.

At the end of the half-hour's vigil the door of Mayfield opened and a man came out and joined the other. Together they walked up the road, and that was the last Mr Stott saw of them.

"Very remarkable!" said Mr Stott profoundly. "I'm glad you called me, Eline. I wouldn't have missed this for the world. But you must say nothing about this, Eline – nothing. The Chinese people are very blood-thirsty. They would think no more of putting you into a barrel full of sharp pointed nails and rolling you down a hill, than I should think of – er – lacing my shoes."

So Maple Manor kept its grisly secret, and none knew of Yeh Ling's visit to the house of death or his search for the tiny lacquer box wherein Jesse Trasmere kept a folded sheet of thin paper elegantly inscribed in Chinese characters by Yeh Ling, in his own hand.

12

"Ursula Ardfern is leaving the stage and is going to live in the country."

Tab made the announcement one evening when he came home from the office.

Rex scarcely seemed interested.

"Oh?" said Rex.

That was all he said. He seemed as disinclined as Tab to discuss the lady.

It was his last night at the Doughty Street flat. He was still suffering from shock, and his doctor had advised a trip abroad. He had suggested that at the end of his vacation he would return to Doughty Street, but on this point Tab was firm.

"You have a lot of money, Babe," he said seriously, "and a man who has a lot of money has also a whole lot of responsibilities. There are about a hundred and forty-five reasons why our little *ménage* should be broken up, and the most important from my point of view is, that I will not be demoralized by living cheek by jowl with a man of millions. You have a certain place to take in society, certain duties to perform, and you can't keep up the position that you are entitled to keep in a half-flat in Doughty Street. I don't suppose you ever want to go to Mayfield to live."

Rex shuddered.

"I don't," he said, with great earnestness. "I shall shut the place up and let it stand for a few years, until the memory of the crime is forgotten, and then perhaps somebody will buy it. I am pretty comfortable here, Tab."

"I am not thinking so much about your comfort as my own," replied Tab calmly. "It isn't going to do me a lot of good in any way. Consider yourself ejected."

Rex grinned.

He sailed for Naples the next afternoon, and Tab went down to the boat to see him off. No mention of Ursula Ardfern was made until the landing bell was ringing.

"I am holding you to your promise, Tab, to introduce me to Miss Ardfern," he said, and frowned as though at some unhappy recollection. "I wish to heaven she hadn't been mixed up in the business at all. How on earth do you account for her jewel-case being in poor Uncle Jesse's vault? By the way, the key of that devil room is in my trunk if the police want it. I don't suppose they will, for they have the other key now."

He had asked this question about Ursula's jewels so many times before that Tab could not keep count of them. Therefore, he did not attempt to supply a satisfactory solution.

Standing on the pier he watched the big ship gliding down the river, and on the whole was glad that the companionship had broken up. He liked Rex and Rex liked him, and they had shared happily the mild vicissitudes which came to young men with large ambitions and limited incomes. Of the two, Tab had been the richer in the old days, and had often helped the other through the morasses which grip the ankles of men who systematically live beyond their means. And now Babe was in calm waters: for evermore superior to the favours of crabbed uncles and businesslike employers; no more would he start at every knock the postman rapped, or scowl at the letters which arrived, knowing that more than half of them were bills he could not hope to satisfy.

Nearly a month had passed since the inquest, and all that Tab had heard about Ursula was that she had been very ill and was now in the country, presumably at the Stone Cottage. He had some idea of going down to see her, but thought better of it.

Meanwhile he had made respectful inquiries about the girl who had so impressed him.

Ursula Ardfern's story was a curious one. She had appeared first in a road company, playing small parts and playing them well. Then, without any warning, she blossomed forth into management, took a lease of the Athenaeum, and appeared playing a secondary rôle in an adaptation of *Tosca* – the lead being in the capable hands of Mary Farrelli. The dramatic critics were mollified by her modesty and pleased with her acting: said they would like to see her in a more important part, and hoped that her season would be prosperous. They asked, amongst themselves, who was the man behind the show, and found no satisfactory answer. Then *Tosca* came off, after a run of three months; she staged *The Tremendous Jones*, which played for a year, and this time she was the leading actress. She had gone from success to success, was on the very threshold of a great career. The simple announcement that she had retired from the stage forever was not very seriously believed. Yet it was true. Ursula Ardfern had appeared for the last time before the footlights.

The day that Rex sailed she saved Tab any further cogitation by writing to him. He found the letter at the office.

"DEAR MR HOLLAND – I wonder if you would come to the Stone Cottage to see me? I promise you rather a sensational 'story,' though I realize that it will lose much of its importance because I will not have my name mentioned in connection."

Tab would have liked to have gone then and there. He was up the next morning at six, and chafed because he could not in decency arrive at the house much before lunch.

It was a glorious June day, warm, with a gentle westerly wind: such a day as every doctor with a convalescent patient in his charge hails with joy and thankfulness.

She was reclining where he had seen her on his first visit to Hertford, but this time she did not rise, but held out a thin white hand, which he took with such exaggerated care that she laughed. She was paler, thinner of face, older looking in some indefinite way.

"You won't break it," she said. "Sit down, Mr Tab."

"I like Mr Tab very much better than I like Mr Holland," said Tab. "It is glorious here. Why do we swelter in the towns?"

"Because the towns pay us our salaries," she said dryly. "Mr Holland, will you do something for me?"

He longed to tell her that if she asked him to stand on his head, or lie down whilst she wiped her feet upon him, she would be gladly obeyed. Instead: "Why, of course," he said.

"Will you sell some jewels for me? They are those which were found – in poor Mr Trasmere's vault."

"Sell your jewels," he said in amazement, "why? Are you – " he checked himself.

"I am not very poor," she said quietly. "I have enough money to live without working again – my last play was a very great success, and happily the profits – " She stopped dead. "At any rate, I am not poor."

"Then why sell your jewellery? Are you going to buy others?" he blurted out.

She shook her head, and a smile dawned in her eyes.

"No, my plan is this: I am going to sell the jewellery for what it is worth, and then I want you to distribute the money to such charities as you think best."

He was too astonished to answer, and she went on: "I know very little about charities and their values. I know in some cases all the money subscribed is swallowed up in officials' salaries. But you will know these."

"Are you serious?" he at last found his voice to ask.

"Quite," she nodded gravely. "I think they are worth from twelve to twenty thousand. I am not sure. They are mine," she went on a little defiantly, and unnecessarily so, thought Tab, "and I may do as I wish with them. I want them to be sold and the money distributed."

"But, my dear Miss Ardfern – " he began.

"My dear Mr Holland!" she mocked him, "you must do as I tell you if you are going to help me at all."

"I'll certainly carry out your wishes," he said; "but it is a weighty lot of money to give away."

"It is a weightier lot of money to keep," she said quietly. "There is another favour I ask – you must not write that I am the donor. You can describe me as a society woman, a retired tradeswoman, or as anything you like; except as an actress; and of course my name must not even be hinted. Will you do this?"

He nodded.

"I have them here," she said. "I kept them at the hotel and had them sent down to me by special messenger yesterday. And now that that business is over, come inside and lunch."

It was very dear to have her leaning on his arm; her dependence thrilled him. He wanted to take her up in his arms and carry her through that sweet-smelling place, slowly and with dignity, as nurses carry sleeping babies. He wondered what she would think and say if she guessed his thoughts. It made him hot to consider the possibility for a second.

She did not go direct to the house, but took him through a sunken patch hidden by low bushes, and he stopped and admired, for here a master hand had laid out a Chinese garden with tiny bridges and dwarf trees and great clumps of waxen rock flowers that harboured a faint and delicate scent, a hint of which came up to him.

"You were thinking of carrying me," she said, *à propos* of nothing.

Tab went a fiery red.

"But for the proprieties, I should like it. Do you like babies, Mr Tab?"

"I love 'em," said he, glad to reach a less embarrassing topic.

"So do I – I have seen so many when I was a child. They are wonderful. It seems to me that they are so near to the source of life, they bring with them the very fragrance of God."

He was silent, impressed, a little bewildered. Where had she seen "so many" babies? Had she been a nurse? She had not been talking for effect… He knew an actress once, the only other one he had interviewed, who had quoted Ovid and Herrick and talked with astonishing ease and fluency on the Byzantine Empire. He learnt from a friend that she possessed an extraordinary memory, and had read up these subjects before he came, in order to get a good story about herself. She had the story.

No, Ursula was different. He wished he had lifted her up in his arms when she had spoken about being carried.

Over the meal the talk took a personal turn.

"Have you many friends?" she asked.

"Only one," smiled Tab, "and he's now so rich that I can scarcely call him a friend. Not that Rex wouldn't repudiate that."

"Rex?"

"Rex Lander," said Tab, "who, by the way, is very anxious to be introduced to you. He is one of your most fervent admirers." Tab felt that he was being very noble indeed, and he experienced quite a virtuous glow at his own unselfishness.

"Who is he?" she asked.

"He is old Trasmere's nephew."

"Why, of course," she said quickly, and went red. "You have spoken about him before."

Tab tried to remember. He was almost certain that he had never mentioned Rex to the girl.

"So he is very rich? Of course he would be. He was Mr Trasmere's only nephew."

"You saw that in the newspaper?"

"No; I guessed, or somebody told me; I haven't read any account of the murder, or any of the proceedings. I was too ill. He must be very rich," she went on. "Is he anything like his uncle?"

Tab smiled.

"I can't imagine two people more dissimilar," he said. "Rex is – well, he's rather stoutish," he said loyally, "and a lazy old horse. Mr Trasmere, on the contrary, was very thin and, for his age, remarkably energetic. When did I mention Rex?" he asked.

She shook her head.

"I can't recall the time and place. Please don't make me think, Mr Holland. Where is Rex now?"

"He has gone to Italy. He sailed yesterday," said Tab, and thereupon the girl's interest in Rex Lander seemed to suffer eclipse.

"I should like to have had Trasmere's real story," said Tab; "he must have lived an interesting life. It is rather curious that we found nothing in the house reminiscent of his Chinese experience but a small lacquer box, which was empty. The Chinese fascinate me."

"Do they?" she looked at him quickly; "they fascinate me in a way by their kindness."

"You know them; have you lived in China?"

She shook her head.

"I know one or two," she said, and paused, as though she were considering whether it was advisable to say any more. "When I first came to town from service – "

He gaped at her.

"I don't quite get that – by 'service'; what do you mean? You don't mean domestic service…you weren't a cook or anything?" he asked jocularly, and to his amazement she nodded.

"I was a sort of tweeny maid; peeled potatoes and washed dishes," she said calmly. "I was only thirteen at the time. But that is another story, as Mr Kipling says. At this age, and before I went to a school, I met a Chinaman whose son was very ill. He lodged in the house where I was staying. The landlady wasn't a very humane sort of person, and being Chinese, she thought the poor little boy had some mysterious Eastern disease which she would 'catch.' I nursed him, in a way," she said apologetically, but Tab knew that the apology was not for her condescension, but for her lack of nursing skill. "The father was very poor then, a waiter in a native restaurant, but he was ever so grateful. Quite an extraordinary man – I have seen him since."

"And the child?"

"Oh, he got better – his father was dosing him with quaint proprietary medicines. I think he was suffering from enteric fever, and nursing is the only thing that cures that. He's in China now – quite an important person."

"I should like to have that other story," said Tab. "Kipling gets my goat. That 'other story' of his is never told. I think he must have had them in his mind when he referred to them, but he got lazy on it."

"My other story must keep," she smiled. "Some day...perhaps... but not now. The father of the boy laid out my little Chinese garden, by the way."

Tab had come by tram, and there was a long walk to the station. He stayed to the very last moment, and then had to hurry to catch the one fast express of the afternoon. He had gone a leisurely hundred yards from the front gate (you cannot walk fast if you turn round at intervals for a glimpse of a cool white figure) when he saw a dusty roadfarer coming toward him. The awkward gait of the walker, his baggy clothes, the huge Derby hat pulled down to his ears, attracted Tab's attention long before he could distinguish the man's features. When he did, it was with a spasm of surprise. The walker was a Chinaman, and carried in his hand a flat packet.

The Oriental deviated from the straight path to cross the road. Without a word he carefully unwrapped a thin paper cover and exposed a letter. It was addressed to "Miss Ursula Ardfern, Stone Cottage," and on the wrapper Tab saw a number of Chinese characters which he guessed were directions to the messenger.

"Tell," said the man laconically. He evidently knew little English.

"That house on the left," said Tab, pointing. "How far have you come, Chink?"

"Velly well," said the man, and taking the letter, folded it again in its covering and trotted off.

Tab looked after him, wondering. How curious a coincidence, he thought, that they should have been talking about the Chinese only half an hour before?

He had to run, and then only caught the train as it was pulling out of the station.

The inexorable and constitutionally discontented news editor was not at all satisfied with the story as Tab wrote it.

"It loses half its value if we can't give her name," he complained; "and after we've started the interest going, *The Herald*, or some other paper, will find out who is the owner of the jewels and get all the fat of the story! Can't you persuade her?"

Tab shook his head.

"What's the great idea – is she going into a convent or something?"

"She didn't mention it," said Tab impatiently. "There it is – take it or leave it, Jacques. It is a good item, and if you don't like it, I'll take it to the chief."

A threat which invariably ended all discussion, for Tab was an important personage on the staff of *The Megaphone*, and his word carried weight.

13

Mr Stott combined the implacable qualities of the feudal lord with an amiable leaning toward the society and approval of his fellow men. There was a café near his office which was extensively patronised by grave business men – directors, bank managers, and superior cashiers. The price of luncheon had been scientifically fixed by the proprietor, so that whilst it was within the means of men of substance and standing, it was just beyond the reach of those whose limited incomes did not permit the luxury of lunching at Toby's, though it was well worth the money to sit at meat with men who had offices labelled "Private," and drove to their businesses in polished limousines.

Mr Stott referred to the wistful folk who passed the door of Toby's to be swallowed up in less exclusive establishments, as the *hoi polloi*, which he understood was an Italian expression. Toby's had almost acquired the status of a club. Occasionally, ignorant strangers wandered in to test the gastronomical excellence of the kitchen, and these were usually accommodated in obscure corners away from the hearing of intimate gossip.

Mr Stott had recently become a person to be listened to with respect, and the necessity for keeping the regular patrons of Toby's aloof from the vulgar herd was doubly urgent by reason of the very important matters that had to be discussed.

"What I can't understand, Stott," said one of his hearers, "is why the devil you didn't send for the police?"

Mr Stott smiled mysteriously.

"The police should have been there," he said, "and by the way, I need not remind you fellows that what I say to you is in absolute confidence. I am scared out of my life lest that babbling servant of mine starts talking. You can never trust these gossiping girls. I confess, though, that I had half a mind, not to send for the police, but to tackle the Chinks myself. I should have done it, too, but the girl was so frightened of being left alone."

"Have they come since?" asked another interested hearer.

"No; nor the woman – you remember that I told you of the woman who used to drive up to Mayfield every night in her car?"

"It seems to me that the police ought to know," interrupted the first speaker. "One of your servants is bound to talk. As you say, you can't trust 'em! And then the authorities will want to know why you haven't reported the matter."

"It is not my business," said Mr Stott pharisaically. "It is for the police to get busy. I'm not at all surprised that the coroner's jury made the remark they did. Here is a man murdered – "

He exhibited the crime graphically.

"At any rate, I'm keeping out of it – these Chinese criminals are dangerous fellows to monkey with."

He had paid his bill and was walking out of the café when somebody touched him on the arm, and he swung round to see a tall, melancholy, and long-faced man.

"Excuse me; Mr Stott, I believe?"

"That is my name. I haven't the pleasure – "

"My name is Carver. I am an Inspector of Police, and I want you to tell me something about what was seen outside Mayfield, both before and after the murder."

Mr Stott's face fell.

"That servant of mine has been talking," he said, annoyed; "I knew she couldn't keep her mouth shut."

"I know nothing about your servant, sir," said Carver sadly, "but I have been sitting in Toby's for the past three days and I have heard quite a lot. It sounded to me almost as if you were the principal speaker on the subject, but maybe I was mistaken."

"I shall say nothing," said Mr Stott firmly, and the detective sighed.

"I shouldn't hurry to make up my mind on that subject if I were you," he said, "it is certain to be a difficult business explaining to the Public Prosecutor why you have kept silence so long…it looks very suspicious, you know, Mr Stott."

Mr Stott was aghast.

"Suspicious…me… Good heavens! Come to my office, Mr Carver …suspicious! I knew I should be dragged into it! I'll fire Eline tonight!"

When Tab in the course of duty called that night at the station, he heard the story from Carver.

"If the poor nut had only had the pluck to telephone to the police when the girl first told him the story, we could have caught those birds. As it is, there's no sense in keeping the house under observation any longer. Who was the woman? That puzzles me. Who was the woman who night after night garaged her car in Trasmere's garden and let herself into the house, carrying a square black bag?"

Tab did not answer. The identity of the woman was no mystery to him. She was Ursula Ardfern.

The fabric of supposition fitted piece to piece. He remembered he had come upon her in the deserted streets at dawn, surveying a burst tyre, and the plainness of her dress. Inside the car was a square black case, but –

Ursula working hand in glove with Chinamen; Ursula privy to these stealthy comings and goings, these midnight burglaries at Mayfield? That was unthinkable.

"…their reason for breaking in after we had left the place is beyond me," Carver was saying. "I can only suppose that they hoped that we had overlooked something of value."

"In Mayfield…there is nothing there now?"

"Only the furniture and one or two articles we took away but have since returned, such as the green lacquer box. As a matter of fact, they only went back yesterday. Mr Lander thought of selling all the furniture and effects by auction, and I believe that before he left he put the matter in the hands of an agent. The Chinamen intrigue me," he said, "though it is by no means certain that both Stott and his servant aren't mistaken. I gather they were considerably panic-stricken, and even I wouldn't undertake to distinguish a Chinaman from a European by the light of a match."

Tab went into Carver's private office, and they sat talking until close on eleven o'clock, at which hour their conversation was violently interrupted by the ring of the telephone.

"Call through for you, sir," said the voice of the sergeant on the desk, and a second later Carver recognized the agitated voice of Mr Stott.

"They're here now! They've just gone in! The woman has opened the door…they've just gone in!"

"Who? Is that Stott – do you mean into Mayfield?" asked Carver quickly.

"Yes! I saw them with my own eyes. The woman's car is outside the door."

"Go and get its number quick," said Carver sharply; "find a policeman and tell him; and if you can't find one detain the woman yourself."

He heard Mr Stott's feeble expostulation, and jumped for his hat.

They boarded the first taxi-cab they could find, and raced through the town at a breakneck pace, turning into one end of the quiet avenue in which Mayfield was situated, just as the tail lights of a car turned the corner at the other end.

Mr Stott was standing on the sidewalk, pointing dumbly, but with hysterical gestures, at the place where the car had been.

"They've gone," he said hollowly. "…couldn't find a policeman: they've gone!"

"So I notice," said Carver. "Did you take the number of the car?"

Mr Stott shook his head and made a choking noise in his throat. Presently he commanded his speech.

"Covered over with black paper," he said.

"Who was it?"

"A Chinaman and a woman," said the other.

"Why in hell didn't you stop them?" snapped Carver.

"A Chinaman and a woman," repeated Stott miserably.

"What was she like?"

"I didn't get near enough to see," Mr Stott made the confession without shame. "There ought to have been police here…lots of police… It is disgraceful. I am going to write to the – "

They left him quivering threats. Carver ran across the concrete garden, unlocked the door and switched on all the lights in the hall. Nothing, so far as he could see, had been disturbed. The door to the vault was locked, and had not been tampered with. Apparently the dining-room had. The fireplace was a broad deep cavity lined with red brick, and pointed with yellow cement. An electric radiator had replaced the stove, and Carver had made a very thorough examination, both of the recess and the wide chimney above. But he saw at a glance that his inspection had been short of perfect. One of the bricks had been taken out. It lay on the table, with its steel lid open, and Carver surveyed it thoughtfully.

"That is one on me," he said. "It looks like the face of a brick, doesn't it? Look at that artistic cement pointing all round the edge? It isn't cement at all, but steel. In fact, this must be about the only secret drawer in the house. I ought to have made more thorough inquiries from the builders."

The box was empty, except for a tiny rubber band. They found its fellow on the table.

"There was something of importance in that box which has been taken out; probably a bundle of papers; more likely two bundles. The rubber bands suggest two. Anyway, they've gone."

He glanced round the room.

"And the green lacquer box has gone," he said. "I know it was here, because I put it on the mantelshelf with my own hands."

He opened the door leading to the vault and satisfied himself that nobody had gained admission to the underground room.

"We had better go along and see this police critic," he said grimly.

It appeared that he had done Mr Stott an injustice, for, greatly fearing, he had crossed the road whilst the people were in the house, and he had made honest attempts to find a policeman, having sent the toothachy Eline on that errand, which was successful, if the success was somewhat belated, for the policeman arrived with her whilst the Inspector was talking to the merchant.

"I not only crossed the road," said Mr Stott, "but I went inside the garden. They must have seen me, for the light in the dining-room went out suddenly, and they came flying down the steps together."

"And passed you, of course?"

"They did not pass me," explained Mr Stott emphatically, "because I was on the other side of the road before they were out of the gate. I do not think anything would have passed me."

"What was the woman like?" asked Carver again.

"I have an idea she was young, but I did not see her face. She was dressed in black, and, as far as I could see, veiled. The other man was small: he only came up to her shoulder."

"That is that," said Carver disconsolately, when they came away. "They ought to have been caught, if that man had the spunk of a rabbit. You are very silent, Tab – what are you thinking?"

"I am wondering," said Tab truthfully, "just wondering."

"What are you wondering?" growled the other.

"I am wondering whether old Trasmere was a much worse man than any of us imagine," said Tab calmly.

14

Early in the morning Tab paid a fruitless visit to Stone Cottage. The woman who acted as caretaker told him that the young lady had returned to town, and it was at the Central Hotel that he saw her.

Never had he approached an inquiry, professional or otherwise, with such reluctance. On most matters Tab had very definite views. His mentality was such that he never hesitated to form a judgment, or wavered in his convictions. That type of mind cannot understand in others the vacillating hesitancy which so often distinguishes them in their judgment of people and things. And yet, strive as he did, he could not reduce to a formula his own chaotic feelings in relation to Ursula Ardfern. One thing he knew. It was no vicarious interest he was showing – he did not even in his own mind regard himself as standing for Rex Lander.

Tab thought best with a pen in his hand, yet when in cold blood he endeavoured to reduce to writing the exact state of his mind in relation to Ursula Ardfern, the white sheet of paper remained white to the end.

The moment he entered her sitting-room Tab felt that Ursula knew the object of his visit.

"You want to see me very badly, don't you?" she said, without preliminary, and he nodded.

"What is it?"

Unless he was dreaming, her voice held a subtle caress, and yet that was a ridiculous exaggeration; perhaps "kindness" were a better word.

"Somebody went into Mayfield last night, accompanied by a Chinaman, and they got away just before the police arrived," said Tab awkwardly. "And that isn't all: that same somebody has been in the habit of visiting Trasmere between eleven at night and two in the morning, and this practice has been going on for a considerable time."

She nodded.

"I told you I did not know Mr Trasmere," she said quietly. "It is the only lie I have told you. I knew Mr Trasmere very well, but there were reasons why it would have been fatal for me to have admitted my friendship with him. No, not one lie – two." She held up her fingers to emphasize her words.

"The other was about the lost jewel-case," said Tab huskily.

"Yes," she replied.

"You didn't lose it at all."

She shook her head.

"No, I didn't lose it at all: I knew where it was all the time; but I was – panic-stricken, and had to make a decision on the spur of the moment. I did not regret it."

There was a pause.

"Do the police know?" she asked.

"About you? No. I think they might find out – not from me."

"Sit down." She was very calm. He thought she was going to explain, and was quite satisfied that the explanation was a very simple one, but she had no such intention, as her first words told him.

"I can't tell you now the why of everything. I am too…what is the word? Too tense. I am not so sure that this is the word, either, but my defences are in being. I dare not relax one of them, or the whole would go. Of course I knew nothing of the murder – you never dreamt I did?"

He shook his head.

"I did not know until Sunday morning, when I was driving out to Stone Cottage," she said. "It was only by accident that I bought a paper in the street, and then I made my decision. I went straight to the police station with my story of the lost jewel-case. I knew it was in the vault, and I had to find some explanation."

"How did it come to be in the vault?" Tab knew that the question was futile before it was half out.

"That is part of the other story," she smiled faintly. "Do you believe me?"

He looked up at her quickly, and their eyes met.

"Does it matter whether I believe or not?" he asked quietly.

"It matters a great deal to me," she said, in the same tone.

It was his gaze that fell first.

Then, in a different and more cheery voice, she went on: "You have to help me, Mr Tab. Not in the matter we have been discussing – I don't mean that."

"I'll help you in that," said Tab.

"I think you will," she answered quickly, "but for the moment, ungracious as it may sound, I do not need help. The other matter is more personal. Do you remember telling me about your friend?"

"Rex?" he asked in surprise.

She nodded.

"He went to Naples, didn't he? I had a letter from him, written on board."

Tab smiled.

"Poor old Rex. What did he want, your photograph?"

"More than that," she said quietly. "You won't think I am horrible if I betray his confidence, but I must if you are to help me. Mr Lander has done me the honour of asking me to marry him."

Tab looked at her open-mouthed.

"Rex?" he said incredulously.

She nodded.

"I won't show you the letter, it would hardly be fair; but he has asked me to give my answer in the agony column of *The Megaphone*. He says that he has an agent in London who will send it by wireless, and I was wondering – " She hesitated.

"If I were the agent?" said Tab. "No, I know nothing whatever about this."

She drew a sigh.

"I'm glad," she said inconsequently. "I mean, I'm glad that you won't be hurt even indirectly."

"Do you intend putting in the advertisement?"

"I have already sent it to the paper," she said. "Here is a copy." She went to her writing-table and brought back a slip of paper, and Tab read: "Rex: What you ask is quite impossible. I shall never make any other reply. U."

"One does get those kind of letters," she said, "and as a rule they are not worth while answering. Had I not known…he was a friend of yours, I don't think I should have taken the trouble – yes I would," she nodded slowly. "Mr Trasmere's nephew has certain claims to refusal."

"Poor old Rex," said Tab softly. "I had a wireless from him this morning, saying that he was enjoying the voyage."

He took up his hat.

"As regards the other matter, Miss Ardfern," he said, "you must tell me in your own time, if you wish to tell me at all. But you must understand that there is a very big chance that the police will trace you, in which case I may be of assistance. As matters stand, I am just a sympathetic observer."

He held out his hand with a smile, and she took it and held it in both of hers.

"For twelve years I have been living in a nightmare," she said: "a nightmare which my own vanity created. I think I am awake now, and when the police trace me – and I am so certain they will trace me that I have left the stage – "

"Was that the reason?" he exclaimed in surprise.

"That is one of the two reasons," she said. "When they trace me, I think I shall be glad. There is still something of the old Eve in me" – she smiled a little sadly – "to make exposure a painful possibility."

One last question he asked as he stood at the door.

"What was in the box? The box that looked like a brick and was hidden in the fireplace?"

"Papers," she replied. "I only know they were papers written in Chinese. I do not know what they were about yet."

"Had they…could they possibly supply a clue to the murder?"

She shook her head, and he was satisfied.

He smiled at her, and with no other word went out. All doubts that he had had as to his feelings toward her were now set at rest. He loved this slim girl with the madonna-like face, whose moods changed as swiftly as April light. He did not think of Rex, or the heartache which her message would bring, until later.

There was no very satisfactory portrait of Wellington Brown in existence. On the ship which brought him from China a fellow passenger had taken a snapshot of a group in which Mr Brown's face, slightly out of focus, loomed foggily. With this to work on, and with the assistance of Tab, something like a near-portrait was constructed and circulated by the police. Every newspaper carried the portrait, every amateur detective in the country was looking for the man with the beard, whose gloves had been found outside the death chamber of Jesse Trasmere.

Less fortunate was the lot of Mr Walter Felling, alias Walters. He had been in prison, and his portraits, full face and profile, were available for immediate distribution. He watched the hunt from one of those densely crowded burrows where humanity swelters and festers on the hot days and nights. In the top room of a crowded tenement, he grew more and more gaunt as the days went by, for the fear of death was in his heart.

Despite the efficient portraiture, it is doubtful whether he would have been recognized by the most lynx-eyed policeman, for his beard had reached a considerable length and suspense and terror had wasted his plump cheeks into hollows and cavities that had changed the very contours of his face. He knew the law; its fatal readiness to accept the most fragmentary evidence when a man was on trial for murder. His every movement had been an acknowledgment of guilt; would be accepted as such by a judge; who would lay out the damning points against him with a cold and remorseless thoroughness.

Sometimes at nights, especially on rainy nights, he would creep out into the streets. Always they seemed to be full of police. He would return in a panic to spend another restless night, when every creak of the stairs, every muffled voice in the rooms below, made him jump to the door.

Walters had doubled back to town, the only safe place of refuge. In the country he would have been a marked man and his liberty of short duration. Avoiding the districts which knew him well, and the friends whose loyalty would not stand the test of a murder charge, he came to the noisy end of Reed Street, posing as an out-of-work engineer.

Here he read every newspaper which he could procure, and in each journal every line that dealt with the murder. What had Wellington Brown to do with it? The appearance of that man in the case bewildered him. He remembered the visitor from China very well. So he, too, was a fugitive. The knowledge brought him a shade of comfort. It was as though a little of the burden of suspicion had been lifted from himself.

One night when he was taking the air, a Chinaman went pad-padding past him, and he recognized Yeh Ling. The proprietor of the Golden Roof was one of the few Chinamen in town who seldom wore European dress, and Walters knew him. Yeh Ling had come to Mayfield on several occasions. He had worn European dress then, and had excited no surprise, for Mr Trasmere's association with the Far East was well known. Yeh Ling must have seen him, for he had passed at a moment when the light of a street lamp fell upon Walters' face. But he made no sign of recognition, and the fugitive hoped that Yeh Ling had been absorbed in his thoughts. Nevertheless he hurried home again, to sit in his darkened room and start painfully at every sound.

Had he known that Yeh Ling had both seen and identified him, he would not have slept at all that night. The Chinaman pursued his course to the unsavoury end of Reed Street; children who saw him screamed derisively; a frowsy woman standing in a doorway yelled a crude witticism, but Yeh Ling passed on unmoved. Turning sharply into a narrow alleyway he stopped before a darkened shop and tapped upon a side door. It was opened at once, and he passed into a thick and pungent darkness. A voice hissed a question, and he answered in the same dialect. Then, without guide, he made his way up the shaky stairs to a back room.

It was illuminated by the light of four candles. The walls were covered by a cheap paper, its crude design mellowed by age, and the only furniture in the room was a broad divan, on which sat a compatriot, a wizened old Chinaman who was engaged in carving a half-shaped block of ivory which he held between his knees.

They greeted one another soberly, and the old man uttered a mechanical politeness.

"Yo Len Fo," said Yeh Ling, "is the man well?"

Yo Len Fo shook his head affirmatively.

"He is well, excellency," he said. "He has been sleeping all the afternoon and he has just taken three pipes. He had also drunk the whisky you sent."

"I will see him," said Yeh Ling, and dropped some money on the divan.

The old man picked this up, uncurled himself, and putting down his ivory carefully, led the way up another flight of stairs. A small oil-lamp burnt on the bare mantelpiece of the room into which Yeh Ling walked. On a discoloured mattress lay a man. He wore only shirt and trousers and his feet were bare. By the side of the mattress was a tray on which rested a pipe, a half-emptied glass, and a watch.

Mr Wellington Brown looked up at the visitor, his glazed eyes showing the faintest light of interest.

"Lo Yeh Ling...come to smoke?"

His language was a queer mixture of Cantonese and English, and it was in the former tongue that Yeh Ling replied.

"I do not smoke, Hsien," he said, and the man chuckled.

"Hsien? – 'The Unemployed One,' eh?... Funny, how names stick...wasser time?"

"It is late," said Yeh Ling, and the head of the man drooped.

"See ol' Jesse tomorrow..." he said drowsily; "got...lot of business..."

Yeh Ling stooped, and his slim fingers encircled the man's wrist. The pulse was weak but regular.

"It is good," he said, turning to the old carver of ivory. "Every morning there must be air in this room. No other smoker must come; you understand, Yo Len Fo? He must be kept here."

"This morning he wanted to go out," said the keeper of the establishment.

"He will stay for a long time. I know him. When he was on the Amur River he did not leave his house for three months. Let there be one pipe always ready. Obey."

He went softly down the stairs and into the night.

Only once did he glance back as he made his unhurried way to the side door of the Golden Roof. But that glance was sufficient. The man he had seen loafing at the entrance of the alleyway was watching him. He saw him now, walking on the other side of the road, a dim, secretive figure. Yeh Ling slipped into his private door, bent down and raised the flap of a letter-slot. The man had come to a halt on the other side of the road. The reflected light from the blazing signs on the main street illuminated his back, but his face was in shadow.

"It is not a policeman," said Yeh Ling softly, and then, as the man strolled back into the darkness, he called his stunted servant.

"Follow that man who wears a cap. You will see him on the other side of the road; he is walking toward the houses of the noisy women."

A quarter of an hour later the stunted man came back with a story of failure, and Yeh Ling was not surprised. But the watcher was neither policeman nor reporter, of this he was sure.

15

In the course of his professional duties Tab Holland had been brought into contact with the master of the Golden Roof on two occasions. The first followed a small scandal, which only remotely touched the restaurant (the woman who was the subject of Tab's investigation had dined there at an important date), and once in connection with a dead-season topic dealing with the nutritive values of food.

He had found the Chinaman reserved to a point of taciturnity, monosyllabic in speech; a most unsatisfactory person.

Tab knew nothing about him except that he was a successful Chinaman who had gravitated into the restaurant business. He asked Jacques for enlightenment, well knowing that if the news editor could not satisfy his curiosity it was because Yeh Ling was altogether uninteresting. Jacques was one of the rarities, to whom reference is so frequently made that it might be imagined they were as common as straws in a stable. He was a veritable "mine of information." The genus occurs sometimes in newspaper offices. Jacques knew everybody and everybody's wife. He knew why they married. He also knew why stars twinkled and the chemical composition of tears. Quote him a line from any classic and he would give you its predecessor and that which followed. He knew the dates of all important earthquakes and was an authority on the Mogul Emperors. He could sketch you with equal facility the position of Frossard's second corps at Rezonville on August 17, 1870, or the military situation at Thermopolae…and dates.

The only serious students of *The Megaphone* reference library were the reporters who went there to confound Jacques. They never succeeded.

"Yeh Ling? Yes…queer bird. An educated Chink…got a son who is quite a swell scholar by Chinese standards. He ought to make a good story some day; that house he is building at Storford – it is on the way to Hertford; says that one day his son will be the Chinese Ambassador here, and he wants him to have a house worthy of his position. That is what he told Stott. Know Stott? He is a dud architect who knows it all. Weird little devil who looks as if he might have been clever with a different kind of brain. Stott laid out the ground work: sort of Chinese temple with two enormous concrete pillars that are going to stand half way down the drive. The Pillar of Cheerful Memories and the Pillar of Grateful Hearts. That's what he is going to call them. Stott thought it was heathenish, and wondered if the bishop would like it. Yes, you ought to see that place, Tab. No, it isn't built. Yeh Ling has nothing but Chink labour. The Secretary of the Builders Union went to see him about it. Yeh Ling said his ancestors had a Union of their own which put the bar upon non-Taoist labour. Taoism – "

"I hate to wade into the foaming torrent of your eloquence," said Tab gently, "but how did you come to meet Stott?"

"Same lodge," said Jacques. "It is not for me to talk down a brother craftsman – are you one of us, by the way?"

Tab shook his head.

"Ought to be. Get a little respect for authority into your system. As I was saying, I don't want to knock Stott, but he's not everybody's meat. Go and see that temple, or whatever it is, Tab. Might be a good story."

On the first idle day he had Tab took his motor-bicycle and went out to Storford. He was not entirely without hope that he would see Ursula – her house was only seven miles beyond Storford Hill, and he had reason to know that she had withdrawn herself to her country home. In a letter telling this she had told him in so many words that when she wanted him she would send for him.

He saw the building from a distance.

He had noticed it before – it was hardly possible to miss seeing it, for it stood on the crest of one of the few hills the country boasted. The walls were half finished and heavy wooden uprights rose like the palings of a fence above the queerly laid courses. And one of the pillars already lifted its lofty head. It flanked on one side a broad pathway, which was half the width of the house, and stood some fifty feet above the ground, being crowned by a small stone dragon.

Tab wondered if this was the Pillar of Grateful Hearts or that which stood, or would stand, for Cheerful Memories.

Its diameter must have been fully five feet. Near at hand was one of the wooden moulds in which it was cast, and a Chinese workman was scraping the interior.

Tab walked through a break in the low hedge which separated Yeh Ling's new home from the road, and now stood regarding with interest the activities of the blue-bloused workmen. Their industry was remarkable. Whether they were running bricks and mortar, or cutting out the garden (already taking shape), or walling up the terraces, they moved quickly, untiringly, wholly absorbed in their occupations. Never once did they stop to lean upon their spades and picks to discuss the chances of the new Administration, or to tell one another how Milligan got his black eye.

Nobody seemed to notice Tab. He strolled farther into the land, and there was none to challenge his right. A gang of men were gravelling and rolling the broad path, and one of these said something which sent the others into a fit of that cluttering laughter which is peculiar to the East. Tab wondered what was the joke.

Turning to walk back to the road, he saw that a car had stopped at the break in the hedge, and his heart gave a leap, for its occupant was Ursula.

"What do you think of it?" she asked.

"It is going to be rather wonderful – how do you like the idea of having a Chinaman for a neighbour? I forgot – you rather like the Chinese."

"Yes," she said shortly. "There could be worse neighbours than Yeh Ling."

"You know him?"

He wondered if she would deny acquaintance or evade the question.

"Very well," she said calmly; "he is the proprietor of the Golden Roof. I often dine there. You know him too?"

"Slightly," said Tab, looking back at the unfinished house. "He must be rich."

"I don't know. One never really knows what money is required to build a place like this. The labour is cheap, and it seems a very simple kind of house."

And then, with a wave of her hand, she drove on. She might at least have asked him to lunch, he thought indignantly.

A week went past, a drab week for a discontented Tab Holland, for now there was neither a likelihood of nor an excuse for a chance meeting.

A sedative week for the hiding Walters. References to the murder seldom appeared now in the newspapers, and he had found a man who had offered to get him a job as a steward on an outward-bound liner.

A week of drugged sleep for a besotted man, curled up on a mattress at the top of Yo Len Fo's house.

But for Inspector Carver an exceptionally busy week, though there was no newspaper record of his activities.

Tab no longer spent his evenings at home. The flat seemed horribly empty now that the love-sick Rex had gone. He had had a radio from him, saying that he was improved in health. The message was cheerful enough, so that Ursula's refusal could not have bitten very hard.

By the end of the week life had become an intolerable dreariness, and to make matters worse nothing was happening in the great world that called for Tab's intervention and interest. He was in that condition of utter boredom when there happened the first of those remarkable incidents which, in his official account of the case, Inspector Carver refers to as "The Second Activity."

The flats, one of which Tab occupied, had originally been apartments in a private house. With little structural alteration they had been turned into self-contained suites. On each of the landings was a door of one of the four flats. Admission to the house was by the front door, and the landlord had so arranged matters that, whilst the key of each flat was different, all keys opened the street door. It was therefore possible to go in and out without observation, unless by chance one of the other tenants happened to be on the stairs or in the passageway at the time.

On Saturday night Tab knew he would be alone in the house; the other three tenants invariably spent the weekend out of town. One was a middle-aged musician who lived on the top floor. Beneath him was a young couple engaged in literary work; then came Tab's flat; and the ground-floor suite was occupied by a man whose profession was unknown, but who was generally believed to be connected with an advertising agency. He was seldom at home, and Tab had only seen him once.

The Saturday night happened to be the occasion of an annual dinner of his club, and Tab dressed and went out early, spent a mildly exhilarating evening, and returned home at half-past twelve. There was nothing in first appearance to suggest that anything unusual had happened in his absence, except that the lights in his sitting-room were burning and he had switched them off before he went out.

His first impression was that the waste of current was due to his own carelessness, but then he recalled very clearly that he had turned out the light and closed the sitting-room door before he went out. Now the sitting-room door was open, as also was the door of Rex's old room.

16

Tab smiled to himself. He who had investigated so many burglaries had never imagined that he would be favoured by the attention of those midnight adventurers. He went into Rex's room, turned the switch, and had only to take one glance to know that somebody had been very busy indeed in his absence. Under the bed which his companion had occupied were two shallow trunks filled with those of Rex Lander's belongings which he had not taken with him. One of these had been pulled out, placed on the bed, and opened. It had been opened unscientifically with a chisel, which Tab knew was his property, and must have been taken from the tool-box in the kitchen. The lock was wrenched off and the contents of the box scattered on the bed. The other trunk had not been touched. Whether the thief had been successful in his quest Tab did not know, because he was ignorant of the box's contents. He guessed he must have been disappointed, for beyond a quantity of underlinen, more or less in a state of disrepair, a few books and drawing instruments, and a packet of letters which Tab saw at a glance were from Jesse Trasmere, there was nothing at all valuable in the trunk.

He went to his own room, but none of his things had been touched. And then he began a careful search of the other rooms in the flat. They yielded, however, no clue as to the identity of the mysterious visitor, and Tab got on to the 'phone to Carver and was lucky to find him.

"Burglars? That's poetic justice, Tab," said Carver's sad voice. "I'll come right along."

The detective was at the house in ten minutes.

"If this had happened in the daytime I could find a fairly simple explanation," said Tab, "because the front door below is left open until nine, and the tenant who comes in or goes out nearest to nine o'clock closes it. We keep the door open, because it saves a lot of running up and down stairs, but the street door was closed when I came home."

"How would it have been a simple matter to burgle the flat?" asked Carver, and Tab explained that there was a window on the landing through which a sure-footed and skilful adventurer might emerge on to a narrow ledge by which the kitchen window could be reached.

"He didn't go that way, I should think," said Carver, after he had inspected the kitchenette. "No; the burglar opened the door like a gentleman. Do you know whether Mr Lander had anything worth stealing in that trunk?"

Tab shook his head.

"I am perfectly certain he hadn't," he said. "Poor old Rex had nothing of value except the money he drew from his uncle's estate just before he left."

Carver went back to Rex's room and carefully emptied the trunk, item by item.

"It was something at the bottom of the trunk. I should imagine it was in this box."

He handled a little wooden box with a sliding lid.

"And here is the top," he said, picking it up from the bed. "Can you get in touch with Mr Lander?"

"He'll be at Naples in a day or two; I'll wire him then; but I shouldn't imagine he had lost anything worth the thief's trouble," said Tab.

They went back to the sitting-room, and Carver stood a long time by the table, tapping its covered surface nervously, his long face puckered in thought.

"Do you know what I think?" he said suddenly.

"Generally," said Tab.

"Do you know what I am thinking now?"

"You think I am giving you a lot of trouble over a happening which wasn't worth mentioning," said Tab.

Carver shook his head.

"I am thinking this," he said slowly and deliberately: "that the man who burgled this flat was the man who killed Jesse Trasmere! If you ask me to give chapter and verse for my conclusion I shall both disappoint you and disappoint myself. I have always found," he went on, "that when one has an instinctive conviction it is a mistake to make too close an examination of one's mind. Every human being was endowed, some time or other, with as powerful and potent an instinct as the most sensitive of wild animals. With the growth of reason, the instinctive quality faded, until today, in humanity, we find only the faintest trace of it. Yet," he said earnestly, "it is possible for humanity to cultivate that germ of instinct so that one can go to a racetrack and pick every winner."

"You are joking," said Tab surprised, but Carver shook his head.

"You get flashes of it at times; you call them 'hunches.' But you won't give it a chance. You slay it with the hands of logic and smother it with argument, and my instinct tells me that the hand that opened Mr Lander's trunk was the hand that destroyed Trasmere. I had a queer feeling when you telephoned to me," he went on – "a queer feeling, as though you or somebody was going to hand to me a ready-made solution of Trasmere's death."

"And you are disappointed. My poor old Carver," said Tab pityingly. "You think too much!"

"We all think too much," said Carver, relapsing into his natural gloom.

The next morning the tenant who occupied the flat below came up whilst Tab was dressing, and Mr Holland was a little taken aback to see one who so seldom put in an appearance on any day. He was a red-faced gentleman, somewhat sportily attired.

"I hope you didn't mind my shouting up at you last night," he said apologetically, "but I had been travelling night and day and I had had no sleep, and naturally I was a little rattled when I heard that noise going on overhead. Did you drop a box or something?"

"To be exact, I didn't drop a box at all," said Tab smiling. "In fact, the noise you heard was made by a burglar."

"A burglar?" said the startled man. "I heard the row, and it woke me up. I got out of bed and yelled up, as I thought, to you."

"What time was this?"

"Between ten and half-past," said the other. "It was just getting dark."

"He must have dropped the box as he was putting it on the bed," said Tab thoughtfully. "You didn't by any chance see him?"

"I heard him go out about a quarter of an hour after I'd made a fuss," said the man from downstairs, "and I was feeling so ashamed of myself for losing my temper that I opened the door to apologize for shouting at him."

"You didn't see him?"

The man shook his head.

"He shut the door quickly, just as I got into the passage. The only thing I saw was his hand on the edge of the door. He was wearing black gloves. Naturally I thought it was you, though the black gloves seemed to be a queer sort of thing for a young man to wear, even if he was in mourning; and taking it for granted that it was you, and that you were mad with me, I thought no more about it."

All this Tab duly reported to Carver.

That ended the episode of Saturday. Sunday's surprise was more pleasant but not less disturbing. It was late in the evening, and Tab was reading by the light of a table-lamp when the bell which connected with the front door rang urgently. This meant that the front door was closed. On the night of Wellington Brown's visit it was open. He unconsciously connected the two visitations, and wondered whether his instinct was working as well as Carver could wish. Putting the book aside he went down and opened the door, and nearly staggered in his astonishment, for his visitor was Ursula Ardfern, and her little car stood by the edge of the sidewalk.

"I am on my way to the Central," she explained. "Can I come in?"

He had seen the two suitcases strapped to the back of the car, and had wondered for what distant and inaccessible spot she was bound.

"Come in, please," he said hastily. "I am afraid this room is rather smoky." He made to pull up the blind, but she stopped him.

"Please don't," she said, "I am all nerves and shivers, and I feel I could swoon on the slightest excuse. It is rather a pity that that delightful practice of our grandmothers' days went out of fashion. It would be such a relief to swoon sometimes." Her tone was half-jesting, but there was a whole lot of seriousness in her face. "I am coming to live at the Central again," she said, "though I really cannot afford that extravagance."

"What has happened?"

"Stone Cottage is haunted," was the staggering reply.

"Haunted?"

She nodded, and a momentary smile came into her eyes, only to fade as quickly as it came.

"Not by a ghost," she said, "but by a very human man – a mysterious individual in black. The woman who looks after me saw him the other night in the garden; I myself have seen him from my window and challenged him. He has been seen by other people pacing the road outside. Now tell me honestly, Tab Holland, am I under the observation of the police?"

The thought had also occurred to Tab.

"I don't think so," he said. "Carver does not tell me everything, but he has never mentioned your name to me as being under the slightest suspicion. In black, you say?"

"Yes," nodded the girl. "From head to foot in black, including black gloves. It was rather spectacular – "

"Black gloves?" interrupted Tab. "I wonder if it is my burglar?" and he told her of the visitor who had come the night before.

"It is extraordinary," she said, "more extraordinary because he was not seen last night. I am not usually nervous, but I must confess that it is a little worrying to know that somebody is watching me."

"How did he come? Had he a car or bicycle, or did he come by train?"

On this point she could not enlighten him.

"I almost wish you had not come up," said Tab. "If you had told me, I would have gone to Stone Cottage and stayed the night, especially after my burglar. I should like to meet the gentleman who treats my flat so unceremoniously."

She made no reply, and then: "Why did I come here, I wonder?" she asked, and it was as though she were speaking to herself, for she laughed. "Poor Mr Tab," she said, with that little hint of mockery in her voice which he adored, "I am laying all my burdens upon you. Mystery upon mystery, some of my own, but this, I promise you, not of my making." She considered, her finger at her lips. "Suppose I return to Stone Cottage on Monday morning and you come down later? My woman will be an efficient chaperon, and I think you should come after dark – that is, if you can spare the time."

Tab wanted to tell her that all eternity, so far as he was concerned, was at her disposal, but very wisely refrained.

He saw her to her car and went back to his room with a sense of exhilaration that he had not felt all that week.

17

It was a delicate matter broaching the subject of police espionage to Carver. In the first place he did not want to give the Inspector the slightest hint that Ursula Ardfern expected to be watched. He compromised by telling that gloomy man, at the first opportunity, that he had seen Miss Ardfern. And then he mentioned casually, and by the way, the story of her watcher.

"Of course it isn't a thief," said Carver promptly. "Thieves do not advertise their presence by alarming the people they hope to rob. Has she complained to the local police?"

Tab did not know, but he guessed that she had not.

"It may be a coincidence," said Carver, "and the man in black may really have nothing whatever to do with the murder of Trasmere, but I am intrigued. You are going down, you say? I wonder if Miss Ardfern would mind my coming too?"

Tab was in a dilemma here. To hesitate would be to give the police officer a wholly wrong impression. To accept was to eclipse the happy evening he had in prospect. For to be alone with Ursula Ardfern, to stand to her in the nature of a protector, would be a wonderful experience which he had no desire to share.

"I am sure Miss Ardfern would be delighted," he said.

"If I can get away I will come," said Carver.

Tab fervently hoped that urgent business would keep his friend in town.

He sent a note round to Ursula putting forward Carver's suggestion, and received a reply by return extending her invitation.

After mature thought, Tab decided that it was not at all a bad idea to have Carver with him. It would give the girl an opportunity of making friends with one who might, in certain circumstances, be a difficult man to satisfy. She could not have too many friends, he thought, and was almost relieved when Carver hurried into the station a few minutes before the last train to Hertford left.

It was dark when they arrived, and by pre-arrangement they did not speak in the long walk which separated them from Stone Cottage, but in single file, keeping to the shadows of the road, they marched forward without meeting with a soul.

When at last they came to the highway in which Stone Cottage was situated, they proceeded with greater caution. But there was nobody in sight and they reached the garden unobserved.

Ursula was standing in the open doorway to welcome them.

"I've had all the blinds pulled down," she said, "and Inspector Carver's coming is rather providential, for my woman has had to go home – her mother has been taken ill. I hope you don't mind appearing in the rôle of a chaperon," she smiled at Carver.

"Even that is not an unusual one," he replied, unsmiling. "Where does she live, the mother of your servant?"

"At Felborough. Poor Margaret only had time to catch the last train."

"How did Margaret know her mother was ill?" asked the Inspector. "Did she have a telegram?"

Ursula nodded.

"Late this afternoon?"

"Yes," said the girl, in surprise. "Why do you ask?"

"She got the telegram in time to catch the train to town; in time, too, to catch a train for Felborough. That was why I asked. You did not see the man last week?"

"I didn't come down until this morning," she answered, troubled. "Do you think that Margaret has been sent for by – somebody – that it was a ruse to get her away?"

"I don't know," said Carver. "In my profession we always apply the worst construction, and we are generally right. What time do you usually go to bed?"

"At ten o'clock in the country," she said.

"Then at ten o'clock, will you go up to your room, put on your lights, and after a reasonable time, put them out again? You may, if you wish, come down, but you must be prepared to sit in the dark; and if you want to talk, you must carry on your conversation in whispers." A rare smile softened his face. "We shall probably all be feeling a little foolish in the morning, but I would rather feel foolish than miss the opportunity of meeting the man in black."

She gave them supper, and after the men had helped clear away the remains of the meal Tab, at her request, filled his pipe. Carver said he did not wish to smoke.

Conversation, for some reason, seemed to flag. They sat silently about the table, each busy with his own thoughts. Suddenly Ursula said: "I am almost inclined to make a restricted confession to you, Mr Carver. I don't think I should ever have dreamt of doing so if I had never met you."

"Restricted confessions are irritating things," said Carver, "so I don't think I should confess if I were you, Miss Ardfern, especially as I know what the restricted confession is all about."

Her eyebrows rose.

"You know?" she said.

He nodded.

"You would tell me," he said, "that you were in the habit of going to Trasmere's house every night, to leave your jewels with him, though that wasn't the object of your visit. You went there," he said, slowly and not looking at her, "to act as his secretary. All the letters that were sent away by Jesse Trasmere were typewritten by you on a portable machine: the make of the machine is a Cortona, its number is 29754, it has one key-cap missing, and the letter 'r' is a little out of alignment."

He enjoyed her consternation for a second, and then went on: "Perhaps you weren't going to tell me that you and Yeh Ling, the proprietor of the Golden Roof, paid a visit to Mayfield the night I nearly caught you? No, I see that you weren't. So we'll restrict the confession to your peculiar occupation."

Tab was speechless.

Ursula Ardfern the old man's secretary! One of the most successful actresses in London acting as amanuensis to that crabbed misanthrope; it was unbelievable. Yet a glance at the girl's face told him that Carver had only spoken the truth.

"How do you know?" she gasped.

Carver smiled again.

'We have very clever people in the police," he said dryly. "You would never imagine it, to read the newspapers. Clever old sixty-nine-inch brains, eh, Tab?"

"I never said that you had a sixty-nine-inch brain," avowed Tab stoutly.

"But – " interrupted the girl, and her voice was agitated, "do you know – do you know anything else? Why we went that night?"

"You went to show Yeh Ling where the old man kept some of his secret documents, in the fake brick in the fireplace. You went hoping that in that box there were some papers which related to you, and you were disappointed. The only thing I am in doubt about is this – was Yeh Ling disappointed too?"

She shook her head.

"I wondered," mused Carver. "Of course I guessed that it was in the little lacquer box, and guessed also that the little lacquer box had a false bottom. Am I right?"

She shook her head again.

"No – Yeh Ling thought it was there; the document he sought was in the brick-box."

"You have the key of Mayfield," said Carver. "I think you had better give it to me. Otherwise you may be getting into serious trouble."

She went out of the room without a word, came back, and handed him the small Yale key, which he glanced at and dropped into his pocket.

"If I were a writing man, which, thank heavens, I am not," he said, "I should call this story of the Trasmere murder, 'The Mystery of the Three Keys.' Here is one solved, and it wasn't much of a mystery. There are two others. The third is the most difficult of all."

"You mean the key that was found on the table in the vault?"

He nodded.

"Yes," he said, and said no more.

In her discretion, Ursula asked no further questions.

Tab was looking at Carver with a new respect.

"Every day, Carver," he said seriously, "you are getting nearer the fictional ideal of a real detective!"

Carver's downturned lips took an upward curve, and then he looked at his watch.

"Ten o'clock, Miss Ardfern," he said with mock severity, and Ursula made a move to the door. 'We must turn these lights out before you leave the room. Everything must be done in order, remembering that somewhere the Black Man is watching."

She shivered.

It was Tab who blew out the light in the drawing-room.

"I think we may draw the curtains," said Carver softly, and pulled back the heavy velvet hangings from the window.

It was a starlight night and there was just sufficient light in the sky to outline the gateway.

"This will do admirably," he said, settling himself in the window-seat. "If you must smoke, Tab, don't bring your pipe within sight of that gate."

Tab groaned and laid his pipe upon the fender.

Ten minutes later Ursula came into the room.

"May I stay?" she whispered. "I have put out my bedroom light most artistically."

They conversed in whispers for an hour, and Tab was beginning to feel sleepy when a hiss from Carver stopped him in the middle of a sentence. Looking out of the window he saw a dark figure by the gate. It was impossible to distinguish more than the outlines. It appeared to be a man of considerable height, but this might have been, and probably was, an illusion. It wore a broad-brimmed hat, presumably dark; more than this they could not see. They waited in silence as the gate opened and the figure stole noiselessly into the garden.

It was half way to the door when another figure appeared. It came from nowhere, seeming to rise up from the ground; and then before the man in the wide-awake hat could draw back, the second man had flung himself upon him. The watchers sat paralysed until Carver, jumping to his feet, ran out of the room, Tab close behind him.

When they flung open the door, both figures had disappeared. Carver sprang toward the gate, and stumbled. His foot had struck a soft bulk which stretched across the garden path; he turned back, flashing an electric lamp upon the object. It was a man, and for a moment they did not see his face.

"Who are you?" Carver pulled the man over on his back. "Well, I'm – "

The man at his feet was Yeh Ling!

18

The Chinaman was unconscious, and Carver looked around for the second visitant. He rushed to the gate, the road was deserted. Flinging himself upon the roadway to secure an artificial skyline, he peered first in one direction and then in the other. Presently he saw his man running swiftly in the cover of the hedges, and started in pursuit.

A hundred yards away from the house was a secondary road, and into this the runner turned. As Carver reached the corner he heard a motor-car engine and dimly saw the bulk of a large touring car retreating rapidly.

He came back to the house, to find Yeh Ling sitting in Ursula's room holding his head in his hands.

"This is the second man; it isn't the wide-awake gentleman," said Carver. "Now, Yeh Ling, give an account of your actions. How are you feeling?"

"Pretty dizzy," said Yeh Ling, and to Tab's surprise his tone was that of a cultured man, his English faultless.

He looked up at the girl reproachfully.

"You did not tell me these gentlemen were coming down, Miss Ardfern, when you wrote to me," he said.

"I hadn't any idea when I wrote that they were coming, Yeh Ling," she answered.

"If I had been here a little earlier I should have seen him," he said. "As it was, I am afraid I have spoilt your evening, Mr Carver." His expressionless brown eyes looked up at the detective.

"I see! You were on guard too, were you?" said Carver good-humouredly. "Yes, we seem to have made a mess of it between us. Did you see the man?"

"I didn't see him," said Yeh Ling, "but," he added, "I felt him," and he rubbed his head. "I think it must have been his fist. I did not notice any weapon."

"You didn't see his face?" persisted Carver.

"No, he had a beard of some kind. I felt it as my hands clutched at him. I am afraid I over-estimated my strength," he said apologetically to the girl, "yet there was a time when I was a star performer at Harvard, in the days when Chinese students were something of a curiosity."

"Harvard?" said Tab, in surprise. "Great Moses! I thought you were a – " he couldn't very well finish his sentence.

But the other helped him.

"You thought I was a very ordinary Chink?" he said. "Possibly I am. I hope I am," he said. "Certainly, Miss Ardfern knew me when I was a very poor Chink! We lodged in the same house, she will remember, and she placed me under an eternal obligation by saving the life of my son."

Then Tab remembered the little Chinese boy Ursula had nursed when she herself was little more than a child. Remembering this, a great many things which had been obscure to him became clear and understandable.

"I had no idea you would come tonight, Yeh Ling, but you begged me if I was in any kind of difficulty to let you know," she said. "You shouldn't have taken the trouble."

"Events seem to prove that," said the Chinaman dryly. "I am merely being consistent, Miss Ardfern. You have been under my personal observation for seven years. Seven years, day and night, either I or one of my servants have been watching you. You never went – " He stopped, and changed the conversation.

"Miss Ardfern never went to Mr Trasmere's house but you weren't watching outside; that is what you were going to say, wasn't it, Yeh

Ling?" smiled Carver. "You need not be reticent, because I know all about it, and Miss Ardfern knows that I know."

"That was what I was going to say," said the other. "I usually followed Miss Ardfern from the theatre to her hotel; from her hotel to Trasmere's house, and home again when she had finished working."

The reporter and detective exchanged glances. This, then, was the explanation of the mysterious Chinaman who had been seen by Mr Stott's servant waiting outside Mayfield smoking a cigar in the cold hours of the morning. It explained, also, the appearance of the cyclist in the roadway that morning when the tyres of Ursula Ardfern's car had burst and Tab had been on hand to render timely assistance.

"I had no idea," breathed the astonished girl; "is that true, Yeh Ling? Oh, how kind you have been!"

Tab saw tears in her eyes, and wished that he, and not this uninteresting Chinaman, had been the person who excited her gratitude.

"Kindness is a relative term," said Yeh Ling. He had brought his feet up on a chair and was rolling a cigarette; he had asked permission with his eyes, and as Ursula nodded he lit it with a quick flick of his fingers, a match having appeared, as it seemed, out of space, and carefully replaced the stalk in a matchbox. "Was it kindness that you saved the life of one who is to me the light of my eyes and the inspiration of my soul, if you will forgive what may seem to you, a writer, Mr Holland, a piece of flowery orientalism, but which is to me the quintessence of sincerity."

Then, without preamble, he told his story: a story which was only half known to the girl.

"I was in this peculiar position," he said, "that I was a rich man or a poor man, whichever way the great law of this country interprets an agreement I made with Shi Soh. Shi Soh you know as 'Trasmere,' and that, of course, is his name. On the Amur River we called him Shi Soh. I came to this country many years ago and worked in the restaurant of which I am now proprietor. I do not mean the Golden Roof, but the little place in Reed Street. The man who owned it lost all his money at Fan-tan, and I bought it a bargain. You may wonder why a man of education, and the son of a great Clan, should be here in this country, playing the humble part of waiter in a Chinese restaurant. I might tell you," he said, simply and without conscious humour, "that education in China, when it is applied to political objectives, is not always popular, and I left China hurriedly. That, however, is all past. The Manchu has gone, the old Empress, the Daughter of Heaven, is dead, and Li Hung is asleep on the Terraces of the Night.

"I was making slow progress when Mr Trasmere came one night. I did not recognize him at first. When I knew him first he was a very strong, healthy man, with a reputation for being cruel to his employees. I have known him to burn men to death in order to make them reveal where they had hidden gold which they had stolen from the diggings. We talked of old times, and then he asked me if there was money to be made in the restaurant business. I told him there was, and that was the beginning of the partnership which lasted until the day of his death. Three-quarters of the profits of the Golden Roof was paid every Monday to Mr Trasmere, and that was our agreement. It was the only agreement that we had, except one which I myself wrote at his dictation and which placed on record this fact: that in the event of his dying, the whole of the property should come to me. It was signed by me with my 'hong,' and by him with his 'hong' which he always carried in his pocket."

"The 'hong'," interrupted Carver, "is a small ivory stamp with a Chinese character at the end. It is carried in a thin ivory case, rather like a pencil-case, isn't it?"

Yeh Ling nodded.

"I kept the document until a few days before his death, when he asked me to let him take it away with him to make a copy. It will be news to you, though not perhaps to you, Miss Ardfern, that Mr Trasmere spoke and wrote Chinese with greater ease than I, who am almost an authority upon Mandarin. A few days later he was murdered. My only hope of saving myself from ruin was to find that agreement, which he had taken away in my little lacquer box."

"But could they touch your restaurant? Are there any other documents in existence which would give Mr Trasmere's heir the right of interfering with you?"

Yeh Ling looked at him steadily.

"It does not need a document," he said quietly. "We Chinese are peculiar people. If Mr Lander came to me on his return from Italy and said, 'Yeh Ling, this property is my uncle's, in which you only have a very small share,' I would reply: 'That is true'; and if the agreement which we two men had not signed was not discovered, I should make no effort at law to preserve my rights."

And he meant it. Tab knew as he spoke that he was telling the truth. He could only marvel that such an exalted code of honour could be held by a man who subconsciously he regarded as of an inferior race and of an inferior civilization.

"You found the agreement?"

"Yes, sir," said Yeh Ling. "It had been taken out of the box in which I gave it to Mr Trasmere and placed – elsewhere. But I found it – and other documents of no immediate interest. As to my coming here tonight – apart from your letter, lady, I was anxious to meet the Black Man also. Yes. He has been watching me for many days. I am certain it is the same." He made a little grimace and rubbed his bruised head. "I met him," he said.

Carver jotted down a few notes in his book and then putting the book away, he turned and faced the Chinaman squarely.

"Yeh Ling," he said, "who murdered Jesse Trasmere?"

The Chinaman shook his head.

"I do not know," he said simply. "To me it is amazing. There must be a secret passage that opens into the vault. I can think of no other way in which the murderer could have got in or out."

"If there is a secret way," said the detective grimly, "then it is the best kept secret I have known. It has certainly been kept a secret from the men who built the house and the vault and the clerk of the works who was on the spot all the time it was being erected. No, Yeh Ling, you must get that idea out of your head. Either the man Brown or

Walters is guilty. We shall know the method they employed when we get them."

"Brown was not guilty," said Yeh Ling quietly, "for I was with him when the murder was committed!"

They heard his pronouncement with astonishment; even the girl seemed surprised.

"Do you know what you are saying?"

"I know what I am saying, and I rather wish I hadn't said it," said the Chinaman with a quick smile. "Nevertheless, it is true. If the murder was committed on Saturday afternoon, then I certainly was with the man called Wellington Brown, but whom we called The Drinker, or The Unemployed One, at that hour. It embarrasses me to say how or where, but it would embarrass me more if you were to ask me whether I know his whereabouts at the present moment. To that question I should answer: 'No.' "

"And you would lie," said Carver quietly.

"I should lie," was the calm answer. "Yet I tell you, Mr Carver, that Wellington Brown was with me, under my eye, from half-past one o'clock in the afternoon of the Saturday on which Jesse Trasmere was killed until night."

Carver eyed him keenly.

"When he came to you," he asked, "how was he dressed?"

The other shrugged his shoulders.

"Poorly. He has always been dressed poorly."

"Did he wear gloves?"

"No. He had no gloves. That was the first thing I noticed, because he was – what do you call it in English? – fastidious to a degree. In the hottest days I have seen him wearing gloves. A shabby dandy! That is the expression I was seeking. I am sorry to disappoint you."

"You haven't disappointed me," said Carver bitterly; "you have merely added another brick wall between me and my objective."

Yeh Ling left soon after. He had bicycled down from town, and cheerfully undertook the long return journey in preference to spending the remainder of the night at the cottage.

It was too late for Ursula to go to her hotel, and they sat up all night, Carver playing an interminable game of solitaire, whilst Tab and the girl walked about the garden in the growing light and talked oddly of incongruous things.

As soon as it was light Carver went out to find the place where the car had stood and to examine wheel-tracks. He gained little from his inspection, except that the tyres were new and that the car was a powerful one, which was hardly a discovery.

"The man who drove was not a skilled driver, or else he was very nervous. Half way up the lane he nearly swerved into a ditch and came into collision with a telegraph pole, winch must have damaged his mudguard severely. I found flakes of brand-new enamel attaching to the damaged wood, so I guessed that the car also had not been long from the makers' hands."

Thus passed the second appearance of the Man in Black.

The third was to come in yet a more dramatic fashion.

19

Mr Wellington Brown woke one morning, feeling extraordinarily refreshed. Usually he woke with a clouded brain and a parched mouth, with no other desire than to satisfy that craving for opium which all his life had kept him poor and eventually had ruined him physically and morally. But on this occasion he opened his eyes, made a quick stock of his surroundings, and uttered a "faugh!" of disgust. He knew himself so well, and was so well acquainted with his idiosyncrasies and the character of these fits which came upon him, that he saw that the end of a bout had come. Some day he would not wake up feeling refreshed, or wake up at all.

He sat up in bed, fingering his beard, and sucked in the breeze that came through the open window. Rising to his feet he found his knees a little unstable, and laughed foolishly. It was Yo Len Fo himself who came in, bearing a tray with a glass of water, a bottle half full of whisky, and the inevitable pipe.

Without a word Wellington poured himself out a stiff dose of the spirit and gulped it down.

"You may take that pipe to the devil," he said. His voice was quavery but determined.

" 'A pipe in the morning makes the sun shine,' " quoted Yo Len Fo.

" 'A pipe in the morning does not go out with the stars,' " replied Wellington Brown, giving proverb for proverb.

"If the Illustrious will stay I will have breakfast sent to him," said the Chinaman urgently.

"I have stayed too long," said Wellington Brown. "What is the day of the month by the foreign reckoning?"

"I do not know the foreign ways," said Yo Len Fo; "but if your Excellency will deign to stay for a few hours in this hovel – "

"My Excellency will not deign to stay in any hovel or palace," said Wellington. "Where is Yeh Ling?"

"I will send for him at once," said the old man eagerly.

"Leave him," replied Mr Brown, with a fine gesture, and began to search his pockets. To his surprise, all his money, which was not much, was intact.

"How much do I owe you?" he asked.

Yo Len Fo nodded, thereby meaning "nothing."

"Running a philanthropic hop joint?" asked the other sarcastically.

"It has all been paid by the excellent Yeh Ling," answered the man.

Brown grunted.

"I suppose that old devil Trasmere is behind this," he said in English; and seeing that the man did not comprehend him he pushed his way past Yo Len Fo and went down the uncarpeted stairs into the street. He felt terribly weak, but his heart was light. Hesitating at the end of a narrow passage, he turned to the left, otherwise he could not have failed to have run into the arms of Inspector Carver, who had made a call that morning upon the proprietor of The Golden Roof.

Mr Brown's day was spent simply. He found his way to the park and, sitting down on a bench, dozed and mused the hours away, basking in the glorious June sunlight and seemingly oblivious to its heat.

Late in the afternoon he felt hungry and went to a refreshment kiosk in the park. Finishing his meal he found the nearest bench and continued his pleasant occupation of doing nothing. Mr Wellington Brown was a born loafer; it is a knack which would prolong many lives in this strenuous age, if it could be acquired.

The stars were corning out in a velvet-blue sky when, with a shiver, he aroused himself and made instinctively for the lights. As he slouched along one of the big main paths that cross the park, he overtook a man who was walking slowly in his direction. The man shot a quick glance at him, and then turned suddenly away.

"Here," said Mr Brown truculently, "I know you. Why in hell are you running away from me? Think I'm a leper or something?"

The man stopped, glanced uneasily left and right.

"I don't know you," he said coldly.

"That's a damned lie," snarled Brown. The reaction of his bout was upon him. He would have quarrelled with anything or anybody. "I know you and I've met you." He groped in his hazy mind for some string that would lead him to the identity of the stranger. "In China, wasn't it? My name's Brown – Wellington Brown."

"Yes, perhaps it was in China," said the other, and of a sudden became friendly, gripped Wellington Brown's arm, and leaving the path, led him across the green spaces of the park.

A courting couple sitting under one of the trees saw them pass, and heard Wellington Brown say: "Don't say that I was his storekeeper, because I wasn't, or his servant! I was his equal, by gad. A partner in the firm, the blamed old swindler…"

So they passed, the Man in Black and the besotted pensioner from China.

At this hour another person deeply interested in Jesse Trasmere's fate was making his final preparations for departure.

He had ventured forth in broad daylight, braved the glances of the purser of the *Arak*, and had signed on as steward of the second saloon on a voyage to South Africa. The end of the long nightmare had come. Walters had to join his ship overnight, an excellent arrangement from his point of view, since it reduced the danger of detection to a minimum.

He carried with him to the big roomy docks a respectable sum of money, the proceeds of his pilfering at Mayfield, and his opportunities had been many, remembering Mr Trasmere's parsimony.

He had sent his bag off to the ship in the afternoon and he had only to convey himself to the docks. He went on foot, keeping to the less-frequented streets, and although this entailed a longer journey he was taking no risks. A month ago he would have trembled at every shadow, and the sight of a policeman would have paralysed his activities, but now the case had been forgotten, one never read a line about it in even the more sensational newspapers, and it was with some confidence that he traversed the wharf and mounted the gangway leading to the ill-lighted decks of the liner.

"Report to the chief steward," said the custodian on duty at the ship end of the plank, and Walters inquired his way forward, went down the broad companion to the broader deck where the chief steward's office is situated, and joined a dozen other men who were lined up in queues waiting to report.

Walters would not have worried if the waiting had occupied the rest of the evening, but in a remarkably short space of time he stepped into the chief steward's cabin, knuckled his forehead, and said: "Reporting for duty, sir. John Williams, steward – " and then he stopped.

On the farther side of the steward's table was Inspector Carver.

Walters turned in a flash, but the doorway was blocked by a detective.

"All right," he said despondently as they snapped the steel handcuffs on his wrist, "but I didn't do it, Mr Carver. I know nothing about the murder. I am as innocent as a babe unborn."

"What I like about you," said Carver unpleasantly, "is your originality."

He followed behind the two men who held the arms of their manacled prisoner, and Tab joined him. As they came off the ship Tab asked: "Well, do you honestly think you have him, Carver?"

"Who – Walters? That's the man all right. I know him very well indeed."

"I mean the murderer," said Tab.

"Oh, the murderer. No, I don't think that this is the gentleman, but he will have some difficulty in proving he isn't. You can say that he's arrested, Tab, but I would rather you didn't say that I charged him with the murder, because I shan't until I have much more information in my possession than I have at present. Perhaps if you come round to the station after you have been to the office, I will be able to tell you a little more, especially if Walters makes a statement, as I think he will."

In this the detective was right, for Mr Walters lost no time in putting his defence on record.

THE STATEMENT OF WALTER FELLING

"My name is Walter John Felling I have sometimes assumed the name of Walters, sometimes MacCarty. I have served three terms of imprisonment for theft and impersonation, and in July 1913 I was sent to prison for five years at Newcastle. I was released from prison in 1917 and served in the army as cook until 1919. On leaving the army I heard from a nose ★ that Mr Trasmere was in want of a valet, and knowing that he was a very rich man and very mean, I applied for the job, producing false references, which were made out by a man named Coleby, who does that kind of job. When Mr Trasmere asked me what salary I wanted, I purposely said a sum which I knew was below the rate usually paid, and he engaged me on the spot. I do not think he wrote for my references. If he had, Coleby would have replied.

"There were two other servants at Mayfield when I went there, a Mr and Mrs Green. Mr Green was an Australian, but I think Mrs Green was born in Canada. He acted as butler to Mr Trasmere, but he did not have a very happy time. He did not like Mr Trasmere, I think. Certainly Mr Trasmere did not like him. My object in securing employment with Mr Trasmere was to find an opportunity for getting away with a good haul. I knew from the first it was going to be very difficult, because of the peculiar habits of the house, but I managed to get a few things together – a gold watch and two silver candlesticks – and was thinking of making a getaway when Mr Trasmere detected

★ "Nose": informer. Either one who betrays or who supplies information to criminals.

Green giving food away to Mrs Green's brother-in-law, and fired them on the spot. Then he discovered the loss of the gold watch and had their boxes searched. I felt very sorry for Green, but of course I could say nothing.

"After the Greens had left I had to do the work of valet and butler, too. I very soon discovered that all the valuables in the house were kept in a room in the cellar. I have never been into that room, but I know it is somewhere in the passage which leads from Mr Trasmere's study, because I have seen the door opened and, by bending down, have been able to look along the corridor.

"I hoped that some day or other I should be able to make a more careful inspection of the place, but that opportunity never came, although it seemed that I was going to have a chance a week or two before Mr Trasmere's death. I managed to get the key from his neck whilst he was in a kind of fit and take an impression, but the fit did not last very long, and I had hardly got the key back before the old gentleman recovered. It was a lucky thing for me that I had wiped the soap from the key on my sleeve, for the first thing he felt for was the chain round his neck. However, I had quite enough to work on, and I started in to make a key that would fit the impression. That is as much as I can tell you about the vault, which I never saw.

"I went to bed every night at ten o'clock, and Mr Trasmere used to lock the door which shut me off from the rest of the house, so that it was impossible for me to see what was going on at night. I complained to him, and he had a key put in a glass box in my room so that in case of emergency I could smash the glass and, with the aid of the key, unlock the door that separated me from the rest of the house. He didn't even agree to this until he was taken ill one night and I was unable to go to his assistance.

"To open the door which locked me in was one thing, to open the little glass cupboard and take out the key was, however, a simpler matter. I used that key several times. The first time I used it I heard voices in the dining-room downstairs, and wondered who it was calling at that late hour. I hadn't the courage to go down and see for fear I should be detected, for there was a light in the hall. But another night, hearing a woman's voice, I went down, the lights being out, and saw a young lady sitting at a table with a typewriter in front of her, tapping the keys whilst Mr Trasmere walked up and down, with his hands behind him, dictating. She was the prettiest young lady I have seen in my life, and somehow I was sure that I had seen her before. I did not recognize her until I saw her photograph in an illustrated paper, and then it seemed to me to be impossible that it could be Miss Ursula Ardfern, the well-known actress. I came down again the next night, and this time they were talking together and Mr Trasmere called her 'Ursula,' and I knew I was right. She used to come from the theatre every night, and sometimes he would keep her there as late as two o'clock.

"One evening, soon after she came, I crept downstairs and, in my stockinged feet, listened to them. I heard him say very sharply: 'Ursula, where is the pin?' The young lady answered, 'It is there, somewhere'; and then I heard him grumbling and grunting, and presently he said, 'Yes, here it is.'

"There was much more to be picked up in the house than I had imagined." (Here Walters enumerated minutely, and as far as can be ascertained exactly, the number and nature of the valuables which he succeeded in acquiring.) "When Mr Trasmere was alone he used to sit at the table with a little porcelain dish in front of him and a brush. I don't know what he was painting, I never saw any of his pictures. I only know that he did this, because I managed to peep at him on several nights, and saw him at work. He did not use a canvas; he always painted paper, and he always used black ink. The paper must have been very thin, because once the window was slightly open and a sheet blew away.

"I managed to see him, because there was a glass fanlight over the door which I used to keep clean, and from the head of the stairs you could look into the room, and if he happened to be sitting in a certain place it was easy to see him.

"On the morning I left the house I was engaged in working at the key I was making, and I could do this without any danger, because Mr Trasmere never came into my room, the door of which I kept locked in case of accidents. I served lunch to my master, and he talked to me about Brown, the man I had turned away from the door. He told me that I had done quite right and that Brown was wanted by the police in this country, and he wondered why he had taken the risk of coming back. He told me that Brown was an opium taker and a drunkard, and that he was a worthless fellow. After lunch he cleared me out of the room and I knew that he was going down to his vault, which he usually did on Saturday afternoons.

"At about ten minutes to three I was in my room working at the key, and had just brought a cup of coffee from the kitchen when the front doorbell rang and I answered it. There was a messenger boy with a telegram, and it was addressed to me. I had never before received telegrams at the house and I was surprised. On opening it I read a message reminding me that I had been convicted at Newcastle eight years before, and telling me that the police were calling at three o'clock.

"I was in a terrible state of mind, for I had in my room a considerable quantity of stolen property and I knew that my next conviction would mean a very long sentence. I rushed up to the room, gathered my stuff together, and was out of the house a little before three. As I opened the door I saw Mr Rex Lander standing by the gate. I had seen Mr Lander before, because he had stayed for a little time in the house a month after I had taken up my position. He had always been very nice to me, and he is a gentleman for whom I have a great deal of respect.

"His uncle, the late Mr Trasmere, did not like him. He told me once that Mr Rex was extravagant and lazy. On seeing Mr Rex at the gate my heart went down into my boots, and I thought that he must immediately detect that something was wrong. He asked me if his uncle was ill, and that gave me a moment to pull myself together, and I told him that I was going on a very urgent errand, and running into the street I had the good luck to find a taxi-cab which drove me to the Central Station. I did not, however, leave town, but made my way to a room which I had once occupied in a house which I knew in Reed Street, where I have been in hiding ever since. I did not see Mr Trasmere again after lunch. He did not come out to inquire who had called when the telegram arrived; there were frequent callers, tradesmen, and others, and I never reported to him unless there was something important or unless letters or telegrams came for him. I have never been in the vault or in the passage leading to the vault, nor have I at any time owned a revolver.

"I made this statement voluntarily, without any pressure, and have answered the questions which Inspector Carver has put to me without any suggestion on his part as to the way they should be answered."

20

"There is the statement," said Carver. "Not a line must be used; only the fact that the statement has been made can be published. What do you think of it?"

"It reads fairly honest to me," said Tab, and the Inspector nodded.

"It does to me also. I never had the slightest doubt in my mind that Walters, or Felling, was innocent. The references to Miss Ardfern's visits are a little obscure, and in one sense rather remarkable, particularly the old man's reference to the pin."

"You are thinking of the pin we found in the corridor?" said Tab quickly.

Carver laughed softly.

"I was and I wasn't," he said. "The pin of which the old man spoke was obviously one of the jewels which were in the box, and as obviously he was taking an inventory of the jewel-case to see that everything was there."

Tab was silent for a while.

"You mean that the jewels really belonged to Trasmere, that he lent them to the girl, and that she had to return them every night?" he asked quietly.

"There is no other explanation," said Carver. "There is no other explanation, either, for her secretarial activities. Trasmere was in a score of enterprises, and I have no doubt that he was the man who put up the money for Ursula Ardfern's season. He was a shrewd old boy and probably had seen her acting. My own impression is that he made a fortune out of this girl – "

"But why should she, a successful actress, consent to act as his midnight secretary? Why should she go on as though she were a slave to this man, instead of being, if your theory is correct, an earner of big money?"

Carver looked at him steadily.

"Because he knew something about Miss Ardfern – something that she did not wish should be known," he said gently. "I am not suggesting it is anything discreditable to her," he went on discreetly, detecting the cloud gathering on Tab's face. "Some day she'll tell us all about it, I daresay. At present, it is unimportant."

He got up from his desk – they were talking in his office – and stretched himself.

"This concludes the day's entertainment, gentlemen," he said, "and if you are dissatisfied, your money will be returned to you at the doors."

There were moments when Carver could be facetious.

"No, I'm not going home. I have a couple of hours' work here. I shan't be disturbed. Happily the station telephone is out of order. A tree fell across a line somewhere between here and the exchange. Remember, Tab, only the briefest notes of Walter's arrest. Nothing about the charge, not a single item of his statement, beyond the fact that he has made one."

Happily Jacques had gone home, or the news editor would have exploded at the meagre details with which Tab supplied his newspaper that night.

He reached home at half-past eleven with a queer little ache at his heart. What was Ursula Ardfern's secret? Why the mystery? Why must her mystery be interwoven with the greater and more sordid mystery of the old man's death?

As he pushed open the door he saw a telegram in the box which was common to the whole of the flats, once the entrance door was closed. It was for him, and he tore open the envelope and unfolded its flimsy contents. It was handed in at Naples, and was from Rex.

"Going on to Egypt; quite recovered. Shall be back in a month."

He smiled to himself, and hoped that "quite recovered" referred to his youthful infatuation as well as his disordered nerves. He paused outside the door to his flat to find his key, and as he did so he thought he heard a sound. It may have come from one of the flats above, but he did not give it any importance, and, inserting the key, he caught a momentary flash of light through the transom of his sitting-room. It was as if at the second he had opened the door the lights in the sitting-room had been extinguished.

It must have been an optical delusion, he thought; but the memory of the burglar came to him as he closed the door slowly behind him. For a second he hesitated, and then pushed open the closed door of the sitting-room. The first thing he noticed was that all the blinds were down, and he had left them up. He heard the sound of heavy breathing.

"Who's there?" he asked, and then reached out his hand for the switch.

Before his fingers could close upon the lever something struck him. He felt no pain, was conscious only of terrific shock that brought him to his knees, incapable of thought or movement. Somebody pushed past him in the darkness. There was a slam of the flat door, a quick patter of feet on the stairs, and the street door slammed.

Still Tab remained on his hands and knees, held there by his own invincible will. There was a trickle of warm blood running over his forehead and into the corner of his eye, and the subsequent smart of it brought him at last to his senses. He got unsteadily to his feet and put on the lights.

It was a chair that had struck him; it lay overturned near the door. Tab felt gingerly at his forehead and then went in search of a mirror. The injury was a very slight one, the wound being superficial. He guessed that the chair must have caught against the wall and eased the blow, for one of the legs was broken and there was a long scratch on the wall. Mechanically he bathed his face, put a rough dressing on his forehead, and then went back to the sitting-room to get a better idea of the confusion which reigned there than he had been able to appreciate at first. Every drawer in his desk had been emptied. One which he kept locked, and which contained his more private papers, had been forcibly broken open and the contents were scattered, some on the floor, a few on the desk. A little bureau by the wall had been treated with the same lack of courtesy, and the floor was littered with its contents.

He found the same in his bedroom; every drawer rummaged except his wardrobe, every box opened.

In Rex's room the only thing that had been touched was the second trunk that the burglar had left on his previous visit. This was on the bed, opened, and its contents had been thrown around in confusion.

Tab's gold watch and chain, which he had inadvertently left behind, was untouched. His cash-box had been wrenched open, but though the money had been emptied out not a cent had been taken. Then he made a curious discovery. In one of the drawers of his desk he had a portfolio of photographs of himself which had been made a year before at the request of his many maiden aunts. This had been removed, and every photograph torn into four pieces. He found the debris with the other papers. It was the only wanton damage that the burglar had done. For what had he been searching? Tab puzzled his brains to remember the possession of something which might interest an outsider. What did Rex own that was worth all the trouble that this unknown visitor had taken?

He got on to the telephone and tried to reach Carver, and then remembered Carver had told him the station 'phone was out of order.

On the stroke of midnight Inspector Carver was tidying his desk preparatory to leaving when a dishevelled and damaged Tab made his appearance.

"Hullo," said Carver, "been fighting?"

"The other fellow did the fighting," said Tab. "Carver, I am going to sue the men who supplied us with our furniture. He said that the chairs were mahogany, and they are only pine."

"Sit down," commanded the detective; "you seem to be a little out of your mind." And then quickly, "You haven't had another visit from your burglar?"

Tab nodded.

"And what is more, I found him at home," he said grimly, and related all that had happened in the flat.

"I'll come along and see the damage, though I don't think it will help us much," said Carver slowly. "So he tore up your photographs, did he? That is rather interesting."

"I guess he didn't like me," said Tab. "I have been trying to remember all the crooks I have annoyed, Carver. It can't be young Harry Bolter, because he must be still in prison; and it can't be Low Sorki, because, if I remember rightly, he got religion in prison and he is now conducting a mission to the submerged. They are the only two people who expressed their intention of cutting short my young life."

"It is neither of those." Carver was emphatic on this point. "Tell me again, Tab, from the moment you opened the door to the moment you lost interest in the proceedings, just what happened. First, did you close the flat door behind you?"

"Yes," said Tab, surprised.

"And then you went into the sitting-room, and he caught you a whack with the chair? There were no lights?"

"None whatever."

"No light on the landing outside the flat door?" asked Carver eagerly.

"None."

"And he just rushed past you and was gone. You remember that very well, I suppose, although you were knocked out?"

"I remember his going and hearing the door slam," said Tab, wondering.

Carver was making notes on his blotting-pad in that strange system of shorthand which nobody understood but Carver.

"Now, Tab, think very carefully before you reply, was there anything in Lander's box, any reference to his uncle, any document respecting his uncle, anything, indeed, that had to do, even remotely, with Trasmere, in that box of Lander's? Because I am perfectly certain that there was the objective and that the search of your room was an afterthought. In fact, it is proved by the circumstance of the thief being in your room when you arrived − he had evidently left that search to the last."

Tab concentrated his mind upon Rex and all Rex's belongings.

"No," he confessed, "I can't remember anything."

Carver nodded.

"Very good," he said, rising; "and now we'll go along and look at this trouble of yours. When did it happen?"

"About half an hour ago; maybe a little more," he looked up at the clock, "yes, it was nearer an hour ago. I tried to get you on the 'phone − "

"The machine is out of order; it always is out of order," said the fatalistic Carver, "when there is real trouble around. In fact, if I obeyed my impulse, I should double the men on duty every time that 'phone falls down."

They were in front of the station, and the cab that Carver had called was pulling up to the kerb when another cab came dashing toward them, swerved to the sidewalk, and stopped dead. Out of the cab's interior tumbled a man who was sketchily attired, and whose pyjama coat showed where his shirt should have been. Mr Stott had arrayed himself hurriedly, and for once in his life was careless of appearance. He fell almost into Carver's arms, and his mouth opened and closed like a fish out of water. When he did speak his voice was a squeak.

"They're at it again! They're at it again!" he piped.

21

Mr John Stott had discovered to his gratification that the association of his name with the Trasmere case had enhanced, rather than detracted from his social standing. It is true that the newspapers, having long ceased to take the slightest interest in the murder, seemed oblivious to the part he had played, or the startling discovery which he had to his credit, but a more important circle of public opinion, that circle which met daily at Toby's and discussed an expensive lunch and such matters of public interest as deserved attention, had applauded Mr Stott's decision to place in the hands of the police authorities the information which, up to that moment, had been confined to some twenty commercial gentlemen, their wives, their wives' families, their servants, the servants of their wives' families, the families of the servants, to say nothing of personal friends of all and each, their servants and attachments.

"So far as I am concerned, the matter is ended," said Mr Stott one day at Toby's. "The police have behaved very shabbily. I have neither been thanked by the Commissioners nor their underlings."

It is true that Mr Stott had never expected thanks; it is true that he had expected a long term of imprisonment, and had shivered every time the doorbell rang lest the callers be minions of the law, armed with warrants for his arrest. It is true that he had dismissed and re-engaged Eline at least twice a day, for having dragged him into this unenviable position. He had expected, at least, the severest censure and condemnation from all those who had to do with the administration of the law, but he had never expected a vote of thanks.

"I told this fellow Carver," said Mr Stott, "and Carver, I might say in passing, is one of those thick-headed, unimaginative men that have made the police force what it is – I told him, 'Don't ever expect any further information from me. If you do, you will be disappointed.'"

"What did Carver say?" asked one of his fascinated audience.

Mr Stott shrugged his broad shoulders.

"What could Carver say?" he asked enigmatically, and nobody seemed to be able to supply an answer on the spur of the moment.

"In my opinion," said Mr Stott impressively, "if a businessman had had charge of this case, we should have had the murderer by the heels and executed by this time!"

Here every one of the businessmen at the long table was in complete agreement. They shared a common faith that a man who can make money by selling sugar, or can acquire a competence by trading in margins, must necessarily be the best type of mind to tackle every problem, however obscure. It was their wont to shake their heads sadly at every mistake the administration made, and hypothesize the same situation if businessmen had been in control. It was accepted, without dispute, that no government or government department came up to the businessman's standard of requirements.

"They had their chance and they missed it," said Mr Stott, "when the Chinaman and the woman were in the house and I was holding them – well, I was practically holding them – the police could have caught the whole gang if they had arrived in time. As it was, they allowed them to slip through their fingers. I hate to say so, though it has struck me since, that probably the police were in it!"

"In the house?" asked a foolish man.

"No," snapped Mr Stott, "in the plot, man! Anyway, I've washed my hands of the whole affair."

Mr Stott was in the habit of washing his hands of the whole affair twice a day, once at lunch and once after dinner. He washed his hands that night to his placid wife, not only of the Trasmere case, but of Eline's tooth; and he washed them with such effect on Eline herself, that she reluctantly agreed to have the offending ivory extracted on the following morning.

She did this after making the most searching inquiries as to whether people told their more intimate secrets when they were under the effects of anaesthetics.

Mr Stott went up to bed at eleven o'clock, had a bath, and got into his pyjamas. The night was warm – indeed it was oppressively hot, and bed was very uninviting. He opened the French window of his room and, stepping out on to the small balcony, he seated himself in a cane chair which occupied exactly one half of the balcony space, and enjoyed what little breeze there was. His partner having gone to bed to sleep, was behaving according to plan. Mr Stott remained contemplating the deserted street, and then crept downstairs and brought back his cigar-case.

He smoked enjoyably for half an hour, watched the Manders return from the theatre, and duly noted that Mr Trammin, who lived three doors away from him, returned home in a state of intoxication and offered to fight the cabman for his fare. He saw old Pursuer's car stop at "Flemington," and when these interests were exhausted, and his cigar was nearly through, he saw two men walking slowly toward him along the opposite sidewalk. He failed to identify them, and had ceased to be interested in their movements when they turned into the gateway of Mayfield.

Instantly Mr Stott was alert. They might be police officers, only – the sound of a large voice came to him.

"Let me tell you, my dear fellow, that Wellington Brown is a good friend and a bad enemy!"

Mr Stott nearly fainted. Wellington Brown! The man whose portrait had been in the newspapers; the man for whom the police were searching!

The other said something in a voice which did not reach the balcony.

"I am not threatening," said the strident voice of Wellington Brown.

They walked up the steps to the door of Mayfield and disappeared from view.

Mr Stott rose with knees that trembled. In the shortest space of time he was at the telephone. Carver's number he knew; he had been on to him several times in connection with the unfortunate little disagreement he had had with the police. But Carver's number was out of order. The operator could not get any reply she said.

Strong as was Mr Stott's repugnance to assist the police in the lawful execution of their duty, he dashed to his bedroom, pulled on his trousers over his pyjama-legs, and with trembling fingers buttoned himself up. There was no time to get into boots, and it was in his bedroom slippers that he shuffled down the street in search of a cab, looking back fearfully from time to time, lest the mysterious men who had entered Mayfield should be upon his track with murder in their hearts.

After an unconscionable time a taxi-cab came past and Mr Stott flung himself into the interior.

"Central Police Station," he gasped, "quick! Double fare if you get me there in ten minutes."

He knew that was the usual thing to say in such circumstances. As even a slow taxi could have covered the distance in five, Mr Stott's instructions were misplaced.

"They're at it again," he quavered as he fell into Carver's arms.

22

"At what again?" asked Carver quickly.

"Mayfield," gurgled Mr Stott; "two men!"

"Two men have gone into Mayfield? When?"

"I don't know how long ago. I saw them. One was Brown."

'Wellington Brown? Are you sure?"

"I heard him speak," said the agitated Mr Stott; "I'll swear to it in a court of law. I was sitting on the balcony smoking a cigar, a box which a friend of mine has given to me – perhaps you know Morrison of the Morrison Gold Corporation – "

But Carver had gone back into the station with a rush, to reappear almost immediately.

He bundled Tab into a taxi and shot a direction at the driver.

"I had to go back to get our own key," he said, "and – " he took something from his coat pocket and Tab heard the snick of an automatic jacket being pulled back. "Unless this man is suffering from delusions, we are going to see developments tonight, Tab."

He looked back through the peep-hole at the back of the cab. The other taxi was following at a distance.

"I brought out every available man," he said. "I wonder if they found room for Stott? Anyway, he can walk," he added cruelly.

Mayfield was in darkness when the cab drove up to the gate. Carver sprang out, ran across the concrete yard and up the steps to the door with Tab at his heels. He flashed a pocket lamp upon the key-hole, flung the door wide open as the second cab drew up at the gate to discharge half a dozen police officers in various stages of attire.

The hall was in darkness, but they had the lights on in a second and Carver ran into the sitting-room. The door leading to the vault was open.

"Oh!" said Carver thoughtfully.

He came back to give instructions to his posse, and then, followed by Tab, he went down the stone steps and along the corridor. The door of the vault was closed and locked and the room was unlighted. Carver felt in his pocket, took out the duplicate key – that upon which Walters had worked so industriously – and snapped back the lock. A touch from his thumb and the vault was flooded with light.

He paused in the open doorway and looked. Wellington Brown was lying face downward in the centre of the room, blood was flowing from under him, *and on the table, in the exact centre, was the key of the vault!*

Carver picked it up. There was no doubt about it; the old bloodstain was still upon it, and he looked blankly at his companion.

"Well, what do you think of that, Tab?" he asked in a hushed voice.

Tab did not reply. He was standing just inside the doorway looking down at his feet, and between his feet was something, the sight of which deprived him of speech. He stooped slowly and picked it up, laying it upon the palm of his hand.

"Another new pin!" said the detective thoughtfully. "This time, inside!"

A thorough search of the house failed to discover the second man. He must have made his escape just before the police arrived, for the smoke of the pistol's explosion still hung in the vaulted roof.

When the doctors came and the body was moved Tab spoke what was in his mind.

"Carver, I have been a fool," he said quietly. "We ought to have been able to prevent this; we should have done if I had only remembered."

"What?" asked Carver, arousing himself from thoughts which did not seem to be particularly pleasant, to judge from his expression.

"That key was in Rex's box. I remember now that he mentioned casually that he put it in his trunk before he went away."

Carver nodded.

"I guessed that," he said. "Probably we both arrived at that solution when we saw the key on the table. The burglary of your flat is, of course, explained. He came the first time for the key and was disturbed by the tenant from the flat beneath, and got away before it had been found. Tonight, the need being urgent, he took a chance, found the key, and – " he shrugged. "How did the key get on the table? The door was locked both sides, yet there is the key – and the new pin," he added half to himself, "the second new pin."

He got up and stretched himself and began to pace up and down old Trasmere's sitting-room.

"No weapon, nothing but the body – and the new pin," he mused, half to himself. "This lets out friend Walters, of course; there isn't a shadow of evidence against him after this second murder. We can hold him for theft on his own confession – but no more. Tab, I am going down to the vault; I don't want you to come with me. There are one or two things that I want to be certain about."

He was gone half an hour, and Tab, whose head was throbbing, was glad to see him when he returned.

Carver said nothing, walked out into the hall where the police constable was sitting.

"Nobody is to be allowed into this house unless they are accompanied by me," he said.

He drove Tab to Doughty Street and went up to see the damage that the burglar had done. But he was less interested in the condition of Rex Lander's wardrobe than he was in the torn photographs. He held their borders to the light.

"No fingerprints: he wore gloves, of course. I wondered if – yes, ah, here it is." He pieced together a torn photograph; scrawled on the face was a heavy black cross. "Yes, I expected that," he said to himself.

"If I were you, Tab, I should put the bolt on the door tonight. I don't want to alarm you unduly, but I rather think you should. The Man in Black is going to stop at nothing. Have you got a gun?"

Tab shook his head, and Carver slipped the automatic from his pocket and laid it on the table.

"Borrow mine," he said; "and take my considered advice – do not hesitate to shoot anybody you find in this flat, or in your room tonight."

"You are a cheerful little soul, Carver."

"Better be cheerful than dead," said the detective cryptically, and left him to puzzle it out.

23

The noise of the roaring presses came up to Tab as he worked in his office. The building shook and trembled, for every machine was running with the story of the mystery of Mayfield. Slip by slip his copy was rushed to the linotype room. Presently the presses would stop and the last city edition would be prepared.

He finished at last, pulled the last sheet from the typewriter, and hunched himself back in the chair.

To the detective's warning he gave no serious attention. He was perfectly satisfied in his own mind that the burglar had come to his flat in order to secure the key. The menace was not against himself, but against Rex Lander. What was that menace? he wondered. Had the old man some other relative who felt himself wronged when the property passed into the hands of the Babe. He was confident that the search of his own belongings had been made in order to find something that had to do with Rex. As to the tearing up of his photographs – he grinned at the thought.

"I never did like those pictures, anyway," he said.

"Which pictures?" asked the solitary reporter in the room.

"I am vocalizing my thoughts and unveiling the tablet of my mind," said Tab politely.

The late-duty man grinned.

"You are a lucky devil," he said, "to be in both these cases. I have been five years on this paper and have never had anything more exciting than a blackmail case which was hushed up before it went into court. What's that drawing?"

"I am trying to draw a plan of the vault and the passage," said Tab.

"Was the body found in exactly the same place?" asked the interested reporter.

"Almost," said Tab.

"And the key?"

Tab nodded.

"Is there a window to the vault?" asked the reporter hopefully.

Tab shook his head.

"If the murderer was a bug he couldn't have got into that vault without unlocking the door," he said.

As he was speaking the chief came in. He very seldom visited the reporters' room, and it was unusual to find him at the office at all after eleven o'clock. But the news of the crime had been telephoned to him and he had driven in. He was a stout man, with grey hair and a disconcerting habit of anticipating excuses. He was at once High Priest and Father Confessor of *The Megaphone* office.

"Come into my room, Holland," he said, and Tab obeyed meekly.

"The Trasmere murder seems to have been repeated in every detail," he said. "Have you found out where this man Brown has been?"

"I gather that he has been in an opium den of some kind," said Tab. "Yeh Ling – "

"The man who owns the Golden Roof?" asked the editor quickly.

"That's the chap. He gave as a hint that that is where Brown had been staying. The man was a notorious drug fiend."

"I understand that two men went into the house together. Nobody saw the second man?"

"Nobody except Stott," said Tab, "and Stott was so scared that he cannot give us anything like a picture of either of them. Certainly nobody saw him come out; he was gone when we arrived."

"And the key on the table – what does this mean?"

Tab made a gesture of despair.

"Of course I know what it means," said the editor thoughtfully. "It is the murderer's defence, prepared with devilish ingenuity in advance. Don't you realize," he said, seeing that his junior was taken aback by this theory, "that before you can convict the man who killed Trasmere, and presumably also killed Brown, you would have to prove that it was possible for him to get into the vault and out again, lock the door, and return the key to the table – and that is just what you could not prove."

That the murderer had this in his mind was a new possibility to Tab. He had regarded the appearance of the key as a piece of whimsical mystifying on the part of the murderer, an act of bravado rather than a serious attempt to save his own neck in the event of his detention.

"Carver says – " he began.

"I know Carver's theory," interrupted the chief. "He thinks that the murderer made a mistake in the first instance and intended leaving the pistol behind, with the idea of conveying the impression that Trasmere committed suicide. He would have been more clever than that; he certainly would not have shot him in the back. No, there is the fact. I was discussing it with a lawyer only last night and he agreed with me. The murderer who killed those two unfortunate fellows is determined that there shall be no conclusive evidence against him, and there will be none until you can prove how that key came to get on the table after the door had been locked from the outside.

"Now, Holland," his manner was very serious, "there is certain to be terrible trouble over this crime, and somebody is going to be badly hurt unless the murderer is brought to justice. That somebody will be your friend Carver, who, presumably, is in charge of this case and was in charge of the other. I like Carver," he went on, "but I must join with the hounds that will put him down unless he can give us something more than theories. And you are in it, too" – he tapped Tab's chest with his plump forefinger – "head, heels, and eyebrows! You are in it from my point of view, especially because it is your job to show the police just where they are wrong, and you have had exceptional opportunity. I am not going to say what will happen to you if you don't get the biggest story of your life out of this murder, because I don't believe in threatening a man who may fall down here and come up smiling on another case, and anyway you are too good a man to threaten. But we've got to get this crime cleared up, Holland."

"I realize that, sir," said Tab.

"And it will be cleared," said the editor, "when you have discovered how that key got on the table. Don't forget that, Holland. Mark that! Puzzle your young brain and get me a solution of that mystery and all the other mysteries will be cleared up."

Tab knew that Carver was still at Mayfield; he had gone back there after inspecting the rack and ruin left by the burglar in Doughty Street, and Tab went straight on from the office to find, as he had expected, that Inspector Carver had by no means completed his investigation.

"The pins are different," were his first words.

The bright little articles were lying on the table before him, and Tab saw at a glance that one was shorter than the other.

"I wonder if our friend missed it," said Carver. "He must have done so on this occasion, though he probably overlooked the loss on the first murder. Anyway, what is a pin more or less?" he added moodily. "Come down to the vault, Tab."

The door of the strongroom was open and the light burning when Tab went in. He looked at the second stain on the floor, and, despite his excellent nerves, shuddered.

"No weapon was found – he did not even attempt to fake a suicide."

Tab told him then his chief's opinion on that matter, and Carver listened with respect and growing interest.

"That never occurred to me," he said, "though it is nevertheless a fact that it would be next to impossible to bring the crime home to the man even if we found him in the passage with a smoking revolver in his hand."

"In that case," said Tab, "we shall never find him at all."

Carver was silent.

"I wouldn't go so far as taking that view," he said at last, "but it is certainly going to be difficult. There are no fingerprints," he said, when Tab looked inquiringly at one of the polished black boxes on the shelf. "Our mysterious Man in Black wore gloves. By the way, I am going to keep an officer on duty in the house for a day or two, to discover whether the murderer returns. I have no hope that he will."

He turned the light out, locked the door of the vault, and then went back to the sitting-room.

"This lets out Felling. I think I have made that remark before," said the detective. "Obviously he was innocent, because at the moment this crime was committed he was under arrest. Incidentally" – he made a little face – "it lets out Brown! In fact, Tab, the only two people who seem to be left in are you and I."

"That occurred to me too," said Tab with a quick smile.

That morning he got up to find a bulky letter in his box. It was unstamped and had been delivered by hand, and recognizing the superscription he opened it with an exclamation of surprise. It was dated Hotel Villa, Palermo, and was from Rex.

"DEAR TAB" (it read). "I am tired of travel and I am coming home. Loud cheers from Doughty Street! The mails here are very erratic, and I have just heard horrific stories of the pilfering that goes on in the Italian post offices, so I am asking one of the stewards of the *Paraka*, the ship on which I came to Naples, and which is leaving here today, to deliver this for me, the enclosed being of some value. I picked it up in a little shop in Rome, and knowing how interested you are in crime and criminals I am sure you will appreciate it. It is a scarab ring, authentically the property of Caesar Borgia. In fact I have with it a guarantee as long as your arm…"

Tab read no farther, but took up the ring that had come out of the envelope and examined it curiously. It was even too small for his little finger, but it was a beautiful piece of work, the beetle being cut from a solid turquoise.

"Don't bother about tipping the steward," (the letter went on), "I am tipping like a Croesus, and I have given him enough money to set himself up for life. I haven't the slightest idea what I shall do when I come back, but I am certainly not going to that charnel-house of Uncle Jesse's; and as you will not have me, I shall probably live luxuriously at the best hotel in town. Forgive me for not writing before, but pleasure is a great business.

Yours ever, REX."

There was a PS.

"If the fast boat calls here on Wednesday, and there is some uncertainty as to whether it will or not, I think I shall come straight away home. If you don't hear from me you will know I have changed my mind. There are some stunning girls in Palermo."

There was a further PS.

"We will have a dinner the night I return. Invite that sixty-nine-inch brain of yours, Carver."

Tab grinned, put the ring and the letter away in his desk, and gave himself over to the serious consideration as to whether it would be advisable for Rex to come back to Doughty Street. He missed him terribly at times. Apparently he had got over his infatuation for Ursula, for the references to the stunning girls at Palermo did not seem to harmonize with a broken heart.

He had arranged to go to tea with Ursula that afternoon, but he had his doubts as to whether he would be able to keep his promise.

The second case was absorbing every minute of his time and he was already regretting the bond of secrecy under which he worked.

On this subject he spoke frankly to Carver when he saw him. Carver saw his point of view.

"There is no reason now why you shouldn't tell everything – the full story if you like, Tab, all except – all except the new pins," he added.

Tab was delighted. So far he had only been able to give the vaguest outlines of the story in print, and the lifting of the embargo simplified his work enormously; incidentally it gave him time to see Ursula.

And she was glad to see him. She threw out two impulsive hands and gripped his as he came into her sitting-room at the Central.

"You poor hard-worked man! You look as if you haven't slept for a week," she said.

"I feel that way," said Tab ruefully, "but if I yawn whilst I am with you, throw a cup at me – not necessarily an expensive cup – I respond to the commonest of crockery."

"Of course you are working on this new crime?" she asked, busy with the teapot. "It is dreadful. Brown is the poor fellow they were trying to discover, weren't they? Isn't he the man that Yeh Ling spoke about?"

Tab nodded.

"Poor soul," she said softly; "he was from China also? I remember. And you have captured Walters. I never thought that Walters was guilty. I did not like the man; I had seen him once and felt instinctively repulsed from him, though I never thought that he would murder Mr Trasmere."

She turned quickly to another topic with relief.

"I have had an offer to go back to the stage, but of course I am not going," she said. "I wonder if you will believe me when I tell you that I hate the stage? It is full of the most unhappy memories for me."

Suddenly a thought struck Tab.

"I heard from Rex this morning," he said. "He is coming back again. You haven't heard from him?"

She shook her head and her eyes were grave.

"Not since he wrote me that letter," she said. "I am dreadfully sorry."

"I shouldn't be," he smiled. "I think Rex has made a very good recovery. Besides, it is the prerogative of youth to fall in love with beautiful actresses."

"Spoken like a grey-beard," she said, with laughter in her eyes. "You are never so amusing as when you are patriarchal, Mr Tab. Did you escape that heartbreaking experience?"

"Falling in love with actresses?" said Tab. "Yes, up to a point."

"What was the point?" she asked.

"Well 'point' doesn't quite express my meaning," said Tab carefully. "I should have said up to a date."

Her eyes caught his and dropped.

"I don't think that I should make any exceptions if I were you," she said in a low voice. "Loving people can be a great nuisance."

"You have found it so?" said Tab, icily polite.

"I have found it so," she repeated, and went on quickly: "What is Rex going to do with life? He is very wealthy. Curiously enough I never dreamt that Mr Trasmere would leave him everything. He used to grumble about Mr Lander's laziness to me, but I suppose he had not made any preparation for his terribly sudden end, and Mr Lander inherited by right of relationship. He was Mr Trasmere's next-of-kin, was he not?"

"I believe he was," said Tab; "but the dear old man made a will, written in his own hand, leaving Rex everything."

He heard a crash and stared stupidly at the cup that had fallen to the floor and broken, and then looked up in amazement at Ursula. She was standing stiffly erect, her face as pale as death, staring at him.

"Say that again," she said hollowly.

"What?" he asked puzzled. "About Rex inheriting the property? You knew that."

She stood with compressed lips and then: "Oh, my God!" she whispered. "Oh, my God, how dreadful!"

In a second he was by her side, his arm about her. "What is it, Ursula?" he asked anxiously, "are you ill?"

She shook her head.

"No, I have had a shock. I have just remembered something. Won't you please forgive me?"

She turned from him quickly and ran out of the room, leaving Tab a prey to various emotions. He waited for fully a quarter of an hour before she reappeared. She was still pale, but she was calm, and her first words were an apology.

"The truth is," she said with a faint smile, "I am a nervous wreck."

"What was it I said that upset you?"

"I don't know…you talked about the will…and it brought it all back," she said hurriedly.

"Ursula, you are not speaking the truth. Accidentally I must have said something that horrified you. What was it?"

She shook her head.

"I am telling you the truth, Tab," she said, and in her distress dropped the prefix.

It was his flush that reminded her.

"I suppose I ought not to call you Tab," she said, a trifle incoherently, "but we actresses are bold and brazen women. I thought with your vast experience you would have known that. Really, I should have begun calling you Tab the first time I met you. And now you want to go…you are trying to tell me that you don't want to go until I explain what it was that distressed me, and you are going to refuse all explanation about my poor nerves, so I can see we are likely to have an interminably quarrelsome evening. Come and see me tomorrow – Tab."

He took her hand and kissed it, and felt awkward and artificial.

"That was very sweet of you," she said gently.

When Tab left her he was feeling amazingly happy.

24

To the left of the vermilion door of Yeh Ling's new house was a tablet let into the brick buttress inscribed with those words which to the old Chinese represent the beginning and end of philosophical piety: *Kuang tsung yu tou*, which in English may be roughly translated: "Let your acts reflect glory upon your ancestors."

Yeh Ling, for all his Western civilization, would one day burn gold paper before a shrine within those vermilion doors and would stand with hidden hands before the family shrine and ask commendation and approval for his important acts.

Now he was sitting on one of the very broad and shallow steps that led from terrace to terrace, watching the primitive system by which his engineer was getting ready the casting of the second concrete pillar. About the site were a number of bottomless tubs, hinged so that they opened like leg-irons open to receive the ankle of a prisoner. Steel brackets on each enabled them to be clamped together to make a long tube. The first of these was in its place, and sticking up from the centre was a rusty steel bar that drooped out of the true – the core of the pillar to be. High above on a crazy scaffolding was a huge wooden vat, connected with the tub by a wooden shoot. All day long an endless chain of buckets, responding to a hand-turned wheel, had been rising to the top of the platform, their contents being turned into the vat.

"Primitive," murmured Yeh Ling; but in a way he liked primitive things and primitive methods.

Down the shoot would run a stream of semi-liquid cement and rubble, and the two toiling labourers would pat and shovel the concrete into place until the tub was filled. Then to the first would be fastened a second mould, the process would be repeated, and the pillar would rise. Then, on a day when the cement had hardened, the connecting wedges would be knocked away, the hinged tubs prised loose, the rough places of the Pillar of Grateful Memories chiselled and polished smooth, and, crowned with a companion lion, the obelisk would stand in harmony with its fellow.

Yeh Ling looked up at the frail scaffolding that supported the vat and the narrow platform, and wondered how many Western building laws he was breaking. The second tub was now brimming with the grey concrete and a third and a fourth were being fixed. All this Yeh Ling saw from his place on the steps, a cigar clenched between his small teeth. He saw the workmen climb down the ladders from the interior of the new tubs, and he glanced at the sun and rose.

A blue-bloused Chinaman, ludicrously handling a fan, came running toward him.

"Yeh Ling, we must wait four days for the water-stone to grow hard. Tomorrow I will strengthen the wall of the terrace."

"You have done well," said Yeh Ling.

"I thought you wrong," said the builder nodding; "it seemed so much money to waste. He that is not offended at being misunderstood is a superior man."

"He that fears to correct a fault is not a brave man," said Yeh Ling, giving one saying of Confucius for another.

The workmen lived on the spot; their fires were burning when he left the ground. On the roadway was a small black car, a noisy testimony to the efficacy of mass production, and into this he stepped.

He did not drive away for a long time, but sat hunched up at the wheel, his head sunk in thought.

Once he glanced at the pillar in making: speculatively, as though his meditations had to do with this. It was growing dark when at last he put his foot upon the starting plug and rattled away into the gloom.

He left the car at the side-door of the restaurant and passed in.

"The lady is in No. 6," said his personal servant; "she wishes to see you."

There was no need for Yeh Ling to ask which lady. Only one had the right of entry to No. 6. He went straight to her, dusty as he was, and found Ursula Ardfern sitting before an untouched meal.

She was very pale, and a shadow lay beneath her grey eyes. She looked up quickly as he came in.

"Yeh Ling, did you read all the papers we found in the house?" she asked.

"Some of them," he said cautiously.

"The other night you said that you had read them all," she said reproachfully, "and you were not speaking the truth!"

He agreed with a gesture.

"There are so many," he said, excusing himself, "and some are very difficult. Lady, you do not realize how many there were – "

"Was there anything about me?" she asked.

"There were references to you," he said. "Much of the writing was in the nature of a diary…it is hard to disentangle item from item…"

She knew he was evading a direct answer.

"Was there any mention of my father or mother?" she challenged him directly.

"No," he said, and her grey eyes searched his face.

"You are not speaking the truth, Yeh Ling," she said in a low voice. "You think if you speak…if you think I know, that I shall be hurt. Isn't that true? And because you would not hurt me, you are lying?"

He showed no evidence of embarrassment at the accusation.

"Lady, how can I say what is in papers which I have not read, or if I have read I cannot understand? Or suppose in his writings one revelation is so mixed up with another that it is impossible to betray one without the other? I will not deceive you. Shi Soh wrote about you. He said that you were the only person in the world he trusted."

She looked her amazement.

"I? But…"

"He said other things… I am puzzled. It is not a simple matter to make a decision. Some day I must give you a translation of everything.

I know that; it troubles me…what is best to do. We Chinese have a word for indecision. Literally it means a straw moving in cross currents – first this way, then that way. My mind is like that. I owe Shi Soh – Trasmere – much…how can I pay him? He was a hard man, but our words, one to the other, have been more binding than sealed papers, and once I said that I would serve his blood. That is my difficulty, a promise which is now…"

Here, such was his emotion that his English failed him. She saw the dull red of his face, the veins of his temples standing out like knotted cords, and was sorry for him.

"I will be patient, Yeh Ling," she said soothingly. "I know you are my friend."

She held out her hand, remembered, and drawing it back quickly took her own and shook it with a delighted gurgle of laughter.

Yeh Ling smiled too, as he followed her example.

"A barbarous custom," he said dryly, "but from a hygienic point of view a very wise one. You are forgiving me, Miss Ardfern?"

"Of course," she nodded. "And now I really am feeling hungry – will you send me some warm food – this is cold?"

He was out of the room before her request was completed.

It was like Yeh Ling that he did not come to the door when she went out. She hoped he would, but Yeh Ling could not have been there, for he was waiting outside, and when she turned the corner he was very near to her though she could not guess this.

25

Rex was home! His telegram, handed in at the docks, preceded him only by half an hour, and his thunderous knock at the door and his long and continuous peal on the bell told Tab the identity of the impatient caller, long before he had thrown open the door and gripped the hand of the returned traveller.

"Yes, I'm back," said Rex heartily, as he dropped himself into a chair and fanned himself with his hat. He was looking thinner, a little more peaked of face, but the colour of health was on his cheeks and his eyes were bright.

"You'll have to put me up, old man," he said; "I simply will *not* go to an hotel while you've an available bed in the flat; and besides, I want to tell you something about my plans for the future."

"Before we start dreaming," said Tab, "listen to a little bit of sordid reality. You have been burgled, my lad!"

"Burgled?" said Rex incredulously. "How do you mean, Tab? I left nothing to be burgled."

"You left a couple of trunks which have been thoroughly and scientifically examined by somebody who has a grudge against you."

"Good God!" said Rex. "Did they find the key? I only saw the story of the second murder when I landed."

"You did leave the key in the trunk?"

Rex nodded.

"I left it in a box – a small wooden box with a sliding lid. There were two of these boxes, I remember, one in each trunk."

"That was the object of the visit. Why he should mutilate poor me I find it difficult to explain."

He told Rex Lander what happened on the night of the second burglary, and Rex listened, fascinated.

"I've lost all the fun being away," he grumbled. "So poor old Brown was the victim, eh? And we thought he was the murderer. And Carver – what has he got to say about it?"

"Carver is rattled, but mysterious," said Tab.

Rex was deep in thought.

"I am going to have that strongroom bricked up," he said; "I made up my mind while I was on the ship. Anyway, I don't suppose anybody will want to buy the beastly place, and I shall have it on my hands for years. But I'll take pretty good care that tragedy number two doesn't become tragedy number three."

"Why not remove the door?" suggested Tab, but Rex shook his head.

"I won't have the vault turned into a show place," he said quietly. "Besides, it will likely enough stop a good sale. My own inclinations are to pull the house down and have it rebuilt; dig it out from foundation to roof and start afresh. But I don't think that even that would induce me to go and live there," he said. "Poor old Jesse's blood would rise up from the ground and find us wherever we were. There is a curse upon the house," he went on solemnly. "Some evil spirit seems to brood over it and inspire innocent men to these hideous crimes."

Tab stared at him in amazement.

"Babe," he said, "you've got poetical. I guess it is the air of Italy."

Rex went red, as he always did when he was embarrassed.

"I feel very strongly about the house," he said curtly, and Tab saw that he had hurt his feelings; but Rex's huff did not last long. He spoke of his voyage, the interesting places he had seen, and then: "You got my ring?"

"Yes, Rex, thank you; it is a beauty," said Tab. "It seems to me to be worth a terrible lot of money."

"It didn't cost so much," said the other carelessly. "I've got a rich way of thinking nowadays, Tab. I shudder at myself sometimes."

They fell to discussing Rex's immediate movements, and Tab succeeded in persuading him to go to the hotel. He had a reason for this; knowing the lazy nature of his former companion, he guessed that if Rex once got himself settled down in the flat he would never leave it.

Rex questioned him closely about the second tragedy, plying him with innumerable questions.

"Yes, I shall certainly have that place bricked up. I will put it in the hands of the builders right away," he said. "And as you decided to chuck me out, perhaps you will come and dine pretty frequently."

He sent for his trunks the following day and made a call upon Carver. Tab heard later that under the personal direction of Rex all the deed-boxes and other movables in the vault had been moved by a gang of workmen, and that immediate preparations were being made to wall up this sinister chamber.

It was like Rex to take up with enthusiasm some unexpected hobby. Carver told him, when next they met, that Rex haunted the builders' yard, was having elaborate plans drawn for a new house, and was himself entering with enthusiasm into the mysteries of mortar-making and bricklaying.

"In fact," said Tab, "poor Rex is making himself an infernal nuisance. He has these spasms. About three years ago he decided, in defiance of his uncle's intentions, to become a great crime reporter, and spent so much time in *The Megaphone* library that the news editor kicked. Whenever he wanted a book, Rex had it; whenever he wanted to look up some old and forgotten crime, there was Rex, in the midst of a chaos of cuttings. The present fit will last exactly three weeks; after that, Rex will buy a large hammock and a large bed and spend his time alternately on one or the other!"

Tab did not see Ursula Ardfern for a week. He wrote to her once, for he was a little worried, remembering her fainting fit on her last night at the theatre, but he received a reassuring, indeed a flippant, message from Stone Cottage.

"I have come back here and am entrenched against all mysterious Men in Black with an aged but active butler, who has served in the army and is acquainted with the use of lethal weapons. The late roses are out – won't you come and see them? They are glorious. And Yeh Ling's Temple of Peace is roofed with shining red tiles, and the villagers are breathing freely again at the prospect of his queer little labourers leaving the neighbourhood.

"I drove over there yesterday and found Yeh Ling very sombre and very quiet, watching the final touches being put on what looked to be a huge barrel, but which I found was the mould in which the second of his great pillars is to be cast. It is the Pillar of Grateful Recollection, or something of the sort, and it is to be dedicated to – me! I feel thrilled! It is hard to believe that all these years Yeh Ling has remembered the trifling services I gave to his son; and isn't it curious, that in all those years, although I have met him many times, for I used to dine regularly at his restaurant (I dined there this week), he has never made one reference to the old days? It is a little eerie, isn't it?

"I am learning to shoot. Forgive this inconsequence, but my butler (how grand that sounds!) is very insistent, and I practise every day in the meadows behind the house. I had no idea that a revolver was so very heavy or jumped so when you pressed the trigger, and the noise is appalling! I was scared almost to death the first day of the practice, but I am getting quite used to it now, and Turner says I shall make a crack shot.

"If you come you will not lack for excitement. Personally I should have preferred that Turner would have given me lessons in archery; it is much more graceful and ladylike. Every time the pistol fires (it is an automatic) it blackens my hands horribly – and it stings!"

Tab read the letter through very many times before he took the Hertford Road. He stopped *en route* to admire the monument which Yeh Ling had erected to his prosperity. He could admire, in all sincerity, for the house presented not only a striking, but a beautiful appearance. Its unusual lines, the quaint setting in which it stood, for the garden had now taken shape, the one lusty pillar that flanked the broad yellow path, made a striking picture.

The workmen had not gone, and presently he spied Yeh Ling himself coming down the broad short flight of steps from the upper terrace.

If he did not distinguish him at first, it was excusable, for he wore the blue blouse and baggy trousers of his workmen; but Yeh Ling had seen him and came straight to where he was standing.

"You've nearly finished," said Tab, with a smile of greeting. "I congratulate you, Yeh Ling."

"You think it is pretty," said Yeh Ling, in his grave cultured voice. "I have had the best builder I could get from China, and I have not stinted him. Some day perhaps you will come and see the interior."

"What are they doing now?" asked Tab.

"In a few days we shall cast a second pillar," said Yeh Ling, "and then the work is finished. You think I am at heart a barbarian?" Yeh Ling seldom smiled, but now his pale lips curled momentarily, "and you will take those pillars as proof?"

"I wouldn't say that – " began Tab.

"Because you are so polite, Mr Holland," said Yeh Ling; "but then, you see, we look at things from a different angle. I think your church steeples are ridiculous! Why is it necessary to stick a great stone spike on to a building to emphasize your reverence?"

He searched in his blouse and brought out a gold cigarette case, and offered it to Tab. Then he lit a cigarette himself, inhaled deeply before he sent a blue cloud into the still air.

"My pillar of Grateful Memories will have a greater significance than all your steeples," he said, "than all your stained-glass windows. It is to me what your War Memorial Crosses are to you, a concrete symbol (literally concrete!) of an intangible sentiment."

"You are a Taoist?" asked Tab, interested. Yeh Ling shrugged his shoulders.

"I am a believer in God," he said, "in 'x,' in something beyond definition. Churches and sects, religions of all kinds are monopolies. God is like the water that flows down the mountainside and fills the brooks and the rivers. There come certain men who bottle the waters, some in ugly bottles, some in beautiful bottles, and these bottles they sell, saying that 'only this water will quench your thirst.' That it does quench thirst we will not deny, but the water is often a little stale and flat and the sparkle has gone out of it. You can drink better from the hollow of your hands kneeling by a brook. In China we bottle it with mystic writings and flavour it with cinnamon and spices. Here it is bottled without any regard to the water, but with punctilious care as to the shape of the bottle! I go always to the brook."

"You are a queer devil," said Tab, surveying the other curiously.

Yeh Ling did not answer for a while, and then he asked: "Is there any news about the murder of Brown?"

"No," said Tab; "where was he, Yeh Ling?"

"He was in a smoke-house," said Yeh Ling, without hesitation. "I took him there at the request of my patron, Mr Trasmere. The man had come over to give him trouble and Trasmere wanted me to look after him and see that he didn't make himself a nuisance. Apparently Brown had these bouts and then recovered, as opium smokers sometimes do, with a distaste for the drug. He must have recovered very suddenly and was gone before I could stop him and before the man who owned the house could let me know. I searched for him, but he disappeared, and I heard no more about him until I read in the newspapers that he was dead."

Tab was thoughtful.

"Had he any friends? You knew him in China?"

Yeh Ling nodded.

"Was there anybody who had a particular grudge against him – or against Trasmere?"

"Many," said the other. "I, for example, did not like Brown."

"But apart from you?"

Yeh Ling shook his head.

"Then you have not the slightest idea who was the murderer?"

Again the inscrutable gaze of Yeh Ling met his.

"I have an idea," he said deliberately, "I know the murderer. I could lay my hands upon him without the slightest difficulty."

26

Tab gasped.

"You're not joking?"

"I am not joking," said Yeh Ling quietly. "I repeat, I know the murderer. He has been within reach of me many times."

"Is he a Chinaman?"

"I repeat he has been within reach of me many times," said Yeh Ling, "but there are reasons why I should not betray him. There are many reasons why I should kill him," he added reflectively. "You are going to see Miss Ardfern?" He changed the subject abruptly. "Do not go there in the afternoons, or if you do approach from the front of the house. Miss Ardfern is taking lessons in revolver shooting, and one of my men, who has been watching the house from the lower meadows, has had several narrow escapes."

Tab laughed and offered his hand.

"You are a strange man, Yeh Ling," he said, "and I don't know what to make of you."

"That is my Oriental mystery," said the Chinaman calmly. "One reads about such things. 'For ways that are dark and for ways that are strange –' you know the stanza?"

Tab went away with an amused feeling that Yeh Ling had been laughing at him, but he had been serious enough when he had been talking about the murder; of that Tab was sure.

Long before he reached the house he saw Ursula Ardfern. She was standing in the middle of the road opposite her gate, waving her hand to him, a dainty figure in grey, her flushed face shaded by a large garden hat.

"I'm such an expert shot, now," she said gaily as he jumped off, "that I thought of putting a few long-range ones in your direction to see how you looked when you were scared."

"I'm glad you didn't, if Yeh Ling's uncomplimentary reference to your shooting is justified," he said, as he tucked her hand under his arm.

"Have you seen Yeh Ling? And was he very rude about my marksmanship?"

"He said you are a danger to life and property," said Tab gravely, and she laughed.

"You would manage your bicycle better if you used both hands," she said, releasing her own. "I want you to see my heliotrope. I have to keep it in a garden by itself; it is a cannibal plant: it kills all the other flowers. How could you spare time to come down?" she asked, her voice changing; "aren't you very busy?"

Tab shook his head.

"I have been instructed to get very busy indeed," he said grimly.

"Over this last case?"

"I can do no more than the police are doing," he said, "and Carver seems to have lost hope, though he is a deceptive bird."

"No clue of any kind has been discovered?"

Tab hesitated here. He had promised Carver that he would not speak of the new pin, but perhaps the restriction was confined only to the printed word.

"The only clues we have," he said, as he sat down by her side under the big maple, "are two very bright and very new pins which we found, one in the passage after the first murder, and one just inside the vault after the second. Both were slightly bent."

She looked at him thoughtfully.

"Two pins?" she repeated slowly. "How strange! Have you any idea of the use that was made of them?"

Tab had no idea, neither had Carver.

"The murderer was, of course, the Man in Black," she said. "I read an account of the case, particularly Mr Stott's statement – he is the scared little man who ran away when Yeh Ling and I went to search the house for our papers. Yes, I say 'our' advisedly."

"By the way, did Yeh Ling really find what he wanted?"

She nodded.

"And what you wanted?"

She bit her lips.

"I don't know," she said. "Sometimes I think he did and is keeping it from me. He swears that there was nothing of interest to me, but I believe he is being…kindly reticent. Some day I am going to have it out with him."

The hand that was nearest to him was playing with a twig on the seat, and summoning his courage he took it in his own and she did not resist.

"Ursula, it isn't easy…you'd think that a man with my enormous nerve could take the hand of a woman…that he loved…without his heart going like an aeroplane propeller, wouldn't you?"

She did not answer.

"Wouldn't you?" he repeated desperately. He could think of nothing else to say.

"I suppose so," she said, not meeting his eyes. "And you'd think that an actress who had been made love to eight days a week, counting matinées, for years on end, would carry through a scene like this without having…an insane desire to burst into tears…if you kiss me, Turner will see you…"

Tab could never remember that moment very clearly. He had a ridiculous recollection that her nose was cold against his cheek and that in some miraculous fashion a wisp of hair came between their lips.

"Lunch is served, madam," said Turner awfully.

He was an elderly, grim-looking man, and apparently he did not trust himself to look at Tab.

"Very well, Turner," said Ursula, with extraordinary courage and coolness. And when he had gone: "Tab, you have realized poor Turner's worst fears; he told me that I was the first actress he had ever taken service with, and I gathered he looks upon the experiment as a dangerous one."

Tab was a little breathless, but he had his line to say.

"The only thing that can save your character, Ursula, is an immediate marriage," he said boldly, and she laughed and pinched his ear.

The confusion of Tab's recollections of that day extended to the golden hours which followed. He came back to town in a desperate hurry – he was aching to write to her! He wrote and he wrote, and an expectant night editor peeped in at him and crept softly away to warn the printer that a big story of the murder was coming along (the night editor had distinctly counted a dozen folios to the left of Tab's elbow), and it was only at almost the eleventh hour that he found he was mistaken.

"I thought you were doing the Mayfield murder. Where's your story?" asked the indignant man.

"It is coming along," said Tab guiltily. He stuffed the unfinished letter into his inside pocket, set his teeth, and tried to fix his mind upon crime. He would stop at the most incongruous moments to conjure up a rosy vision of that day, only to turn with a groan to…

"…the position of the body removes any doubt there may have been as to the manner in which the man met his death. The features of the two crimes are almost identical…"

So he wrote at feverish haste for half an hour, and the night editor, cutting out the superfluous "darlings" that appeared mysteriously in the copy, formed a pretty clear idea as to what Tab had been writing when he was interrupted.

Tab posted the letter, went home, and began another, this being the way of youth.

It was all a dream, he told himself when the morning came. It could not be true. And yet there was a fat envelope containing the letter he had written overnight, awaiting the post…

Tab opened the letter and added seven pages of postscript.

Later in the morning he asked Jacques, the news editor, if he believed in long engagements. He asked this casually, as one who was seeking information for business purposes.

"No," said Jacques decisively, "I don't. I believe after a man has been two or three years on a newspaper he gets stale, and ought to be fired."

Tab had not the moral courage to explain the kind of engagement he meant.

That day the weather broke. The rain shot down from low-hanging clouds, the temperature fell twelve degrees. Nevertheless, he thought longingly of the garden of Stone Cottage. It would be snug under the trees, snugger still in that long low-ceilinged sitting-room of hers. Tab heaved a deep sigh and strolled off to fulfil his promise to Rex.

Rex was full of his new scheme, and dragged his visitor into the bedroom, where blue prints and maps and plans seemed to cover every available surface.

"I'm going to build a veritable mansion in the skies," he said; "I have chosen the site. It is just this side of where Ursula Ardfern has her cottage. The only rising ground in the country."

"I know the only hill in that part of the world," said Tab, with sudden interest, "but unfortunately you have been forestalled, Rex."

"You mean by Yeh Ling," said the other carelessly; "I'll buy him off. After all, it is only a freak on his part to put up a house there."

Tab shook his head.

"You will have some difficulty in persuading him to sell," he said quietly. "I happen to know that he is almost as keen on his house as you are on yours."

"Stuff," laughed Rex. "You seem to forget that I am made of money!"

Tab shook his head.

"I didn't forget that," he said, "but I repeat I know Yeh Ling."

Rex scratched his head irritably.

"It will be a shame if I can't get it," he said. "Could you persuade him – I've rather set my heart on that site. I saw it once in the old days, long before I ever knew that Ursula Ardfern lived nearby, and I said to myself: 'One of these days I'll build a house on that hill.' How is my adored one, by the way?"

The opportunity which Tab had wanted.

"Your adored one is my adored one," he said quietly. "I am going to marry Ursula Ardfern."

Rex fell into the nearest chair, looking at him with eyes and mouth wide open.

"You lucky dog!" he said at last, and then he came to his feet with his hand outflung. "I go away on a holiday and you steal my beloved," he said, wringing Tab's hand. "No, I am not feeling at all bad about it – you are a lucky man. We must have a bottle on this."

Tab was relieved, to an extent greater than he had anticipated. He had rather dreaded telling the love-sick youth that the object of his passion had agreed to bestow herself upon the best friend of the man who was responsible for their meeting.

"You are going to tell me all about this," said Rex, busy with the wire-cutters; "and of course I'll be your best man and take in hand the arrangements for the swellest wedding this little village has seen in years," he babbled on, and Tab was glad to let him talk.

Presently they came back to the subject of the house. Rex made no attempt to hide his disappointment that the ideal site was taken.

"I should have given it to you, old man," he said impulsively. "What a wedding gift for a pal! But you shall have a house that is worthy of you, if I have to build the darned thing myself! As an architect I am a failure," he went on; "my views are too eccentric. Poor old Stott swooned at the sight of some of my designs," he chuckled to himself. "I'm not going to give up the attempt to carry my great idea into effect," he told Tab at parting, "I shall see Yeh Ling at the earliest opportunity. I may be able to persuade him to sell."

Tab went down to Hertford the next afternoon, and never had his bicycle moved more leisurely.

"I told Rex," he blurted out, and he saw her face fall.

"He wasn't hurt," said Tab, anxious to relieve her mind; "in fact, he behaved like a brick! Do you mind very much? My telling him, I mean?"

"No," she said quietly. "He wasn't hurt?"

Tab laughed.

"It may sound uncomplimentary to you, but I am sure that Rex was only temporarily infatuated."

He saw a smile dawning and took her face between his hands.

"If I were Rex," he said, "I should hate Tab Holland."

"Rex is stronger minded," she said. "Let us go into the garden. I have been thinking things out, and I feel that there is something that you ought to know, and the longer I put it off the harder it will be to tell."

He followed her, carrying an armful of cushions, arranged her chair, and sat upon its arm; and then, in the most unconcerned voice, holding no hint of the tremendous statement she was to make, she said:

"I killed Jesse Trasmere."

27

He leapt to his feet.

"What?" he gasped.

"I killed Jesse Trasmere," she repeated; "not directly, not with my hands, but I am responsible for his death, almost as assuredly as if I had shot him." She caught his hand and held it. "How white you are! I was a brute to put it that way. In our profession we love these dramatic – no, I don't mean that, Tab."

"Will you tell me what you do mean?"

She signalled him to sit on the footrest of the chair.

"I'll tell you something, but I don't think I'll tell you any more about the murder," she said, "and this is the something which you ought to know, and which I intended you should know. I had not the slightest intention of saying what I did. The spirit of tragedy seems to haunt me," she said, staring straight ahead; "I was cradled in that atmosphere of violence and wickedness. I once told you, Tab, that I had been in service as a tweeny-maid, and I think you were startled. I went there from a public orphan's home, an institution where little children are taught to be born old. Tab…my mother was murdered, my father was hanged for her murder!"

There was no pain in her eyes, just a little hardness. He took both her hands in his and held them.

"I don't remember anything about it," she went on; "my earliest recollection was the long dormitory where about forty little girls used to sleep, a very fat matron, and two iron-faced nurses; and the why and wherefore of my being at Parkington's Institute only came to me late in life. One of the little girls had heard the matron tell the nurse, and

I had to piece together the fact that I was an orphan by the act of my father, and that after his trial and execution I had been sent to this home to be brought up and educated for the profession which all good little girls follow, and which had, as its supreme reward, an appointment as under-cook. I was not so fortunate. I am afraid my cooking was rather vile, for when I came out of the Institute it was to take a place as under-housemaid and general help in the kitchen of a great society leader, who spent thousands of pounds upon charity, but weighed the very bread that her servants ate. I had only been in this place for three months when Mr Trasmere made his appearance. It was on a cold windy afternoon – I remember it as distinctly as though it were yesterday – when one of the parlour-maids came and said I was to go up into the drawing-room. I found Mr Trasmere alone, and I was rather frightened at the sight of him, for he did not speak, but sat with a little scowl on his face, taking me in from head to foot.

"I was between twelve and thirteen then, a sensitive child, to whom life, as it came to me, was a veritable hell. He asked me what was my age, and whether I was happy, and I told him the truth. Apparently he had seen the authorities at the Institute, for I was allowed to go away with him, and he took me to a poor apartment house and placed me under the care of a woman who either owned or rented the house, and sub-let the rooms furnished to the queerest lot of people I have ever seen congregated under one roof. Knowing him now much better, I am inclined to think that Mr Trasmere owned the house himself and that the woman was his nominee. I did not see him again for nearly two months. I had a room to myself and he sent me school books to read and study, and it was whilst I was here that I first met Yeh Ling, who, as I have told you, was a poor waiter at a Chinese restaurant.

"At the end of the two months Mr Trasmere came for me, and his coming was heralded by the arrival of a huge box of clothes, the like of which I had never seen, let alone worn. He left a message that I was to be dressed and ready to go with him, and that afternoon he called and took me down into the country, to a preparatory school which, after the Institute, was heaven upon earth. On the way down he told me he had heard about me from some friends of his, and he wanted to give me an education which would fit me to take the position which he had for me, and I was so overcome by his kindness that I cried all the way to our destination.

"The three years that I spent at St Helen's seem, even now, like a beautiful dream. I was happy, I made many friends, and my whole outlook on life changed. The year I left, Mr Trasmere came down to our Commemoration and saw me acting in a play which the school dramatic society had produced, and from what he saw was evolved this extraordinary arrangement. Knowing what I do, I know he was not wholly disinterested. It was his practice to take up projects and finance likely people. Once he told me that he had intended settling in this country and living the life of a gentleman – to use his own words – but that he was so unutterably bored that to give himself an interest he took up the most extraordinary of schemes.

"Do you know at one time he financed twelve tea-rooms and collected his share of the takings every day? Do you know that he was behind three doctors and took his profits from each? He was Yeh Ling's backer, and in time he came to be mine. I was with him six months, acting as his secretary in a tiny office he hired for the purpose, and to which he never came until five o'clock in the afternoon.

"Then it was that he suggested that I should go on to the stage, and sent me away with a touring company. Of course he was financially interested in it, and it was my duty to send him a daily return showing the amount of money we took every night. On Saturdays I paid the salaries and expenses and remitted the remainder to him. When the tour was finished I came back to town, to find that he had already made arrangements in his furtive, secretive way, to start a season with me as the principal attraction. My salary! You would laugh if I told you. It was hardly enough to keep body and soul together, only, as an excuse for his parsimony, he agreed that he would pay me one half of the profits over a certain amount.

"To my astonishment, as well as to his, I became not only a respectable success, but a great financial success. The profits on my seasons were enormous; they exceeded to an incredible extent the amount he had fixed. And of course he paid. Jesse Trasmere's word was more than his bond. It was his oath.

"His code was the code of the Chinese businessman. When you know what that means, Tab, you will realize how very punctilious he was in such matters. He made exactly the same arrangements with Yeh Ling. There was the curious bond which bound us together, Yeh Ling and I – our shares were enormously in excess of his estimate. But he paid loyally. Between him and me there was never an agreement of any kind. In the case of Yeh Ling there was an agreement, as you know. But the most bizarre aspect of my success was that I was compelled to continue as his secretary. Every night, when the theatre was closed, I motored to his house, dealt with his correspondence, and answered his letters. Sometimes I was so weary after a heavy evening that I could scarcely drag myself up the steps of Mayfield. But Jesse was inexorable. He never let up on any bargain he made, any more than he evaded the terms of any agreement which proved adverse to him.

"When I began to get talked about he insisted upon my making a 'show,' as he called it, and bought a lot of jewels which he told me should be mine at his death. Whether he bought them – they did not look new to me – or whether he acquired them in one of those deals of his which nobody knew anything about, I am unable to say with certainty. They were beautiful – but they were not mine until his death. Every night I dined with him at Yeh Ling's, and he handed to me the jewel-case which he had taken from his bag, and every night I carried those jewels back to the house and gave them into his care."

"Did the old man ever tell you how he came to seek you out?"

She nodded, and a faint smile came and went.

"Jesse Trasmere was very frank. That was one of his charms. He told me he knew my deplorable history, and he wanted somebody about whom he knew a few discreditable facts! He said that in almost those identical words. 'You'll have to go along as I want you,' he said; 'and the higher you get, and the more successful you become, the less you will want the news published that your father was a murderer.' And yet, curiously enough, he never objected to my taking my own name, for Ardfern is my name, for professional purposes. I don't suppose anybody at that dingy Institute associates me with the skinny little girl who used to scrub and peel and toil at uninteresting lessons from morning until night."

"What was your father?" asked Tab, with an effort, for he expected that any reference to her parents must still wound her.

To his surprise she answered readily.

"He was an actor," she said, "and I think he was a clever actor until he took to drink. It was in drink that he murdered my mother. That much I learnt at the home – I have not troubled to inquire since. What are you thinking about, Tab?"

His forehead was knit.

"I am trying to recall the execution of any person named Ardfern in the last twenty years; I know them all by name," he said slowly. "Have you a telephone?"

She nodded.

In three minutes Tab was talking to the news editor of *The Megaphone*.

"Jacques," he said, "I want some information. Do you remember any person named Ardfern being executed for murder in the last" – he looked round at the girl – "seventeen or eighteen years?"

"No," was the instant reply. "There was a man named Ardfern against whom a coroner's verdict of manslaughter was returned, but he skipped the country."

"What was his first name?" asked Tab eagerly.

"I am not sure that it was Francis or Robert. No, it was Willard – Willard Ardfern. I remember there were two 'ards' in it," said the information-bureau.

"In what town was this crime committed?"

Jacques answered without hesitation, giving the name of a small country town that Tab knew well.

He hung up the receiver and turned to the girl.

"What was your father's name?" he asked.

"Willard," she replied, without hesitation.

"Phew!" whistled Tab, and wiped his streaming forehead. "Your father was not hanged."

He saw her go red and white.

"Are you sure?" she asked.

"Perfectly sure. Old Jacques never makes a mistake. Besides which he had the name pat when I asked him. Willard Ardfern. He was indicted for manslaughter. I fear that your unhappy mother died of his violence, but Willard Ardfern himself left the country and was never arrested or tried."

His arm went round her in support, she had gone suddenly white and ill-looking.

"Thank God," she whispered. "That seemed worse than killing my poor mother. Oh, Tab, it has been such a nightmare to me! Such a dreadful, dreadful weight. You can't know how I felt about it."

"Was it that?" – he hesitated – "something I had said that made you feel bad when we talked of Mr Trasmere's will?"

She looked at him steadily, but did not give an answer.

"I used to hate this nightly borrowing of jewels" – she went back to her relations with Jesse Trasmere – "I had enough money to buy my own, though I have no particular leaning toward jewellery, but old Trasmere would not hear of it. Any movement towards my independence he checked ruthlessly." She stopped suddenly, and her mouth made a little O of surprise. "I wonder if he heard...in China?" she asked. "Yes, that is it! He must have met my father. That is how he came to know about me! I am sure Yeh Ling knows, because Mr Trasmere had a habit of making elaborate notes – I wonder," she said, speaking to herself. Impulsively she threw out her hands and caught his. "Tab, the night you came into my dressing-room I felt instinctively that you were a factor in my life. I could never have dreamt how big a part you were going to be."

For once in his life Tab could not think of an appropriate rejoinder.

28

There came to police headquarters a tall, ruddy-skinned man of middle age. He wore a suit which was evidently not made for him, and he seemed a little depressed by his surroundings.

"I have an appointment with Inspector Carver," he said, and passed a letter across the desk to the police clerk, who read it and nodded.

"Inspector Carver is expecting you," he said, and called a messenger.

Carver looked round as the door opened and viewed his caller with a speculative eye. Then he jumped up.

"Of course!" he said. "Sit down, please."

"I hope," began the man, "there isn't going to be any trouble."

"Not for you," said Carver, "but I rather fancy there is trouble coming for somebody."

The messenger closed the door and left them together.

Half an hour later Inspector Carver telephoned for the office stenographer, and when the harassed man with the fresh face and ill-fitting clothes left the police office after a three-hour examination, Inspector Carver had material for much cogitation.

Tab called in the ordinary way of duty and they discussed the latest tragedy, but never once did Inspector Carver make reference to his visitor of the morning. That was his secret, and too precious a one, in the circumstances, to breathe to a soul.

He drove down that afternoon to the detention prison where Walters was awaiting trial and had a long talk with him.

Yeh Ling was in his parlour, half way through his long weekly letter to his son, when Inspector Carver was announced. He put down his brush and gazed impassively upon the servant who had brought in the Inspector's card.

"Is this man alone?" he asked.

"Yes, Yeh Ling. There is no one with him."

Yeh Ling tapped his white teeth with his well-manicured nails.

"Come," he said laconically, and there was something in Carver's face which told Yeh Ling all that he wanted to know. But there was a fight to be made yet, and he was not without hope that this matter of the Trasmere murder, and the tragedy that had followed, would be settled in a manner more consonant with his keen sense of obligation.

The Inspector did not come to the point at once. He accepted a cigar that the Chinaman offered to him, spoke jocularly of Yeh Ling's letter-writing, asked a question or two about Ursula Ardfern, and at last hinted at the object of his visit.

"Yeh Ling," he said, "I think the Trasmere case is coming to a solution."

Yeh Ling's eyelids did not so much as flicker.

"In fact," said the Inspector, carefully examining the ash of his cigar, "I have found the murderer."

Yeh Ling said nothing.

"I need very little confirmatory evidence to put the man who killed Jesse Trasmere on the trap," Carver went on.

"And you have come to me to furnish that evidence," said Yeh Ling, with a touch of irony.

Carver shook his head and smiled.

"I don't know... I didn't think you would," he said, and then almost sharply: "Where are the documents you took from the Trasmere house the night you went there with Miss Ardfern?"

The Chinaman got up without hesitation, unlocked a small safe in the corner of the room and brought out a thick packet of papers.

"They are all there?" asked Carver, shooting a suspicious glance at the other.

"All except two," was the cool reply; "one of which has reference to my interest in the Golden Roof and that is with my lawyer – "

"And the other?" asked the detective.

"That deals with matters of a sacred nature," said Yeh Ling, in that precise English that sounded almost affected.

Carver bit his lip.

"You know that this is the document I particularly want?" he asked.

"I guessed that," was the reply. "Nevertheless, Mr Carver, I cannot give it to you; and if you know so much" – for a second a ghost of a smile lit his brown eyes – "then you will also know why it is not forthcoming."

"Does Miss Ardfern know?"

Yeh Ling shook his head.

"She is the one person who must not know," he said emphatically. "If it were not for her" – he shrugged his shoulders – "you might see it."

Carver knew that he was opposed by a will greater than his own, and that neither threats nor promises would move this impassive man from the attitude he had taken up.

"What does it matter whether you see this paper or not?" asked Yeh Ling. "You say you know the murderer, that you have sufficient evidence to put him on the trap – but have you?"

His look was a challenge.

"You cannot convict a man on supposition, Mr Carver. You must prove beyond any doubt whatever that Jesse Trasmere was killed by somebody who had the means of getting in and out that locked vault, and leaving the key on the table. It is not enough to say: 'I am certain that this prisoner killed his – benefactor!' It is not sufficient that you can show motives. You must produce the means! Until you can say the murderer obtained admission to the vault by this or that door, in this or that way, or that he employed these or those means to restore the key to the table from the outside of a locked door through which no key could pass, you cannot secure a conviction. That is the law. I studied law at Harvard, and I have the rules of evidence at my fingertips." He smiled faintly. "You see, Mr Carver, that the confirmatory evidence you require cannot possibly be supplied by me."

Carver knew that he was speaking no more than the truth; that he was against a dead wall unless some human eye had witnessed the murder, and the method by which the murderer escaped.

The logic of the Chinaman's criticism was irresistible, and Carver, who had seen success within reach, experienced a sense of failure at the very moment when he thought that all his efforts were coming to fruition.

"Then tell me this," he said. "I understand that on several occasions you have been followed by the Man in Black. Have you any idea who he is?"

"Yes," said the other, without hesitation; "but what is the value of my ideas? I could not swear to any facts, and facts are the meat and drink of juries, Mr Carver."

Carver got up and sighed heavily, and hearing him, Yeh Ling broke into a fit of silent laughter.

"I am sorry," he apologized, "but I am thinking of my favourite poem," his eyes twinkled. "You remember the other gentleman who 'rose with a sigh, and he said can this be? We are ruined by Chinese cheap labour…'"

"I shall certainly not 'go for the Heathen Chinee,'" said Carver good-humouredly, "not for the moment. What I like about you, Yeh Ling, is your refreshing sanity. I don't know that I have ever dealt with a man – shall I say fought with a man? – who would have given me greater pleasure to fence."

The Chinaman performed a deep kow-tow, and his mock humility amused Carver long after he had left the shadow of the Golden Roof.

Yeh Ling, who seldom made any personal effort for the comfort of his guests, paid particular attention to the preparations which were being made in No. 6 that night. The Italian waiters, to whom the proprietor was almost unknown, were both nervous and annoyed, for nothing seemed to please Yeh Ling. He had the flowers changed half a dozen times. He had new cloths brought, and at the last minute insisted upon the table being laid all over again. He brought the rarest of glass to adorn the board, unearthed unsuspected treasures of chinaware and substituted them for the crockery of the restaurant. This done, he summoned to his room the *maître d'hôtel* and the wine chef, and chose the dinner with the most exquisite care.

"Yeh Ling has really done himself proud," said Tab, admiring the table.

The girl nodded. She had hoped that Yeh Ling would have chosen another room, but she had no real feeling of repugnance; and besides, she had been here since Trasmere's death.

"It is very thrilling to be dining alone with a young man," she said, handing her wrap to the waiter. "And I can only hope the scandal of it doesn't get into the newspapers!"

"Shall we see Yeh Ling?" asked Tab, half way through the dinner.

She shook her head.

"He never appears. He has only been in this room twice to my recollection."

"It is our first appearance together in public," said Tab solemnly. "I can count on our boys, but if any of those *Herald* thugs hear and catch a glimpse of your expensive ring, there are going to be scare lines in that deplorable rag – *The Herald* has no reticence or decency."

She laughed softly and looked at the "expensive ring" that glittered and sparkled in the light of the shaded lamp.

"I asked Carver if he would come along after dinner," said Tab, "but he is busy. He sent the most flowery and poetical messages to you – really Carver is a surprising person; there is a whole world of romance hidden behind that somewhat unpleasing exterior, if you will pardon the journalese."

But if Carver could not come, they had a visitor. There came a tap and the door opened slowly.

"Great Moses!" said Tab, springing up. "How the dickens did you know that we were here, Rex?"

"I spotted you," said Rex Lander reproachfully, "slinking in at the side door like two guilty souls! May I offer my congratulations, Miss Ardfern, and lay at your feet the fragments of a broken heart?"

She laughed nervously at his jest.

"No, I can't stay," said Rex, "I have a party; and, moreover, I am entertaining a man with terrific ideas on architecture. Isn't it queer? Now that I am no longer arc-ing, I have conceived a passion for that unhallowed profession! Even old Stott is becoming an admirable personage in my eyes. Have you forgiven me, Miss Ardfern?"

"Oh, yes," she said quietly, "I have forgiven you a very long time ago."

Rex's baby eyes were very kindly, his plump face was wrinkled in a smile of amiable reflection.

" 'When a young man's fancy – ' " he began, and caught a reflection in the mirror.

From where Tab and the girl sat they could see nothing. Rex saw reflected the half-open door and a figure that stood motionless outside. He spun round with an exclamation.

29

"Good lord, Yeh Ling, you gave me a fright! What a creeping old devil you are."

"I came to see whether the dinner was successful," said Yeh Ling softly. His hands were covered in his wide sleeves, a little black skull cap was pushed on the back of his head, his shabby silk suit and white-soled slippers seemed remarkably out of place in that very modern setting.

"It was a great success, Yeh Ling," said Tab, "wasn't it?"

He turned to the girl, and she nodded and her eyes met Yeh Ling's and for the fraction of a second held them.

"I think I'll go," said Rex awkwardly, and gripped the girl's hand again. "Good night, old man, you are a lucky old thief." He wrung Tab's hand and was gone.

"Was the wine to your liking?" said Yeh Ling's soft voice.

"Everything was beautiful," said Ursula.

There was a touch of colour in her cheeks that had not been there before. "Thank you, Yeh Ling, you gave us a wonderful feast. We shall be late for the theatre, Tab," she said, getting up hurriedly.

She was very silent in the car that drove them to the Athenaeum, and Tab felt a little of the gloom which had suddenly come into their festivity.

"Yeh Ling is a creepy sort of fellow, isn't he?" he said.

"Yes, I suppose he is," was her reply, and that was all she said.

Ten minutes later she was sitting in a box, intent upon a stage which she had once adorned, and seemingly oblivious to everything except the play. Tab decided that she was a little temperamental, and loved her for it.

Going out to smoke between the first two acts (she insisted upon his going) he saw Carver standing by a tape machine in the vestibule of the theatre. His attention was concentrated on a very prosy account of a yacht race which was coming through, but he saw Tab out of the corner of his eye, and signalled him.

"I am going home with you tonight," he said surprisingly. "What time will you leave Miss Ardfern?"

"I am seeing her to her hotel immediately after the show."

"You are not going to supper anywhere?" asked the other carelessly.

"No," said Tab; "why do you ask?"

"Then I will be waiting at the Central Hotel for you. I wish to see you about a nephew of mine who wants to become a newspaper reporter. Perhaps you can give me a few hints."

Tab glanced at him suspiciously.

"I have suspected you of many weaknesses, but never of nepotism!" he said. "You told me a few weeks back that you hadn't a relation in the world."

"I have acquired a nephew since then," said Carver calmly, his eyes still upon the tape; "it is a poor kind of detective who can't discover a nephew or two. I may fall down on a murderer, but when it comes to unearthing distant relations I am at the top of my class. You will find me somewhere in the shadows of the Central," he added.

Tab did not see the detective again until he had left the girl in the vestibule of her hotel. Coming out into the street, Carver, true to his word, appeared from the night and took his arm.

"We will walk home. You don't take enough exercise," he said. "Lack of exercise is bad for the old, but it is fatal for the young."

"You are very chatty this evening," said Tab; "tell me something about your little nephew."

"I haven't a nephew," said the detective shamelessly, "but I am feeling kind of lonely tonight. I have had a very disappointing day, Tab, and I want to pour my woes into a sympathetic ear."

"Faugh!" said Tab.

Carver showed no inclination to find a sympathetic listener, even when they were back at the flat and he had a modest whisky and soda before him.

"The truth is," he said at last, in answer to a direct question, "I have reason to believe that I am being most carefully watched."

"By whom?" asked the startled Tab.

"By the murderer of Trasmere," said the detective quietly. "It is a humiliating confession for a man of my experience and proved courage to make, but I am afraid to go home tonight, for I have a large premonition that our unknown friend is preparing something particularly startling in the way of trouble for me."

"Then you really want to stay the night here?" said Tab, as the fact dawned upon him.

Carver nodded.

"Your instinct is marvellously developed," said he. "That is just what I want to do, if it is not inconvenient. The fact is, I had not the moral courage to ask you before. It isn't very pleasant to admit – "

"Oh shush!" said Tab scornfully. "You are no more scared of the murderer than I am."

"I am more accessible to him in my own lodgings," said the detective, and that sounded fairly true. "If I stayed in an hotel I should be even more accessible, so I am going to make use of you, Tab. How do you feel about it?"

"You can bring your belongings and stay here until the case is over," invited Tab. "I don't think that Rex's old bed is made up."

"I prefer the sofa, anyway. Luxury enfeebles and vitiates a man as it enfeebles and vitiates a nation – "

"If you are going to be oracular, I am retiring to bed," said Tab.

He went into his room, brought out a rug and a pillow and threw them on to the broad settee.

"I'd like to say," said Carver, as Tab was leaving him for the last time, "how surprisingly good you look in evening kit. The difficulties of making a reporter look like a gentleman must be almost insuperable, but you have succeeded beyond my most sanguine expectations."

Tab chuckled.

"You're indecently humorous tonight," he said.

He hadn't been in bed five minutes before the light went out in the sitting-room. Mr Carver was apparently settling himself to sleep.

Tab's dreams were happy, but they were strangely mixed. Within five minutes of his head touching the pillow he was carrying Ursula through her scented garden and his heart was full of gratitude to providence that this great and wonderful prize had come to him. And then in his dream be began to feel uncomfortable. Glancing over his shoulder he saw the sinister figure of Yeh Ling watching him, and he was in the garden no longer, but on the slope of a hill flanked by two huge pillars, and Yeh Ling stood at the entrance of his queer house, arrayed in dull gold brocade.

"*Bang… Bang!*"

Two shots in rapid succession.

30

He woke with a start. There was a rush of feet in the sitting-room, and then − crash.

He was out of bed in a second and into the sitting-room. Carver was nowhere to be seen and he felt by the draught that the door of the flat was wide open. He put his hand on the light switch and a voice from the darkness said:

"Don't touch that light!"

It came from outside the door, and it was Carver who was speaking.

Below came the thud of the street door closing.

Carver came hurriedly into the room, passed him, ran to the window and looked out.

"You can put it on now," said Carver. A red weal was slashed across his face, and it was bleeding slightly. He put up his hand and looked at it.

"That was a narrow squeak," he said. "Yes, he's gone. I could have taken a chance and run downstairs after the door slammed, but even that might have been a fake to lure me into the open."

The whole building was awake now. Tab heard the sound of unlocking doors and voices speaking from above and below.

"It was the cigar that gave me away," said Carver ruefully. "I was a fool to smoke. He must have seen the red end in the darkness, and on the whole I think he shot pretty accurately."

There was a small Medici print hanging by the side of the window. The glass was shattered. A round bullet-hole showed on the white shoulder of Beatrice D'Este.

Carver fingered the hole carefully.

"That looks to me like an automatic," he said. "He is getting quite modern. The last time he killed a man he used a type of revolver which was issued by the Chinese Government to its officers some fifteen years ago. We know that from the shape of the bullet," he went on unconcerned. "There is somebody at the door, Tab. You had better go and explain we have had another attack of burglaritis."

Tab was gone some ten minutes, disquieting the tenants of the flats. When he returned he found Carver examining the track of the second bullet, which had struck the lower window sash and which had drilled a neat little hole.

"Probably hit the wall opposite," said Carver, squinting through.

"The man below found this on the stairs," said Tab.

It was a small green-handled knife in a lacquered scabbard.

"Pseudo-Chinese," said Carver. "It may even be the genuine article." He pulled out the knife, tested the razor-like edge. "And sharp," he added. "I had an idea he didn't mean to use his gun."

"Now," said Tab, facing the detective squarely, "we will dispense with all light and airy persiflage and come down to sober affidavits. You expected this attack. That is why you came tonight with your fake story of a literary-minded nephew."

"I did and I didn't," said Carver frankly. 'When I told you that the attack would be made on me I half believed it, but as I couldn't find an excuse for getting you to stay with me, and, moreover, as I have no accommodation for a man of your luxurious habits, I decided on the whole I'd take a chance by staying here." He looked at his watch. "Two o'clock," he said. "He must have come about a quarter of an hour ago, and I will give him this credit, that I did not hear the door open. Fortunately there was a clothes hook behind the door, and some time or other you hung an old hat there. It was hearing this hat fall that made me realize that either I was growing deaf or else the stealthy personage was unusually soft-footed. He must have seen first my cigar, and then my outline as I rose, for, like a fool, I hadn't pulled the settee away from the window. He was back in the lobby in a flash, and before

I knew what had happened he had fired twice, slammed the door, and gone. He was still in the hall when I went out, but it was so dark that I could see nothing."

"I thought I heard the door first."

"Because you were asleep," smiled the detective, "and you hear the last sound first. No, I will give you a guarantee that he shot at me before he shut the door." His eyes narrowed. "I wonder," he said softly.

"What?"

"I wonder if your friend has had a duplicate of this attack? Where is he staying?"

"I think we ought to warn him, anyway," said Tab. "Our visitor came in the first place to burgle Rex's trunks, and probably he doesn't know that Rex isn't staying here. He is at the Pitts Hotel."

Carver got the telephone directory and discovered the number. It was some time before he had an answer, for the clerks at the Pitts Hotel are not accustomed to calls at that hour of the morning. Presently he got into touch with a porter.

"I don't know whether he is staying here, but I will find out," said that official.

It was ten minutes before he had made the discovery.

"Yes, he is in Room 180. Shall I put you through?"

"If you please," said Carver. He heard the click and clug of the connection being made, and after an appreciable delay Rex's sleepy voice answered him.

"Hullo! who is that? What the devil do you want?"

"I'll talk to him," whispered Tab, and took the receiver from the detective's hands.

"Is that you, Rex?"

"Hullo! who is that – Tab? What's the idea?"

"We have had a visitor," said Tab. "You remember I told you about the burglar? Well, he came again tonight."

"The devil he did."

"In fact, we've turned the old flat into a shooting gallery," said Tab, "and Carver wonders whether you have had a similar experience."

"Not I," was the cheerful reply. "It is as much as a man's life's worth to wake me out of my sleep."

Tab grinned.

"Keep your door locked."

"And my telephone receiver off," said the other. "I'll let you know if anything happens. Is Carver there?"

"Yes," said Tab.

Carver went to the phone.

"He wants to speak to you."

Carver had made a signal, and now he took the receiver in his hand.

"I am sorry you have been disturbed, Mr Lander," he said, "but I'd like you to know officially that we warn you that an attempt has been made to get into this flat at – well, ten minutes ago. What time would that be?"

"That would be about a quarter to two, I guess," said Rex's voice. "Thank you for telling me, Inspector, but I am not at all scared."

Carver put the receiver on the hook and rubbed his hands.

"Do you think they will go there? What on earth is amusing you?" asked Tab irritably.

"I am intensely amused, I admit," said Carver, "at the queer, simple, and tragic error that our murderer made."

Early in the morning Carver called at the Pitts Hotel and personally interviewed a sleepy-eyed Rex, who sat up in bed in violently striped pyjamas and expostulated with commendable mildness upon the interruption to his night's sleep.

"I am one of those people," he said severely, "who require at least twelve hours' heavy slumber. Heaven having endowed me with the means whereby I can gratify my wishes in this respect, it is a little short of an outrage that Tab and you should call me up even to tell me that the flat has been burgled again."

Reporting his interview on his return to the flat, Carver offered a few remarks on the vagaries of masculine fashions, particularly in relation to pyjamas, and came back at a tangent to the very serious events of the past twelve hours.

"I think you'll be all right tonight," he said. "At any rate I am leaving you to your own devices. Bolt the door and put a tripwire between a couple of chairs."

"Oh, nonsense!" said Tab. "He will not come again tonight."

Carver scratched his chin.

"What is tonight?"

"Saturday."

"The fatal Saturday, eh?" he said. "No, perhaps not. What are you doing today?"

"I am driving a friend into the country, or rather she is driving me," said Tab promptly. "It is my weekend off, but I shall be back in town tonight."

Carver nodded.

"Ring me up the moment you are back. Will you promise that?"

And Tab laughed.

"Certainly I will if it is any satisfaction to you."

"If you don't ring me I shall ring you at intervals throughout the night," threatened Carver. "I have already warned Lander. Above all, Lander must not sleep at this flat."

"Don't you think that by now they will have discovered that he is no longer living in the flat?" asked Tab.

"They may or may not," was the reply, "and" – he hesitated – "I don't think I should talk about this to Miss Ardfern. In fact, I would rather you didn't."

Tab had no intention of alarming Ursula, and he could make that promise without reservation.

31

She came to Doughty Street and picked him up, and they were at Stone Cottage in time for lunch. The weather was still unsettled, but Tab had passed the stage where weather made any difference to him.

Though he did not tell her of his sensational experience, he did mention his dream.

"Ursula," he asked, "you like Yeh Ling, don't you? So do I, as a matter of fact, but do you absolutely trust him?"

She considered before she spoke.

"Yes, I think I do," she said. "He has been a most faithful friend. Think, Tab, without my knowledge, all these years he has been watching over me. I should be a most ungrateful girl if his loyalty did not move me."

Tab thought that there might be some other explanation of Yeh Ling's devotion, but wisely said nothing.

"Do you know," she said, "that he keeps a man watching this house day and night? I only discovered it by accident when I was engaged in revolver shooting. Perhaps Yeh Ling told you that I nearly shot one of his sentinels."

"He is a strange man," admitted Tab, "but my dream rather impressed me – "

"Even the first part of your dream hasn't come true yet," she suggested demurely, and he picked her up in his arms there and then.

Happily the so-easily scandalized Mr Turner was engaged elsewhere.

Tab's heart was full of love and gratitude when he left her in the sweet-smelling dusk, and mounting his bicycle, which he had brought strapped to the back of Ursula's car, started on his leisurely way home.

Half way he had a puncture which delayed him, and it was nearly ten o'clock when he wheeled the machine into the garage where it was maintained.

The last part of the journey was made through a heavy driving rain and he was wet through by the time he reached Doughty Street.

A hot bath and a change of clothing brightened him, and he was filling his cigarette case preparatory to going out to take a meal when he was called to the telephone. He expected to be greeted by Carver, but it was Rex who was speaking, and his voice was eager and urgent.

"Is that you, Tab? My boy, I've made the most wonderful discovery!"

"What is that?" asked Tab, wondering.

"You are not to breathe a word to Carver, you understand, Tab? This is the most extraordinary discovery, Tab!" His voice shook. "I have found out how the murder was committed!"

"The Trasmere murder?"

"Yes," came the quick reply. "I know how the man got in and out of the vault. I was in there this afternoon inspecting the work that has been done, and I found it by accident. It is all so simple, Tab, how the key got on to the table and...everything. Can you meet me at Mayfield?"

"At Mayfield?"

"I'll be waiting outside the door for you. I don't want any of Carver's men to see us."

"Why not?" asked Tab.

"Because," said Rex's voice deliberately, "Carver is in this murder up to his neck!"

Tab nearly dropped the receiver from his hands.

"You are mad," he said.

"Am I? You shall judge for yourself. And Yeh Ling is in it – hurry!"

Tab ran to the larder and pushed a handful of biscuits into his pocket, put on his raincoat, and went out into the vile night, his mind in a state of chaos.

Carver!

And Yeh Ling was in it too!

The wind had risen and half a gale swept through the deserted Peak Avenue as he strode along to the house of mystery. He did not see Rex until he passed through the gate. That young man was standing under the shelter of the portico by the door. Nearby in the concrete yard Tab saw a car.

"We'll find our way in the dark. I've got a pocket-lamp," he whispered, and Tab stepped into the dark deserted hall, with its fusty scent and its strangely oppressive atmosphere of decay and neglect.

Rex's voice was trembling with excitement.

"We can put the lights on after we get into the corridor," he said.

He found his way across the room by the light of the lamp, unlocked the door, and led the way into the passage.

"Shut that door, Tab," he hissed, and when Tab had obeyed he turned on all the lights.

Near to the end of the corridor Tab saw a great heap of bricks and a board covered with mortar; the work of bricking up the vault had begun, and the first course stretched across the open doorway of the vault.

Rex stepped over the brickwork and illuminated the empty interior.

"There!" said Rex triumphantly, and pointed to the table.

"What is it?" asked Tab, in amazement.

"Hold both sides of the table and pull."

"But the table is fixed on to the floor; we noticed that before," said Tab.

"Do as I tell you," said Rex impatiently.

Tab leant over the table, and gripping both edges, firmly pulled...

187

32

He awoke to consciousness with a sense of a dull pain at the back of his neck and a feeling of restriction. He was sitting against the wall, propped up, and when he tried to bring up a hand to rub his aching neck he found they would not move. He opened his eyes and looked around, and the first thing he noticed was that his feet were strapped together. He stared stupidly at the fastening and tried to move his hands – but they were in a curious position. He was handcuffed behind. To the connecting links a cord had been fastened and passed under him to the strap.

"What – " he began, and heard somebody laugh softly.

Looking up he saw Rex. That young man was sitting on the edge of the table, smoking.

"Feel better?" he asked politely.

"What is the meaning of this, Rex?"

"It means that, as I promised, you have found the murderer of dear Uncle Jesse," said Rex, his baby blue eyes gleaming. "I killed Jesse Trasmere. I also killed that drunken beast Brown. I didn't intend killing Brown," he went on reflectively. "Unfortunately he left me no alternative. He recognized me in the park at the time when I was supposed to be in Naples."

"Didn't you go abroad?" gasped Tab, the minor deception for the moment bulking largely.

Rex shook his head.

"I didn't go any farther than the mouth of the river," he said. "I came off with the pilot. The cables and wireless messages that I sent were despatched by the steward, whom I paid for that purpose. I never left town."

Tab could say nothing.

"If you had done as I wished," said Rex, with an odd note of reproach in his voice, "I should have made you a rich man, Tab; but like the sneaking swine you are, you took the woman who was fore-ordained to be my wife! Your beastly lips have touched hers, my goddess!" His voice quavered.

Tab, staring at him, realized that he was in the presence of a madman.

"You think I am mad," said Rex, as though he was guessing the other's thoughts. "Perhaps I am, but I adore her. I killed Jesse Trasmere because I wanted her, could not wait for her, needed the money to possess her."

In a flash there came to Tab Ursula's words: "I killed Jesse Trasmere. I was the indirect cause."

So she knew! That was the explanation of her strange attitude when Rex had come into the room.

And Yeh Ling knew, and had come soft-footed to the door of the private dining-room, ready to leap upon the visitor if he showed any sign of hostility. Yeh Ling, the watchful, the soft-footed one, the everlasting guardian – in his heart Tab Holland thanked God for Yeh Ling.

Rex went out of the vault and was gone for five minutes. When he came back he was carrying a writing-pad, which he put on the table, pulling up a chair and sat down.

"I am going to give you the scoop of your life, Tab," he said. There was no mockery in his voice; it was, if anything, very serious and gentle.

"I am going to write a full confession of how I killed all three of you."

Tab said nothing. The whimsical act of the man was in keeping with the theory of lunacy. For half an hour he listened to the scratching of a pen and the rustle of paper as one by one the sheets were covered, blotted, and neatly put aside. What was his end to be?

Rex would kill him; he had no doubt whatever on this score. The man was impervious to appeal, and it was senseless to call for help. His voice would never escape the confinement of that underground room.

Carver and he had made an experiment after Trasmere's death. He had stayed in the vault and fired a blank cartridge whilst Carver was outside the house listening, but no sound had come out.

Tab looked round for the sign of a weapon, but if Lander had brought one it was not visible.

"There, I've said everything, and here it shall stay on the table, and when they find your bones they will know why you died."

Watching him, Tab saw him sign his name with a flourish, the old flourish, which had often amused him.

"What are you going to do, Lander?" he asked quietly, and Lander smiled.

"Have no fear," he said, "I am not going to disfigure your athletic body or do you any violence. You are going to stay here and die."

Tab fixed him with an unwavering glance.

"You don't suppose – " he began, but thought better of it.

"I don't suppose that your friend Mr Carver will not come in search of you; that was what you were going to say; but believe me, Mr Carver will never find you. In the first place he would not come here, for nobody knows that you are here. He didn't even suspect that I was your visitor last night."

"Have you a clock in your room?" said Tab, a light dawning on him.

The other frowned.

"In my bedroom, at the hotel?" he was surprised into saying.

"You haven't!" said Tab triumphantly. "Good old Carver! He asked you the time when he was talking on the telephone, didn't he? And you replied. He knew you were the man who came into the flat. He knew that when he called you up you would be fully dressed and have a watch in your pocket."

"Oh," said the other blankly, and then: "He came to see me this morning, damn him! It was to discover whether there was a clock in the room, eh?" he grinned, but there was no humour in those bared teeth. "He doesn't know you are here, anyway," he said. "Goodbye, Tab. Do you remember how you tried to make a reporter of me, and how I used to sit at the office studying crime? Well, I found a new trick in those cuttings, and I have been waiting years to put it into practice."

No other word he spoke, but took something from his pocket: it was a reel of stout cotton. Then from his waistcoat he produced a new pin, and with great care and solemnity tied the thread to the end of the pin, Tab watching him intently. And all the time he was working, Rex Lander was humming a little tune, as though he were engaged in the most innocent occupation. Presently he stuck the point of the pin in the centre of the table, and pulled at it by the thread he had fastened.

Apparently he was satisfied. He unwound a further length of cotton, and when he had sufficient he threaded the key upon it, carrying it well outside the door. The end he brought back into the vault, pushing it through one of the air holes. Then he closed the door carefully. He had left plenty of slack for his purpose and Tab heard the click of the lock as it was fastened, and his heart sank. He watched the door fascinated, and saw that Lander was pulling the slack of the cotton through the air hole. Presently the key came in sight under the door. Higher and higher came the sagging line of cotton and the key rose until it was at the table's level, slid down the taut cotton, and came to rest on the table. Tighter drew the strain of the thread, and presently the pin came out, passed through the hole in the key, leaving it in the exact centre of the table.

Tab watched the bright pin as it was pulled across the floor and through the ventilator.

That was the secret of the pin!

The last time the thread must have slipped, or possibly the point of the pin had caught in the woodwork of the door and had fallen where he had found it. Or the man may have left it in the vault, and it had been left in the passage after Trasmere's death to add mystery to mystery.

"Did you see?" Lander's voice shook with pride. "Simple, eh? And quick…Tab?"

Tab did not answer.

"I am a rotten architect, eh, Tab, but by Jingo, I'm a good bricklayer! Have you seen me lay bricks, Tab…? I know so much about it that I fired the two workmen today, and said I was going to get somebody else to finish the job… Tab, I'm finishing it…"

Tab crossed his hands and tried to snap the connecting links of the cuff, but he could not get purchase. He had been so tied that he could hardly move. His head was aching terribly, and he knew the cause; one of the first things he had seen on recovering consciousness was the sandbag which Rex Lander had used as he was leaning across the table, fooled into believing that some secret passage would be revealed when he pulled.

Rex was singing softly, and mingled with his voice came the click and ring of trowel on brick, that scraping sound that bricklayers make, that tap, tap, tap of the trowel as it knocked the bricks into place.

"I shall probably be working all night," Lander interrupted his singing to say, talking with his mouth against the ventilator. "I ought to have put the light out, but it is too late now."

"You poor lout," said Tab contemptuously. "You poor cheap lunatic! I can't be angry with you, you unspeakable fat man!"

He heard the quick intake of the other's breath, and knew that he had touched him on the raw.

"Don't you realize," said Tab remorselessly, "that the very first place Carver will look will be this vault, and when he finds it bricked up, the very first thing he will do will be to tear it down, and all your fine explanations will not stop him. And then what will he find? The confession which, in your crazy vanity, you have made, and my statement."

"You'll be dead," howled Lander, and went to work frantically.

33

Tab's brain was clearing now; he was taking a cold survey of the position. Rex Lander was mad – up to a point. Mad as men of abnormal vanity are mad. Vanity inspired the bravado which made him leave in the death-room a statement which would surely hang him when it was found. Vanity and hurt pride led him to his present dreadful act, even as it had led him to search amongst Tab's papers at the flat for Ursula's non-existent love letters and to tear and mutilate the portrait of the man who had won her love.

Rex was the burglar. Who else could have found his way unerringly in the dark? And Carver had known!

Madness in relation to crime fascinated Tab. In his younger and more confident days he had written a monograph on the subject, which, amidst much profitless speculation, had contained one gem of reasoning – the demand for corroborative evidence of criminal insanity. "Not evidence of a number of acts showing that an accused person is insanely cruel or pursues some one, apparently mad, course; but proof that in other relations he is abnormal. It is corroboration of homicidal tendencies that a man insists on wearing odd boots of a different colour, or that he is in the habit of walking in the street without his trousers."

By this standard Rex was sane.

So thought Tab with one half of his brain; the other half was taking stock of his immediate hope of escape. He was handcuffed behind; around his legs was a strap that was beyond the reach of his teeth. Between the links of the handcuffs and the strap a cord had been fastened and pulled tight, so that his knees were doubled up without hope of straightening unless he could succeed in breaking the cord. If that were possible, there was the key within reach. He made one effort, pulling up his legs still farther and then jerking out his feet violently. The pain of it nearly made him faint, tough as he was. It seemed as if both his shoulders were dislocated. He could feel the cord; it was stout…perhaps with finger and nail he could pick it into shreds, fibre by fibre, or cut it with his thumbnail…

After the wall was up his time would be very short unless the vault contained some other ventilator which neither Carver nor he had discovered. And yet, even if the cord was broken he must wait until Lander had completed his work. It would be fatal, handcuffed as he was, to break out whilst Rex was on hand. His only chance was to free himself of the trussing cord whilst the work outside was in progress, get the key, and by some contortion unlock the door and employ his great strength to push through the newly laid bricks. The time would be short…but the cord was unbreakable.

He rolled over on one side, and bracing his feet against the leg of the table and his head against the wall succeeded in getting on to his knees. Bound as he was, his eyes were at the level of the table-top. Shelves, steel shelves…perhaps there was a rough edge somewhere. He hobbled along on his knees and saw a promising place.

Again he rolled over, this time on his back, raising his feet until, by straining, he brought the cord against the shelf. And all the time came the ring of the trowel and the crooning song of Rex Lander. He knew at once that it was a hopeless proposition. The sharp edge was beneath the shelf, he could only reach the upper surface. Crossing his legs to get a better purchase, he felt the strap slip upward. By pushing at the strap he brought it to below his knees, and he could have yelled his delight, for now the cord was slack and he would, he thought, at least be able to stand.

The sound of amateur bricklaying ceased suddenly, and Rex came to the grating.

"You're wasting your time doing all those funny tricks," he said confidently. "I practised that tie all one evening and you'll not get away. If you come out you'll be sorry!"

"Avaunt, fat man!" snarled Tab. "Get to your flesh pots, gross feeder!"

Rex chuckled.

"Partial to tab lines, eh?"

"Get out of my sight," said Tab, "you theatrical poseur! All the money you have couldn't make you a gentleman – "

He was interrupted by the torrent of rage which swept down upon him from the impotent man outside.

"I wish I'd killed you," he screamed. "My God, if I could get in – "

"But you can't," said Tab, "that is why the position is so remarkably free from anxiety. Carver knows – don't forget that. Carver will have you on the trap – he has promised himself that treat, though I can't see how they'll hang a crazy man," he went on. Lander clawed at the steel plate, sobbing in his rage.

"I'm not mad, I'm not mad," he screamed. "I'm sane! Nobody can put me away... I'm not mad, Tab; you know I'm not mad."

"You are just the maddest thing that ever lived," said Tab inflexibly. "Thank God I saved Ursula – " the words were hardly out of his lips before he regretted them.

He had turned the mind of the man at the door in the last direction he wanted it to go.

"Ursula...mine! Do you hear, she's mine now..."

Tab heard the clash of the trowel as it was thrown down and the sound of hurrying feet growing fainter.

Tab wriggled himself to his knees, threw back his weight, and came to his feet. It was a terrible strain to support himself, but he was standing, doubled up grotesquely, but free to move his feet a few inches at a time. So he crept to the table, and leaning over, pulled the key toward him with his chin. He brought it carefully to the edge, then gripped the handle in his teeth and shuffled to the door. But the lock was set so close to the wall that he could not get his head into position to insert the key. He tried twice, and then, what he feared happened. The key dropped from his teeth with a clang to the floor.

He was on the point of kneeling when he heard somebody moving about. Rex opened the door to the sitting-room and shouted something; what it was, Tab could not hear, but there came to him a noise as if somebody was breaking sticks. Crack, crack, crack! it went, and then he sniffed. It was a faint smell of burning petrol he had detected and he knew that for him the worst had happened. Mayfield was on fire.

34

"No answer," said Exchange.

Mr Carver rubbed his nose irritably and glanced up at the clock. Then he lifted the instrument again.

"Give me Hertford 906," he said.

In five minutes the call was signalled.

"Miss Ardfern... Carver speaking. I'm very, very sorry...got you out of bed, did I...so sorry! What time did Tab leave?... Half-past eight...you don't say so? Oh yes, he's all right...gone to the office... oh yes, he does some Saturday nights. Don't worry...not at all. Only he promised to call...can't trust love-smitten young men, eh... certainly I'd call you if there was anything wrong."

He put the instrument back and looked up at the clock. Then he pressed a bell. The sergeant who answered was dressed as if he expected to go out into the storm at any moment.

"Men ready...good. Pitts Hotel; two men to each entrance, one to the upper floor, in case he breaks that way. Four good men for his room...men sharp enough to dodge his quick-firing batteries...he'll shoot."

"Who is the man, sir?"

"Mr Rex Lander. I want him for murder and forgery; attempted murder and burglary. If he's not at home it will be easy...we'll take him as he comes into the hotel. One of the night porters is probably being well paid by him. He was the fellow who stalled me last night and gave Lander a chance to get to his room and use the telephone. So we'd better get there before the room clerk goes off duty. And don't forget to impress upon the men that Lander will shoot! If the night porter is on duty we'll take him. He's not to get to the telephone…beat his head off if he tries. I'll be with you in five minutes."

He made another attempt to get in touch with Tab, but was no more successful. Then a thought struck him. He remembered that Tab had told him the name of the sporting tenant who occupied the flat below. But Tab had also told him that this gentleman was seldom at home. Still, there was a chance.

He waited, the receiver at his ear.

"Is that Mr Cowling…why, I am sorry to disturb you… I'm Inspector Carver, a friend of Holland's, who lives above you. You haven't any idea whether he is at home? I've been trying to get him… you've heard the 'phone going, have you? Yes, that was me."

"He came in about an hour ago," said the tenant's voice, "then somebody called him. I can hear the 'phone very plainly from my room. Bex or Wex or some such name."

"Rex?" asked the Inspector quickly; "yes, yes…he went out, did he? – thank you."

He sat staring down at his blotting-pad for a minute, then he got up and pulled on his raincoat.

His squad were getting into cabs as he came out of the station, and he entered the first of these.

Had he left it too long? he wondered. The warrant had been issued after he had taken the sworn statement of the man Green, formerly butler to Jesse Trasmere. He had brought this witness from Australia; had cabled to him the very day that Trasmere was found murdered. Green's reply had confirmed his suspicions.

Too late now to regret his delay. Accompanied by his sergeant, he strolled into the hotel. The lounge was empty, half the lights had been extinguished, and, as he had expected, the room clerk had gone, leaving a stalwart night porter in charge.

"Mr Lander, sir? No, I don't think he is in. I'll get through to his room."

"Don't touch that telephone!" said the Inspector, "I am an officer of the police. Show me to his room."

The man hesitated the fraction of a second, and then:

"If you monkey with the switchboard I'll put you where the rats won't bite you," said Carver sharply. "Come out of that!"

The man obeyed sulkily.

"I've done no wrong," he said; "I was only trying to – "

"Watch this man," said Carver. "Now give me the key of Lander's room."

The man took down a key from a hook and threw it on the counter.

Rex Lander's suite was empty, as Carver had expected.

"I want a thorough search made of these rooms," he said to the sergeant. "I will leave you a man to help you. All stations must be maintained until they are withdrawn. He may come in late."

He waited for half an hour inside the hall, but though there was a constant procession of cars and cabs laden with people returning from the theatres, there was no sign of Rex Lander.

The hall porter became informative.

"I've got a wife and three children. I don't want to get into any trouble. What do you want Mr Lander for?"

"I'll not tell you," said Carver curtly.

"If it is anything very serious I know nothing about it," said the porter. "I might as well tell you that I did him a favour the other night."

"Last night, was it?"

"Yes. He was in the hall when somebody telephoned through for him, and he asked me to keep them waiting whilst he went up to his room. He told me it was a lady friend that he wasn't on good terms with. That's all I know about it. He is a very nice man," he added in justification.

"A perfect peach," agreed Carver sardonically. "Well?"

One of the men he had left to search the room was coming hurriedly across the lounge. He drew Carver aside and produced from his pocket a long-barrelled revolver of an old-fashioned make.

"We found this in one of the drawers," he said.

Carver examined it curiously. The moment he saw it he knew what it was, even before he found the Chinese characters engraved on the steel of the butt.

"I thought so," he said. "It is a Chinese issue, the sort they served out to their Army officers about twelve years ago. I think you'll find it was the property of Trasmere." He snapped it open. It was fully loaded; containing four live and two used cartridges. "Keep that carefully apart. Wrap it in paper and have it photographed for finger-prints," he ordered. "You found nothing else?"

"There's a receipted bill from Burbridge's for a sapphire ring," said the man, and Carver smiled faintly.

The present which Rex had bought "in Rome" for his friend had been purchased within a few miles of Doughty Street and was intended to emphasize the fact that Rex was abroad.

It was nearing twelve o'clock when a 'phone message came through from police headquarters and Carver went to the instrument.

"Is that you, Mr Carver… Mayfield is burning…the brigade have just had a call."

Carver dropped the receiver as if it were red-hot and flew to the door. A cab had just set down some guests at the hotel and he pushed unceremoniously past them.

"Peak Avenue," he said.

What a fool not to have thought of Mayfield before! He cursed volubly in the darkness of the taxi. And after he knew that Rex Lander had called Tab on the 'phone, and that Tab had gone out! Of course, that was where he would have taken Tab – to Mayfield. Tab would have gone cheerfully, having no suspicion of his friend, and – Carver shuddered.

He had read only too clearly the significance of the torn photographs. The man was insanely jealous; would stop at nothing. With two murders to his discredit, a third would be simple.

Long before he reached Peak Avenue he saw the red glow in the sky, and groaned. Amidst that blazing hell Rex Lander had destroyed not only his rival but half the evidence of his crime.

The cab dashed through the police line into the Avenue, crowded now with half-dressed inhabitants, and brightly lit by the flames that mounted above the doomed house. The roof fell in as he sprang from the cab; a column of sparks leapt into the dark sky, and Carver could only stand speechless and sorrowful beyond expression.

Then it was that somebody tapped his elbow, and looking round he saw a man in a soaked and bedraggled dressing-gown. At first he did not recognize him, for the little man's face was blackened and scorched, his eyes were red and wild.

"My father was a fireman," said Mr Stott solemnly. "We Stotts are a hard bit'n race. Heroes all of us!"

Carver looked at the man aghast.

Mr Stott was very drunk!

35

Eline Simpson, with a large handkerchief tied round her face, turned on her bed and groaned. It was unfortunate for all concerned that Eline's bedroom was immediately above that occupied by Mr John Stott and his wife, although Eline's groans had no serious effect upon that lady.

Mr Stott had reached the stage where he waited with agonized expectancy for the next boom of anguish; when it did not come he was frantic, when it finally shivered the walls of his room he was maddened. Eline was an irregular groaner.

"Eline goes tomorrow!" he roared, and even Mrs Stott heard him.

"She's had her tooth out," said Mrs Stott sleepily.

"Go upstairs and tell that girl to get up and walk about...no, no, not to walk about, to sit still."

"M'm," said Mrs Stott, and sighed happily.

Mr Stott glared at her and then came another groan from above. He got out of bed and into his dressing-gown – it was really a kimono – and trotted up the stairs.

"Eline!" he called, in a hushed, intense voice, suitable to the hour and the occasion.

"Yes, sir," pathetically.

"What the he – why are you making such a...such a hullabaloo?"

"Oh...my...tooth...does ache, sir!" she wailed jerkily.

"Nonsense!" said Mr Stott; "how can it ache when it is at the dentist's? Don't be a baby. Get up and take something...come downstairs...dress yourself decently," he warned her.

He went down into the dining-room and from a secret cupboard produced a bottle with a boastful label. Into a tumbler he splashed a very generous portion.

Eline came in a flannel dressing-gown and skirt. She looked scarcely human.

"Drink this," commanded Mr Stott.

Eline took the glass timidly and examined it. "I could never drink that, sir," she said, awe-stricken.

"Drink it!" commanded Mr Stott fiercely; "it is nothing."

To prove that it was nothing he poured himself out an even more impressive quantity and tossed it down. In retaliation, the whisky almost tossed down Mr Stott. At any rate, he staggered under the shock. Fortunately for his reputation as a hard and easy drinker Eline was oblivious to everything except a sense of complete suffocation, accompanied by a feeling that she had swallowed a large ladleful of molten lead. So she did not see Mr Stott gasping like a fish and clutching his throat.

"Oh, sir…what was it?" she found voice to ask.

"Whisky," said Mr Stott, in a strangled voice, "neat whisky! It is nothing."

Eline had never drunk neat whisky before. It seemed to her, as whisky, distinctly untidy. It had sharp edges. She could only look upon her employer with a new-born respect.

"It is nothing," said Mr Stott again. Now that it was all over it seemed, at any rate, easy. He was an abstemious man, and in truth had never tasted whisky in its undiluted state. Bravado had made him do it, but now that it was done he had no regrets.

"How's your tooth?"

"Fine, sir," said Eline gratefully. She experienced a wonderful sense of exhilaration. So did Mr Stott.

"Sit down, Eline." He pointed grandly to a chair.

Eline smiled foolishly, and sat.

"I have always been a very heavy drinker," said Mr Stott gravely. "My father was before me. I am what is known as a three-bottle man."

He wondered at himself as he spoke. His maligned parent had been a Baptist minister.

"Goodness!" said Eline impressed; "and there are only two bottles on the sideboard!"

Mr Stott looked.

"There is only one, Eline," he said severely, and looked again. "Yes, perhaps you're right." He closed first one eye and then the other. "Only one," he said.

"Two," murmured Eline defiantly.

"We Stotts have always been devil-may-care fellows," said Mr Stott moodily. "Into one scrape and out of another. Hard-drinking, hard-riding, hard-living men, the salt of the earth, Eline."

"There are three bottles!" said Eline, in wonderment.

"My father fought Kid McGinty for twenty-five rounds." Mr Stott shook his head. "And beat him to…to…a jelly. Hard fighters every one of us. By heaven," he said, his pugilistic mood reviving certain memories, "if I had laid my hands on that scoun'rel…!"

He frowned heavily, rose, and walked with long strides into the hall. Eline, scenting action, followed. Her strides were not so long, but longer than she expected. Mr Stott was standing on the doorstep, his hands on his hips, his legs apart, and he was looking disparagingly at Mayfield.

"Come any more of your tricks – and look out!" he challenged. "You'll find a Stott – "

Eline clutched his arm frenziedly.

"Oh, sir…there's somebody there!"

Undoubtedly there was somebody there: a light was showing in the front room – a red and uncertain light. And then a door closed loudly. "Somebody there…?

Mr Stott strode down the steps furiously. Even when he strode down a step that wasn't there, he did not lose his poise.

"Somebody there…?"

He remembered mistily that the gardener had a lazy habit of leaving his spade beneath the trimmed hedge that marked the boundaries of his property.

"You'll catch your death of cold, dear," wailed Eline outrageously.

But Mr Stott neither observed the uncalled-for endearment, nor the rain that soaked him, nor the wind that flapped his dressing-gown loose. He groped for the spade and found it, just as a car came smashing through the frail gate of Mayfield.

"Hi, you sir," shouted Mr Stott fiercely, "what in hell do you mean, sir?"

He stood in the centre of the road, brandishing his spade – the mudguard of the car just missed him.

Mr Stott turned and stared after.

"Disgusting…no lights!" he said.

But there were lights in Mayfield, white and red and yellow lights, that flickered up in long caressing tongues.

"Fire!" said Mr Stott thickly.

He staggered up to the door of Mayfield and brought his spade down upon the narrow glass panel with a crash. Putting in his hand he found the knob of the door and fell into the passage.

"Fire!" boomed Mr Stott.

He had an idea that something ought to be done…a feeling that somebody should be rescued. The dining-room was blazing at the window end, and by the light he saw an open door. Below was a glow of steady illumination.

"Anybody there?" shouted Mr Stott.

And then a shiver ran down his spine, for a distant voice called: "Here!"

"Fire!" yelled Mr Stott, and stumbled down the steps. The voice came from a door.

"Wait… I'll kick out the key…"

There was a sound of metallic scraping and something hit the brickwork at his feet.

Mr Stott frowned at it. A key.

"Open the door," said the voice urgently.

Mr Stott stooped and picked it up, made three shots at the keyhole, and at last got it.

A man, doubled up as if in pain, shuffled out.

"Unfasten the strap," he commanded.

"There's a fire," said Mr Stott impressively.

"So I observe…quick."

Stott unbuckled the strap and the man stood up.

"Get those papers…on the table," said the strange man. "I can't touch them, I'm handcuffed behind."

The rescuer obeyed.

The passage was thick with smoke, and suddenly all the lights went out.

"Now run!" hissed Tab, and Mr Stott, still gripping his spade, groped forward. At the foot of the steps he paused. The heat was fierce, the flames were curling down over the top step.

"Whack the floor…the carpet with your spade and run…don't worry about me!"

Mr Stott made a wild rush up the stairs, striking more wildly at the floor. The smoke blinded him: he was scorched, he felt his few locks shrivel in the heat.

And then Tab Holland behind pushed him with his shoulder, and it seemed to Mr Stott that he was being thrown into the fiery furnace. He uttered one yell and leapt. In a fraction of a second he was in the passage…gasping and alive.

"Outside…!"

Tab thrust his shoulder again at the dazed man, and Mr Stott walked out into the rain just as the first fire-engine came clanging into the street.

"There *is* a fire," said Mr Stott, with satisfaction. "Come and have a drink."

Tab wanted something more than a drink. He saw a running policeman, and hailed him.

"Officer…can you unlock these handcuffs. I'm Holland of *The Megaphone*. Good business!"

A turn of a key and he was free.

He stretched his aching arms.

"Com'n have a drink," urged Mr Stott, and Tab thought that the suggestion was not altogether foolish.

They came to Mr Stott's dining-room, to find Eline singing in a high falsetto voice, a voice which had aroused even Mrs Stott, for that good lady, in deshabille, was regarding the musical Eline with wonder and shame when they arrived.

The good lady staggered at the appearance of her husband. Tab seemed a less notable phenomenon – even the vocal Eline faded from the picture.

"What is the meaning of this?" she asked tearfully.

"There's been a fire," murmured her husband.

He glared at Eline fiendishly, and pointed to the door.

"Shut up, girl! Go to bed! You're fired – you're the secon' fire tonight!"

He was so overcome by his witticism that he relapsed into what promised to be continuous laughter. The clang of another engine arrested his merriment, and he stalked out of the house.

"I don't think Mr Stott is quite well," said Mrs Stott, in a tremulous voice. "I – be quiet, Eline! Singing sacred songs at this hour of the morning!"

And then came Mr Stott in a hurry, and behind him, Carver.

"Thank God, my boy… I never expected…!"

Carver found a difficulty in speaking.

"I rescued 'm," said Mr Stott loudly.

His face was black, what of his dressing-gown was not singed was sodden. He flourished the spade.

"I rescued 'm," said Mr Stott, with dignity. 'We Stotts come of a hard bit'n race. My father was a firem'n – he rescued thousan's from burnin'."

Here he was getting near to the truth, for, as has been before remarked, Mr Stott's father was a Baptist minister.

36

"We must warn Miss Ardfern at once. I have been on the telephone with her this evening. I was enquiring about you, and the chances are that I so thoroughly alarmed her that she is awake. I only hope to God she is!" said Carver.

But whilst it was easy earlier in the evening to get into touch with Hertford 906, it was now impossible. The Hertford operator, after the second attempt, signalled through that there was an interruption.

Carver came back to Mr Stott's dining-room with a grave face. They could speak without interruption, because Mrs Stott and the errant Eline had disappeared. Mr Stott, his hands clasped across his stomach, was fast asleep in a chair, a touch of a smile on his lips. Probably he was dreaming of his heroic and hard bit'n ancestors.

"Tab," said Carver, "you know Stone Cottage? Have you any recollection of the telephone arrangements? Is it a dead-end connection or is it connected from the road?"

"I think it is from the road," said Tab: "The wire runs by the house and the connection crosses the garden. I remember, because Ursula said how unsightly it was."

Carver nodded.

"Then he's there," he said, "and the wire has been cut. I'll get the nearest police station and see what we can do," he said. "In the meantime we will find somebody with a car; make a few quick inquiries, Tab."

Tab's inquiries were particularly fortunate. In the very next house was a young man whose joy in life it was to exceed all speed limits on a sporting Spans, and he accepted the commission which would enable him to break the laws with the approval of the police, with alacrity and enthusiasm.

When Tab returned, the Inspector was waiting at the garden gate. "Is that the car?" he said. "Our friend knows the way?"

"I could find it blindfold," said the amateur chauffeur...

It was a wild ride. Even Tab, who treated all speed regulations with scorn, admitted that the driver erred on the side of recklessness.

They spun through driving rain that stung and smarted like needles, that fell so fast that the two powerful lamps created fantastic nebulae and halos in the darkness ahead. They skidded round greasy corners, thundered along narrow roads...once Tab could have sworn he glimpsed a black car drawn up under a hedge...they passed before he could be sure.

The garden gate was open when Tab leapt out from his precarious seat. As he came through the gate a dangling wire struck him across the face.

There was no need to look for evidence of a visitor...the door was open wide.

His heart was beating thunderously as he stood in the quiet hall, where the only sound that came to him was the sober ticking of a clock. He struck a match and lit one of the candles that he knew Ursula kept ready on a side table. By its faint light he saw that a chair in the hall had been overturned and lay on the carpet, which had been dragged up as though in a struggle. He held on to the wall for support.

"I'll go alone," he whispered hoarsely, and went up the stairs slowly. Every movement required an effort.

On the landing above a dim night-light burnt. It was a broad landing, carpeted with a square blue carpet, and there were two easy-chairs and a small table-nest. Ursula had told him she sometimes read there, for there was a sky-light overhead which could be opened on hot days. Here, again, the carpet was in disorder and on the blue settee –

He bit his lip to stop the cry that came.

Blood! A great patch near one end. He touched it frightfully, and looked at the tips of his fingers. Blood!

His knees gave way under him, and he sat down for a second, then with a tremendous effort rose again and went to the door of Ursula's room and turned the knob.

Shading the candle with his hands he walked into the room. A figure was lying on the bed: the brown hair lay fan-like across the pillow, the face was turned away from him, and then... His heart stood still.

"Who is that?" said a sleepy voice.

Ursula turned on her elbow, shading her eyes from the light of the candle.

"Ursula!" he breathed.

"Why – it is Tab!"

He caught a glitter of steel as she thrust something back under the pillow that she had half withdrawn.

"Tab!" She sat up in bed. "Why, Tab, what is wrong?"

The candlestick was shaking in his hand, and he put it down on the table.

"What is wrong, dear?" she asked.

He could not answer; falling to his knees by the bedside he trembled his relief into the crook of his arm.

37

Rex Lander was smiling as he drove through the rain, for it seemed to him that a great trouble had passed from his mind. The solution of all his difficulties had appeared miraculously. He did not hurry, the end was sure now, and the woman who had completely occupied his mind for four years, whose portraits by the hundred he had secretly treasured, whose face he had watched, to whose voice he had listened night after night, until she had become an obsession that excluded all other thoughts and fancies, was his!

He had hated his sometime friend since the day Tab had made a mock of his adoration. He had loathed him when the incredible fact had been proved beyond doubting that Tab had stolen into the girl's heart, and had won her in his absence.

He had planned his life on this supposition. Wealth! The possession of great power, the ability to bestow upon the object of his choice all that human vanity or human weakness could desire.

Tab was dead now, he thought complacently, and his confession was ashes. He regretted the impulse which had made him write. He had had no intention of doing that when he brought Tab to Mayfield, and he was rather puzzled at his own stupidity. It was a mad thing to do. Mad? He frowned. He was not mad. It was very sane to desire a woman of Ursula Ardfern's grace and beauty. It was sane enough to want money, and to go to extremes to obtain what he wanted. Throughout all the ages men had killed others that their position might be enhanced. They were not madmen. And he was not mad. He had a definite plan, and madmen do not have definite plans.

Ursula would this night consent to marry him, and would be glad, if she refused, to reconsider her decision. He would be her accepted lover before he left the house, and the thought took his breath away.

"Am I mad?" he asked aloud, as he parked his car in the side turning where Carver had almost found it once.

Madmen did not take such elaborate precautions. Madmen did not remember that by some mischance her servant might telephone for the police, nor carry in their pockets a weighted cord to throw over the telephone wire and bring it down. They did not even buy the cord of such and such a length – so much to bind Tab Holland, so much to break the wire – and buy just sufficient for the purpose.

"I am not mad," said Rex Lander, as he went in through the gate.

The house was in darkness; no lights glowed from the upper window where she was sleeping.

He had made a very careful reconnaissance of the house, and he knew its vulnerable points. He opened the casement window of the drawing-room, and had stepped softly inside the room before, in ordinary circumstances, a servant could have answered his ring at the door.

He was in her room! Her sitting-room! It held the very charm of her presence, and he would have been content to sit here, absorbing the atmosphere which she lent to everything she touched, dreaming dreams as he had dreamt so often in the night watches at Doughty Street, at his office when he should have been working, in the solitary walk home from the theatre after he had been listening entranced to her wonderful voice.

He took from his pocket a large electric torch and flashed it round. On the little cottage piano was a bowl of roses; reverently he drew one out, nipped off its stalk, and threaded it tenderly in his buttonhole. Her hand had placed it there. She had taken it from the garden, kissed it perhaps – he bent his head, and his lips touched the velvety petals.

The door was not locked. He was in the hall, the wide-flagged hall. In the corner was a grandfather's clock that ticked sedately.

Her room was in the front of the house: he knew he could not miss it, but must stand on the landing in an ecstasy of anticipation. He put down his torch upon the settee, and mechanically smoothed his hair. Then he tiptoed forward. His hand was on the knob of the door when an arm came round his neck, a lithe sinewy arm that strangled the cry which rose in his throat.

Such was the man's strength that he lifted his assailant bodily from the ground, and, twisting, would have flung him down, but Yeh Ling's leg gripped his, and then Rex Lander wrenched his hands free and dived for his pocket. Yeh Ling saw the gleam of the automatic.

"Sorry," he breathed.

It seemed to Rex Lander that he felt a momentary spasm of pain in his left side.

"You…!" he gurgled. He coughed deeply once, and Yeh Ling eased him down to the settee.

The Chinaman stood, his head bent forward, listening. No sound but the "clac-cloc, clac-cloc" from the hall below. He lifted Lander's eyelids and touched the ball of the eye gently. The man was dead.

Yeh Ling pulled a blue silk handkerchief from his sleeve and wiped the perspiration from his face and eyes, replacing the handkerchief carefully. Then, bending down, he brought the limp arm of Lander about his neck, and with a jerk lifted him to his shoulder. Slowly, painfully, he passed down the stairs with his burden. At the foot of the stairs he was compelled to lay the man down. He tried to find a chair, but without success. Sitting on the floor by the side of his victim, Yeh Ling recovered his breath, and getting up noiselessly opened the door wide.

Black as the night was there was sufficient light to distinguish objects faintly. He could not hoist the man again: he could only drag him across the hall. He knocked over a chair in the process, but fortunately it fell on the carpet and made no sound. Into the garden, along the paved path, out into the road…

Yeh Ling's breath came in a thin whistle. He had to stop again to recover himself. He made another effort to lift the body, and was partially successful. He staggered up the road, his knees giving way under him, but his will dominated; and when he reached a safe distance from the house he put his burden down and went in search of Lander's car. This he found with no trouble: it was unlikely that he should fail, for he had seen the man arrive. He started the engine and brought the car backward along the road until it was level with the Thing. Then he got down and hoisted it into the back of the car, lit a cigarette, put on the lights, and drove slowly along the road toward Storford.

Half a mile from where his new house was situated he turned off the lights, and covered the remainder of the distance without their assistance. Drawing the car up close to a hedge, he gathered the limp figure on his shoulder, and tramped across the muddy ground until he came to the uprights that supported the cement vats. There was a flicker of lightning on the horizon. Yeh Ling could see in that flash (even if he had not known) that no progress had been made in the construction of his Pillar of Grateful Memories: the tub-like moulds stood in place, the steel core, like an attenuated tree-trunk, leaned and swayed in the gale drunkenly.

After much seeking he found the end of a rope fastened to one of the cross-pieces of the platform, and this he tied about the Thing's waist, and went to the windlass. A growl of thunder, a more prolonged quiver and splash of blue light. Looking up, Yeh Ling saw a bundle suspended in mid-air, and took another turn of the wheel.

The wind was blowing fiercely, sending that limp weight at the rope's end swaying to and fro, and Yeh Ling peered up, striving to follow its every movement. Presently came another flash, and another, and yet another. The body had swung over the edge of the mould. Yeh Ling released the primitive brake and the body dropped. From his breast pocket he took the torch that he had found on the settee and flashed a light up at the wooden mould. Yes, it had disappeared.

There was a ladder against the wooden casing, and he climbed up, found another ladder inside, and descended the eight feet which intervened between the mould and the top of the hardening concrete beneath. Without loosening the rope he dragged the body to its feet, and with quick, strong hands, lashed it to the steel core, winding the rope round and round. Presently he cut and knotted the binding, and climbed up again to the top of the woodwork, looking down in an effort to see the sagging figure. The lightning was now incessant, the thunder growing in intensity. He saw, and was satisfied. Pulling up the inside ladder, he dropped over, and in a few moments was himself back on ground level.

And now he made a search. He had to find the rope which controlled the shoot, and he discovered it at last. Pulling it gingerly, he heard the rush of the viscid concrete as it flowed down the shoot into the mould. He pulled the sluice gate wider yet, and heard the "swish, swish" of the flood as it gained in volume. After a while he released the rope, found a shovel, and climbed up the ladder again. The concrete had nearly reached the top of the mould. There was no sign of Rex Lander. Plying the tool, he levelled down the uneven surface of the cement and descended for the last time.

The storm was local and passing, but if it had been the most cataclysmic disturbance of Nature Yeh Ling would not have noticed. He sat on the running-board of Lander's car, wet to the skin, his hands raw and bleeding, every bone aching, and he smoked a cigarette and thought. So thinking he heard the roar of an oncoming car, and ran to the cover of the hedge. It passed in a flash.

"I cannot afford to wait," said Yeh Ling.

He got into the car and drove off, avoiding Storford village and taking, instead, a road which led by the river. Here he stopped and got out, keeping his engine running. With his hands he released the clutch and the car tumbled down the bank into the black water. Then Yeh Ling went back for his own rattling machine.

When day was breaking Yeh Ling lay in a hot scented bath in his apartment overlooking Reed Street. His hands, free from the water, held a thin selection of Browning's poems; he was reading "Pippa Passes."

215

38

"There are bloodstains on the stairs," said Carver, "and on the garden path outside. There is also the mark of car wheels which have evidently been backed from the lane where Lander usually keeps his car, but beyond that all trace is lost."

He looked at Tab and Tab looked at him.

"What do you think?" asked Tab quietly.

"I am not putting my thoughts into words," said the Inspector; "and I tell you honestly, Tab, that I'd rather have that confession of Lander's — wild and incoherent as it is — than I'd have Lander himself."

Dawn was breaking and Ursula had come down to make them coffee, a silent but absorbed listener.

"It is perfectly certain that Lander came here," said Carver. "He destroyed the telephone connection, he made an entrance by the window in the sitting-room, and he went upstairs. You heard nothing, Miss Ardfern?"

"Nothing." She shook her head. "I am not a very light sleeper, but I am sure if there had been any kind of struggle outside my door I should have heard."

"It all depends on who controlled the struggle," said Carver dryly. "My own belief is — however, that is nothing to do with the matter. There is the fact that Lander's hat was found in the roadway, Lander came here, his car marks are distinguishable, and that Lander himself has gone. Turner heard nothing?"

"Nothing," she said. "That isn't remarkable: he sleeps at the back of the house, in a room opening from the kitchen. Does the confession tell you much?"

"A whole lot," said Carver emphatically, "and with Tab's explanation as to how the key was put back on the table the thing is as clear as daylight. It seems that Lander has for years been planning to get his uncle's money, and his scheme was hurried when he learnt – probably from the old man's lips when he was staying with him – that Trasmere intended leaving his money away from the family. Whilst Rex Lander was a guest at Mayfield he must have taken the revolver, which was undoubtedly Trasmere's property, and I have an idea that he took something else."

"I can tell you what it was," said Ursula quietly. "He took away with him some Mayfield notepaper."

Tab looked at her in astonishment.

"Why should he do that, Ursula?"

She did not answer him at once, because here Carver interposed a question.

"How long have you known, Miss Ardfern, that Lander was the murderer of Jesse Trasmere?"

Tab expected her to say that she did not know at all, and that the news had come in the nature of a dreadful shock. Instead:

"I knew he was the murderer the day that Tab told me about the will Mr Trasmere had left."

"But why?" asked Tab.

"Because," said Ursula, "Mr Trasmere could not read or write English!"

The full significance of the simple statement came more quickly to Carver than to Tab.

"I see. I've known the will was a fake all the time," he said, "but I thought it was just a forgery, and that Lander had imitated the writing of the letters that used to come for him from the old man."

"They never came from the old man. Mr Lander wrote them himself," said the girl. "I rather think he wrote them with the intention of establishing the authenticity of the signature when the will was discovered. He had guessed the old gentleman's secret. Mr Trasmere was very sensitive on the point. He used to complain that although he could write and read Chinese without any difficulty – in fact I have learnt since that he was scholarly in that direction – he could not write two words of English. That is the principal explanation as to why he employed me for his secretary, and why he must have somebody upon whom he could place the utmost reliance, and on whom he had some sort of pull."

"Do you mean to tell me that Rex was writing letters to himself?" asked Tab incredulously.

She nodded.

"There is no doubt at all," she said. "When you told me Mr Trasmere had left a will in his own handwriting, I nearly fainted. I knew then just what had happened, who was the murderer, and why Mr Trasmere had been murdered."

Carver rubbed his unshaven chin.

"I wish I could find Lander," he said, half to himself.

"How long did Rex have this idea?"

Tab broke the silence which followed.

"For years; ever since – " he hesitated.

"Ever since he first saw me?" said the girl miserably.

"Before then. There was another lady upon whom he set his heart," replied Carver. "Lander, as I say, had to hurry up his scheme when he found that the money was going to be left away. He was only waiting his opportunity. The plan had been completed to the smallest detail. He had practised with the key trick assiduously, and he decided to put the plan into operation on the day the murder was committed. He knew that his uncle generally spent his Saturday afternoons in the vault, that the doors leading to the vault would be open. His first job was to get rid of the servant. By some means he discovered that Walters was a crook: I have an idea that there was a time when Lander was an industrious student of crime, and I seem to remember somebody telling me that he used to spend hours at *The Megaphone* library and made himself very unpopular in consequence."

Tab nodded.

"That is where he might have become acquainted with Walters, or Felling, though I am not going to dogmatize on the subject. It is sufficient that he found that Walters was a convicted thief, and that on the afternoon of the murder he sent a telegram (which I have been able to trace) to Walters, telling him the police were coming for him at three. From the moment he saw that telegram delivered, and he must have been watching, to the moment that Walters left the house, Lander was somewhere handy. As soon as he saw the door opened, and Walters came out, he made his appearance. When Walters had gone he went into the house, passed down the steps into the passage, and found, as he had expected, his uncle working at the table, probably checking some money that had come in during the week – a favourite occupation of his. Without warning, he shot the old man dead. Then looking round for the key, he found that it was not, as he had expected, in the lock, but on the chain about Trasmere's neck. He broke the chain and took out the key, which was bloodstained. He had a pin and thread ready, which he fastened to the centre of the table, put the other end through the air hole after threading the key, pulling the door to, locked it, and drew on the slack in exactly the same way as you saw and described, Tab.

"I noticed one little bloodstain near the bottom of the door when I first inspected the cell, but could not make head nor tail of it. Nor could I understand the appearance of a tiny piece of grit in the ward of the key. Both these mysteries have been solved. When the key was back on the table he pulled out the pin, removed it from the cotton, which he put back in his pocket, and by some mischance dropped the pin in the passageway."

There was another long pause, and then: "Where is he now?" asked Carver irritably.

The only man who could have supplied him with exact information was at that moment sleeping peacefully on a hard and narrow bed.

39

Yeh Ling wrote:

> "DEAR MISS ARDFERN — I am giving what you call a house-
> warming on Monday next. Will you not come? And please, if
> you can, will you persuade Mr Carver and Mr Holland also to
> be my guests for this festivity?"

The girl wrote instantly, accepting the invitation, both on her own
and Tab's behalf.

"It is a great idea," said the news editor; "there is a story in that
house, Tab. Now, boy, see if for once in your young life you can turn
in a really informative column! There is something gone wrong with
your stuff lately — the night editors are complaining bitterly about the
slush that finds its way into your literary efforts. You are not supposed
to refer to the Secretary of State as 'darling,' and it is not usual to speak
of a judge as 'beloved.' "

Tab went very red.

"Do I do that, Jacques?" he asked conscience-stricken.

"You do worse than that," said Jacques. "Now...a good story about
these pillars of Yeh Ling's. Get a touch of the flaming East into your
mundane exercises, will you?"

Tab promised faithfully that he would.

He had the unexpected pleasure of meeting Mr Stott at the house-
warming, and introduced that gentleman to Ursula. Mr Stott had a
particular interest in Yeh Ling's fabric, for, as he explained some dozen
times, he had put in the foundations.

"I owe you a very great deal, Mr Stott," said Ursula warmly. "Tab – Mr Holland has told me how splendidly brave you were on the night of the fire."

Mr Stott coughed.

"There is some talk in town of presenting me with a piece of plate," he said deprecatingly; "I have done my best to stop it. I hate a fuss about a trifle of that description. The curious thing is, all my family have disliked that kind of fuss… Our family has always hated publicity. My father, who was perhaps the best minister in the Baptist movement, might have gone into the church and become a bishop – in fact, they practically offered him a bishopric – he was just the same. I remember…"

Yeh Ling led them through the house, showing them his art treasures, accumulated with some labour and now seeing the light of day for the first time.

Ursula felt very happy, was childishly appreciative and enthusiastic over every beautiful little statuette, over every example of the native painters' art which Yeh Ling showed her.

"Yeh Ling," she said, when they were alone for a second, "have you heard any news of Mr Lander?"

He shook his head.

"Do you think he has got away to another country?" she asked.

"I think not," said Yeh Ling.

"Do you know, Yeh Ling?" she said meaningly.

"I can only assure you, Miss Ardfern," said Yeh Ling, waving the cool air into his face with a beautifully painted fan, "that I have never looked upon Mr Lander's face since the night I saw him at the Golden Roof."

She was content with this, but –

"Who was Wellington Brown?" she asked, in a strained voice.

"Lady," said Yeh Ling gently, "he is dead; it was better that he died so than in the way you feared."

She passed her hand before her eyes and nodded.

"We Chinese forgive our fathers much," said Yeh Ling, and left her to her grief.

From the house he took his guests to the terrace gardens, and then down the broad yellow avenue to the two massive grey pillars that stood guard at the entrance of his domain.

"You had a lot of trouble with these, I am sure," said Stott, casting a professional eye upward.

"With one only," said Yeh Ling, and his fan moved to and fro languidly. "With the Pillar of Grateful Memories there was a hitch. Somebody came into the ground one night whilst it was raining and let cement into the mould, cut off the hauling rope, and did other trivial damage. My builder thought that the pillar would not set, but it has."

He looked up at the smooth face of the concrete, and his eyes rested some dozen feet above the ground.

"I have dedicated this to all who have helped me: to the old man Shi Soh; to you, Miss Ardfern…to all gods, Western and Eastern; to all who love and are loved."

When his guests had gone Yeh Ling, in his blue-and-gold satin dress of ceremony, came back to the pillar, and there was a little book in his hand. His finger was inserted midway.

The servant who accompanied him he dismissed.

"I believe," said Yeh Ling, "I shall be happier…" He stood facing the pillar, bowed, then opening the book, he began to read in his deep rich voice. He was reading the service for the burial of the dead.

When he had finished he lit three joss sticks which stood in the blue vase the servant had carried, and placed them before the pillar, kow-towing deeply. Then from his capacious sleeve he produced some strips of gold paper suitably inscribed, and these he burnt.

"I think those are all the gods I know," said Yeh Ling, dusting his fingers daintily.

EDGAR WALLACE

BIG FOOT

Footprints and a dead woman bring together Superintendent Minton and the amateur sleuth Mr Cardew. Who is the man in the shrubbery? Who is the singer of the haunting Moorish tune? Why is Hannah Shaw so determined to go to Pawsy, 'a dog lonely place' she had previously detested? Death lurks in the dark and someone must solve the mystery before BIG FOOT strikes again, in a yet more fiendish manner.

BONES IN LONDON

The new Managing Director of Schemes Ltd has an elegant London office and a theatrically dressed assistant – however, Bones, as he is better known, is bored. Luckily there is a slump in the shipping market and it is not long before Joe and Fred Pole pay Bones a visit. They are totally unprepared for Bones' unnerving style of doing business, unprepared for his unique style of innocent and endearing mischief.

EDGAR WALLACE

BONES OF THE RIVER

'Taking the little paper from the pigeon's leg, Hamilton saw it was from Sanders and marked URGENT. *Send Bones instantly to Lujamalababa… Arrest and bring to headquarters the witch doctor.*'

It is a time when the world's most powerful nations are vying for colonial honour, a time of trading steamers and tribal chiefs. In the mysterious African territories administered by Commissioner Sanders, Bones persistently manages to create his own unique style of innocent and endearing mischief.

THE DAFFODIL MYSTERY

When Mr Thomas Lyne, poet, poseur and owner of Lyne's Emporium insults a cashier, Odette Rider, she resigns. Having summoned detective Jack Tarling to investigate another employee, Mr Milburgh, Lyne now changes his plans. Tarling and his Chinese companion refuse to become involved. They pay a visit to Odette's flat and in the hall Tarling meets Sam, convicted felon and protégé of Lyne. Next morning Tarling discovers a body. The hands are crossed on the breast, adorned with a handful of daffodils.

EDGAR WALLACE

THE JOKER
(USA: THE COLOSSUS)

While the millionaire Stratford Harlow is in Princetown, not only does he meet with his lawyer Mr Ellenbury but he gets his first glimpse of the beautiful Aileen Rivers, niece of the actor and convicted felon Arthur Ingle. When Aileen is involved in a car accident on the Thames Embankment, the driver is James Carlton of Scotland Yard. Later that evening Carlton gets a call. It is Aileen. She needs help.

THE SQUARE EMERALD
(USA: THE GIRL FROM SCOTLAND YARD)

'Suicide on the left,' says Chief Inspector Coldwell pleasantly, as he and Leslie Maughan stride along the Thames Embankment during a brutally cold night. A gaunt figure is sprawled across the parapet. But Coldwell soon discovers that Peter Dawlish, fresh out of prison for forgery, is not considering suicide but murder. Coldwell suspects Druze as the intended victim. Maughan disagrees. If Druze dies, she says, 'It will be because he does not love children!'